Readers' comments about Amorous Accident

Gary Young, **AKP Review**: 'Keating has proved you can create good art and have a dog in it. Well written, thought provoking and challenging.

J.M. Frank, **FIREPAW**: "An entertaining novel which highlights the important issue of animal research. Amorous Accident never becomes preachy or strays from being an entertaining novel while still delivering an important message."

Jay Bail, **BookReader**: "Impressive mystery with compelling characters, love of animals and a strong opposition to using dogs in laboratory experiments. Keating has a sharp eye for atmosphere. If you don't love dogs after this novel, you're hopeless.."

Joy Burch, *Chesapeake Style Magazine*: "Jean brings her ability to organize and analyze to her mystery. She is lively and humorous, and these traits are also found in her writing."

Melissa Simpson, **Daily Press**: "Keating weaves a good tale. Her passion for animal rights in laboratories comes across clearly – as does her love and understanding of dogs."

Paul Aron, The Virginia Gazette: ".. A book for mystery lovers and dog lovers under one cover."

Shelley Glodowsik, **Midwest Book Review**: "The story is compelling and well planned. The plot moves along briskly. Keating hides the killer where no one thinks to look. The characters (including the four-legged furry kind) are sweet beyond compare. "

"If you know someone who likes whodunits and loves papillons, you've got to consider giving them this book. Keating artfully portrays both the elegance and intelligence of the papillon, the intricacies of relationships and false leads. I got close to guessing the person whodunit, but no brass ring. Yet, even if you do guess the person, you'll be in for a surprise at the end, because Amorous Accident has a supremely satisfying ending. Absolutely! Amorous Accident comes to a very satisfying conclusion."
---- Carol

"What a thriller! I was totally surprised by the ending, though all the clues were there, weren't they!"
---- Jean Pomfrey and Sparky

"I started reading it and couldn't close my eyes until I finished your book and closed the cover. I love mysteries, but your book is more than that. I learned a lot about taking care of our latest family member named Twinkles. You inserted many little details into your story that I gleaned and put to use. Thank you for a wonderful day of reading and for an excellent mystery."
----Carolyn B. Grubb and Twinkles

"Your book appears to be a much more serious type of mystery than those others written by Conant, Barenson, etc. I like yours best because of the fact that it has a Papillon in it."
---- Betty and Bill Martin

"Wow! I expected a cute, lighthearted murder to go with the angelic face on the cover of your book. How gruesome – right up there with Patricia Cornwell. How did you think of it? I am enjoying your book a great deal."
----Janet Baumgardner and Skye

"You really had me guessing. There were all kinds of possibilities of who done it. What an ending! I was surprised and delighted. I really , really liked the book. I read it all the way through, even the Acknowledgments. It is truly a great book!!!!"
— Ken and Nana Ridgeway

"It's fascinating! Completely unexpected ending – had no idea who the murderer was. It is a wonderful book. I hope you have several more in mind or in the pipeline."
---- Beth Riandre

"I was glued to your book until I finished. And it's phenomenal, just excellent. I can't wait for you to write another one."
---- Carol Matteini and Harley (black lab)

"I wanted to write and say how much I enjoyed reading Amorous Accident. My Jack Russell Terrier, Pippin, enjoyed it too, since I read a good chunk of it out on the couch in the garage with him. When is the next mystery due out? I want to see Kevin and Blackie move in together!!! The mystery was lovely."
— Angela Wade and Pippin

"I started your mystery this morning, I didn't want to put it down. My Lily is a black German Shepherd, so I'm taking Blackie's plight very personally. If she goes back to those people (the institute), I will never forgive you!!! You really have a very endearing and vivid description of Sky. I like Uncle Kev, and the sprinklers at the Porters' home were really cool. I was supposed to give the house a good cleaning, but I have done nothing but read your book. The poem gave me chills. It still makes me feel a little misty. It really makes you think too."
—Heidi Griswold and Lily (German Shepherd)

Beguiling Bundle

Death Takes Best of Breed

To Richard .
Best Wishes

Jean C. Keating

Jean C. Keating
and
Puff

Astra Publishers
Williamsburg, Virginia

Library of Congress Catalog Card Number:
ISBN -10: 0-9674016-5-8
ISBN -13: 978-0-9674016-5-2

First printing: November, 2007
10 9 8 7 6 5 4 3 2 1

Astra logo by Beverly Abbott, For Arts Sake

Copies available from the publisher:

Astra Publishers
209 Matoaka Court
Williamsburg, VA 23185
(757) 220-3385
www.Astrapublishers.com

Acknowledgments

I offer my sincere appreciation to five wonderful and talented friends, Dorothy Bryant, Carol Chapman, Margaret Van Cleve, John Harrell, and Peg Quarto, who read and corrected the text and story logic of this book. Without them, this book would never have happened.

I am also indebted to Richard Bailey and the other members of my critique group which Rick chairs for their support, encouragement, and helpful advice with character names and dialogue creation.

As usual Beverly and Ira Abbott have been staunch allies in the creation and art work of the cover. You can see their talents as well as the cover of this book on Bev's new web site at **bevabbottartist.com.**

I am deeply grateful and indebted to my wonderful veterinarian, Dr. Mark Sullivan, for hours of coaching in the dangers and symptoms of chocolate poisoning in toy dogs. I offer my thanks, as well, to the many friends on my internet links relating to Papillons who responded to my request for advice regarding experiences with raisins and chocolate ingestion with their own dogs. To them all, my thanks for making this book possible.

Last but certainly not least, my love and thanks to the past and present members of the Astra pack, canine and feline, whose daily antics furnish the characters in my books with fresh and vivid activities to portray.

Jean C. Keating

About the Author

Jean C. Keating is an award winning author, speaker and freelance writer. She has been writing books and stories about companion animals for ten years. Her most recent book won the Virginia Press Award. Her novel about life with six generations of her beloved Papillons was nominated for a Pulitzer Prize and was a national finalist for the coveted Merrill award as best work depicting the human/animal bond.

She holds degrees in mathematics, physics, and information systems. Named Virginia's Outstanding Young Woman of the Year in 1970 for her civic as well as professional efforts as an aerospace engineer with NASA, she authored more than 50 scientific and educational administrative reports during her years with NASA and subsequent service as head of research for Virginia's Higher Education Council.

She retired from government service in 1998 and began writing fiction. In addition to this fifth book, her short stories have been published in numerous magazines. She frequently travels, doing speeches and book reviews with one of her papillons in his persona of Sherlock Bones. The past president of the Chesapeake Bay Writers Club, Jean lives in Williamsburg, Virginia with two ancient cats and an ever-changing number of show Papillons and rescues. She and her muse, Puff, are hard at work on the third mystery in the series entitled *Cricket Catcher*.

Dedication

This book is dedicated to my ever faithful muse, sidekick on numerous book signings and speeches, and foot warmer during my long hours of writing.

Astra's Coffee'n Cream
My beloved Puff

a.k.a.

Sherlock Bones
Blackeared the Pirate
Little Santa Paws
Captain John Sniff
General George Barkington

Illustrations

Airee's Riding Shotgun and Airee's Driving Miss Abby pose at one day of age in the photo on page 28. The picture is courtesy of Linda Knight, the proud owner and photographer.

Anna Schwarz's Asia Time to Fly appears in the picture on page 107 standing in the dishwasher to prove that Papillons are not just pretty faces but highly inventive service dogs as well. The picture appears with the gracious permission of Anna.

By Jean C. Keating

Fiction:
    Amorous Accident
    Pawprints On My Heart
    Paw Prints Through the Years

Non-fiction:
    Published! Now $ell It!

Foreword

Each year, the marvels of television bring special dog shows like the annual Westminster Kennel Club show into homes all over the globe. This Superbowl of the dog world is a black-tie event that features the top ranked stars of dogdom and is open only to dogs who have acquired the title of Champion at registered shows sanctioned by the American Kennel Club. Except for dog show enthusiast, TV viewers never see the grass root adventures of the five to eleven dog shows that entertain and challenge some two million of Americans each weekend. At these shows puppies as young as six months of age compete in a multitude of classes to first acquire the coveted title of Champion, and dogs role up the wins as Best-in-Show title holders that are referenced in Westminster announcers introductions.

The fictional murder in this book is set at one such grass-roots show, and provides a humorous glimpse at characters and dialogue that might be expected at such a show.

It also provides a look at the admirable work undertaken by the national breed clubs in America to provide protection and aid to purebred dogs who fall on hard times. Each breed recognized by the American Kennel Club has a national breed club. All have rescue arms that work to support, protect and place dogs of their breed in suitable situations, keep them out of shelters, and insure that they find forever homes. The segment of this mystery which relates to the little puppy named Bunny is based on actual efforts by the Rescue Committee of the Papillon Club of America.

x

Beguiling Bundle

Death Takes Best of Breed

CHAPTER ONE

The weekend started off badly even before the murder.

Genna Colt's grip on her mechanical pencil tightened sufficiently to break off the fragile plastic clip as her green-banded hazel eyes squinted in agitation. Trying to keep her voice reasonable and assertive rather than aggressive, she repeated, "As I've told you for the last two months, I am taking a holiday beginning tonight and will not be available until after the Memorial Day Weekend."

The cause of her agitation sat next to her in the small conference room at NASA-Langley's Spacecraft Payload Research Division. John Hunter, the assistant project engineer for the star tracker, which was her current assignment, continued his outline of her altered work efforts as though she had not spoken.

"I'm sure that Ms. Colt can accelerate her evaluation of your prototype and have a report to me by tomorrow afternoon. And I'll be able to certify the satisfactory delivery of your model and get you a check cut for at least the 40% advance you were promised."

Hunter's thin elongated face gave no evidence that he even noted Genna's existence. As usual, he treated her as some unnecessary and barely tolerated part of the proceedings. Also as usual, Genna's temper was rising at the insult in direct proportion to the number of minutes she was required to endure his behavior.

She silently cursed Paul Carter, her boss and the owner of the small company for which she worked. By some miracle Carter and CtimesTwo, Inc. had won the contract to evaluate the two payload prototypes for the Sirius project. Carter had smoothly talked her into joining forces with him in this little company and the responsibilities for the science rested on Carter and herself. The rest of the company consisted of two secretaries, one being Carter's wife. Most people thought the company name of CtimesTwo stood for Carter and Colt, but the other half of the company was Carter's wife. He liked to keep things in the family.

At the moment, Genna was considering mayhem on her fellow professional colleague. A broken crown had forced Carter to seek a tooth implant, which had been scheduled for today. She had agreed to this hastily called meeting with Hunter, with whom Genna mixed like molten lava and cold sea water, only after Carter had done a lot of begging over the phone. She was heartily regretting her concession. In fact, she momentarily nursed the idea of smacking the absent Carter in his surgical site when next she saw him for deciding to go ahead with his tooth implant on this day of all days. As a result, she had to put up with Hunter and his insensitive behavior.

Hunter's high forehead showed the peeling

effect of too much sun. An avid gardener, he'd spent most of the previous weekend in his yard despite what had proved to be an exceptionally hot and humid May weekend in Tidewater Virginia. The sun sensitive scalp of his receding hairline only added to the problem, so that now Hunter's semi-balding head was red and scaly. Genna gained momentary control of her temper by reminding herself that if she ignored his cold, china-blue eyes, he looked like a Chinese Crested with a bad case of mange.

"I'm sorry, but my personal plans cannot be altered at this late date," Genna said more calmly than she felt.

Hunter continued to ignore Genna and her comments and to address his remarks to a third individual seated at the table. Carlton Swinson, the president of CS Industries, was well nourished and muscular rather than fat. He was probably close to six feet in height, but his thick build made him appear shorter. At the moment he looked as though he'd be more comfortable standing than sitting. His girth was obviously not suited to the width of the standard government-issue conference chair in which he was stuffed.

Genna focused her attentions on an appraisal of the developer of the prototypes she would be evaluating. She found she liked what she saw. Maybe it was the expensively tailored suit that fit his frame to perfection. Maybe it was the faint scent of Old Spice that he gave off. It reminded her of her father, and she wondered briefly at the choice of such a traditional scent by a man whose dress otherwise reflected the latest in fashion: the beautiful weave of a suit that was more almond than brown, the fashionable stripped shirt of blue and almond on white, and the patterned tie that reflected the same tones.

Jean C. Keating

Genna was suddenly conscious that her attire and Hunter's were dowdy by comparison. The teal blazer she'd thrown on over white slacks and a white blouse put beautiful green lights in her eyes, but it sported a few white dog hairs, courtesy of last minute hugs of her dogs before leaving for the meeting. Hunter had thrown a plaid jacket over a jarring mismatch of open-collared shirt and pants and looked, as usual, as though he'd been interrupted as he was trying to dress in the men's toilet. "*I will not allow feelings of inferiority to alter my position,*" she told herself. "*I am not working this weekend.*"

This was her first meeting with Swinson. Contact between the two contractors was not considered proper policy until Swinson delivered the prototypes and Paul and Genna assumed responsibility for validating their compliance with design specifications. Any prior communications had been conducted through Hunter, and Genna tried always to insure that Paul handled those, because Hunter's attitude never failed to raise her blood pressure.

She sympathized with Swinson. She didn't want to feel any emotional involvement, but she did. She applauded his openness in admitting his need for an early evaluation and his willingness to acknowledge the financial crunch that drove his action. She also appreciated his treatment of her as a fellow professional. But it didn't mean she was going to penalize others to get him out of his self-induced trouble.

In desperation, she picked up the coffee cup sitting in front of her and took a big gulp before she remembered it was both unpleasantly strong and nearly cold.

Swinson seemed unconscious of the direction of her thoughts. He chewed on a short-trimmed mustache and beard from time to time, and the salt

4

and pepper coloring of his facial adornments reminded Genna of a Schnauzer.

"I am spending way too much time thinking about dogs and the dog shows this weekend, and not focusing nearly enough on the conversation at hand," she reminded herself. Then she immediately consoled herself that a pregnant and needy dog at home and guests arriving for the four days of all-breed dog shows at Jamestown were exactly why she'd insisted on time off this weekend. *"Damned if Hunter is going to change my plans,"* she silently vowed.

"I would be most grateful for your speedy processing of the advance on payment," Swinson said. "I realize that I'm delivering it days early and just before a three-day holiday weekend, but your indulgence would mean the world to my company." He glanced nervously at Genna, very aware even if Hunter was not of the hostility in her body language. "As I've explained, I need to make payroll by Tuesday, the actual due date of the prototype, and will be hard pressed to do so without the payment of the first installment."

The brown eyes Swinson turned toward Genna pleaded for her help, understanding and cooperation. But unfortunately for Swinson, his eyes only reminded her of one of the major reasons for her insistence on having this weekend free and strengthened her determination to resist Hunter's efforts to alter her schedule.

Six weeks before, Genna had taken in a pregnant female Papillon from a rescue organization. She had accepted the responsibilities for easing the frightened and malnourished animal through the stress of delivering and raising her litter of puppies. She'd called the little rescue Twinkle because of the happy lights that seem to shine in the

5

small creature's eyes at any little act of kindness extended to her.

Against the memory of Twinkle's appealing and innocent eyes and the little dog's needs for Genna's time and attention, neither Hunter nor Swinson had a snowball's chance in a live volcano of getting their way. Neither man seemed to understand that for differing reasons: Swinson because he was accustomed to getting his way around women through his smooth people-skills, and Hunter because he never assumed any woman was allowed an opinion that differed from his own.

Swinson seems to have some idea of his lack of success, however. He turned to Hunter with a question. "Would this be something you might handle without the need to bother Ms. Colt?"

Hunter paused a bit too long in answering, torn between his dislike at admitting that there was anything he could not do without Genna's help and his interest in getting his way about ordering Genna to perform work to his schedule.

Genna answered for him. "I'm afraid you're out of luck on that score, Mr. Swinson. I'm the only specialist in navigational astronomy on this project, and the star tracker's performance will have to be tested and validated by me."

For once, Hunter kept his mouth shut, but his eyebrows drew a bit closer together as he scowled at the accuracy of Genna's statement.

"What about the infrared horizon sensor?" Swinson was nothing if not focused on getting what he wanted. "Maybe that portion of the payload could be validated and paid for early. It wouldn't completely get me off the hook with my payroll, but it would go a ways toward helping," he said with a pleading smile at Genna.

"Sorry," Genna replied swiftly before she could

allow his smile to make her feel any guiltier or any more obligated to help him out. "The payloads have to work together, and I'll have to validate that they do."

"*Damn that man,*" she told herself. "*I am not responsible for his getting his company into such a negative cash-flow problem.*" Still, she did feel guilty and frustrated that she felt guilt. Only the thought of Twinkle waiting at home and one houseguest already there, who was sitting with Twinkle, allowed her to continue her insistence on her leave schedule being honored.

"But I will promise you this," she finally temporized. "I will review your evaluation reports during the long weekend, and make certain that the evaluation and validation efforts are completed by end of business on Tuesday."

"I should hope so," Hunter injected. "This man is an honored military veteran, an Army Ranger, and we should do all we can to help him with making his company a success."

"Well, I didn't know about his specialty," Genna said, "but I do remember his military background was mentioned in his vita."

"Well, Paul Carter told me about his fine record, so I'm sure he must have told you too," Hunter snapped.

Genna ignored the argumentative injection. She would not rise to the bait of Hunter as much as calling her a liar. She flashed Swinson her most supportive smile. "Is that where you got your training in navigational devices and infrared technology?" She remembered that his degree was in some business field rather than engineering or scientific one, but couldn't remember much else. She'd planned to brush up on the background of all the key people in CS Industries before next Tuesday. But

Paul Carter's hurried phone call had left her little time to do anything but rush off to this meeting.

"Something like that," Swinson temporized, "and a lot of work and study since forming the company. I'm also blessed with a lot of good people who work for me." He smiled at Genna again, and then added, "So you can understand why I hate to let them down with payroll difficulties."

"Most of the time, we have to worry about contractors going over the time scheduled for delivery of payload modules. You're a bit early, which is all to our good. We should be able to help you out with validating your delivery," Hunter said.

In the face of Genna's determined stance and negative head nodding, Hunter threatened, "I'll talk to Paul Carter and see what we can do."

Genna extracted a folder from her briefcase and handed it to Hunter. "By all means talk to Paul as you wish. I'll leave you with another copy of the measurements we'd agreed were needed on the prototypes. If you'll have an electronics tech run the measurements and send the file to my home computer, I'll validate the performance statistics and get them to you before the end of business on Tuesday at the latest. But I can't promise anything any sooner. I have a house full of guests and commitments to them for the weekend."

Hunter took the folder reluctantly as she closed her briefcase and rose to leave. She nodded curtly at Hunter, shook Swinson's reluctant hand with a bit more warmth, and exited before either man could think of any more pressure tactics.

CHAPTER TWO

Thirty-odd miles later, Genna's nerves were still in knots. Although traffic on I-64 West had been light and even the 199 cut across to Route 5 had gone smoothly for once, she was still tense and frustrated. She turned easily on to Route 5, but even that beautiful scenic drive, running parallel with the James River, did little to relax her mood after her battle of wills with Hunter. She felt sorry for Swinson; guilty that she'd been so uncompromising, and annoyed that she'd been put in the position in the first place.

"Drat!" she muttered. "I plan ahead. Why can't they?"

She took the turn off Route 5 into the long drive leading to home and Heron's Rest too sharply, and her little PT Cruiser complained with squealing wheels.

"Darn, it, PeeWee! Don't you give me trouble too," she muttered to the car. But she slowed her speed and willed herself to relax and appreciate the beauty of the shade afforded by the trees that overhung both sides of the lane. As always, she enjoyed the pride of belonging as the modest, red brick and cedar-clad, two-storied home nestled against a backdrop of pines and tall tulip poplars came into view.

Heron's Rest was her childhood home, a peaceful spread of woodland acres along the James River, in which she'd shared many wonderful years with a father she'd adored. For some time after her father's death, she'd wondered if it could ever feel warm and cozy again, but marriage to Jonathan Colt had changed all that. Now Jonathan, his cat and his extended family, along with the assorted canines who claimed Genna and Jonathan as their humans, filled the home once again with love and laughter.

She maneuvered her little Chrysler around a dark blue sedan belonging to her guest that was parked in the circular drive and eased the little silver hatchback into the waiting bay of her double car garage. A long wall of shelves along the outer wall was lined with blue plastic bins, partially marked with white labels that testified to her good intentions but losing battle with keeping clutter at bay.

Home! It had a soothing impact on her frustrated nerves. The sound of barking from several dogs brought a smile to her face as she opened her car door. She made certain the garage door had completely closed and that the area was secure, before rushing to open the door into the house and respond to the happy greetings of three small Papillons and a larger black shepherd mix waiting just inside the door to the laundry and dog room.

"Hello, little people," she greeted the four. "Sky, have you been a good host while I was away?" she voiced, her hands struggling with trying to hold her purse while stroking the head of a wiggling, dark red and white bundle of energy. Her fingers traced a brilliant half-mask of black, which accentuated a wide white blaze and muzzle on the tiny canine's head. Heavily fringed ears and tail beat a swift affirmative to her question. A lightening-fast tongue covered her hand with doggie kisses and happy yodels answered her greeting.

"And how are you this evening, little Rusty?" The second little bundle of fur she addressed was doing his best to emulate a tiny gazelle, jumping upward so that all four feet were off the floor. The abundant black and white hairs of his coat and the long trailing black fringes on his ears were standing out on all sides due to the wind stirred up by his activity. Rusty found it hard to reach Genna's outstretched arms, since his sire who'd taught him the jumping trick kept pushing him aside, but his happy yips left no doubt of his joy at her return.

The black shepherd mix utilized her larger bulk to push through the two exuberant smaller dogs and succeeded in bouncing against Genna so hard that she dropped the brief case and purse she was carrying. Just as well! It left both her hands free to attempt to give three pairs of ears and three heads the pats and scratching the three were demanding.

"Blacky is a gooooood girl," Genna crooned to the larger black dog. "Have you been helping Uncle Kevin look after Twinkle?"

The fourth member of Genna's reception committee stood patiently with regal posture, waiting for her three pushier companions to finish their greetings. The black on white markings of the fourth dog's coat were enhanced by reddish-brown accents which came alive with fiery highlights as a shaft of sunlight from the small windows over the washer-dryer washed the tiny Papillon in light, proving once again

11

the appropriateness of her name: Amber Fire.

Genna reached past the two male Papillons and Blacky, to open her arms to Amber, who responded with a swift leap upward to land in her human's arms. Sky squealed at having been outmaneuvered and stood on his hind legs, his front paws reaching upward to be included in Genna's arms, his hind legs flexing in tiny upward leaps as he debated trying to jump into Genna's arms also.

Genna's happy chuckle overlaid a querulous human voice from somewhere in the house beyond.

"It's about time you got home," a strained voice said. "And no, Blacky has not been any help at all, thank you very much."

"And how are you and Twinkle doing?" Genna responded as she returned Amber to the floor, picked up purse and briefcase, and like the Pied Piper led the assembled collection of sixteen dancing canine feet through the laundry room and kitchen into the great room. The sight that greeted her brought a soft laugh.

A bear of a man dressed in a loose denim shirt and faded jeans arose from the comfortable chair in front of the television where he'd been sitting. Neither he nor the apprehensive figure in a dog bed beside him looked especially comfortable or interested in TV. A silvery, portable wire fencing arrangement completely enclosed his chair and the dog bed with its tense occupant. The three-foot segments of the portable fencing were angled at the point of joining to allow a freestanding enclosure that walled Andrews and a fourth tiny dog away from the rest of the room and house.

Kevin Andrews crossed the short space of floor to the limit of the silvery fencing to envelope Genna in a hug. His stern face could bring terror to a lawless felon and had often done so in his capacity of senior

12

homicide detective in Richmond. Now the laugh lines around his light hazel eyes softened the craggy countenance which greeted his returning hostess.

"Well, no wonder you didn't greet me in person. What gives with the fencing?" Genna asked as she extracted herself from his hug.

"Twinkle kept trying to wander off, Blacky and Sky were nosing her and making her growl, so I found this portable fence in your dog room and just locked us up together," the amply padded man replied.

The fourth tiny canine had left the safety of her bed to rush to the limit of the portable pen upon Genna's entrance into the room. She watched Andrews with signs of nervousness, but continued to crowd as close to Genna as the protective fencing would allow. Her large black ears and general outline were sufficient to identify her as another Papillon, but her sparse coat, drooping tail and fearful attitude all bespoke a sad story of ill usage.

Genna dumped her purse and briefcase on the floor again and reached over the thirty-inch high confining barrier to gently scoop up the fearful animal. "Twinkle, it's all right!" she assured the little dog that snuggled tightly against her body.

Six weeks of loving care, nutritional food and needed medicine had filled in many of the sharp planes in the little dog's frail frame. Gentle handling and plenty of love had eased some but not all of Twinkle's fears of people. Imminently approaching motherhood had produced the big belly. Only time would bring this little waif the happy assuredness and confidence of the three that danced around Genna's feet.

"I'm certainly glad you're home. Twinkle was beginning to worry that I'd have to deliver her pups," he said.

"Do you think she trusts you enough to let you do

that?" Genna countered with a chuckle.

"I doubt it; I think she's too smart for that. I know I don't trust myself to get involved," Andrews admitted.

Genna smiled at the relief in the big man's voice. He was the only father she and her husband Jonathan could now claim as their own. Genna's father was dead long before she'd met and married Jonathan Colt. One of the many gifts Genna had acquired upon her marriage to her author husband was the addition of this steady soul to her extended family.

Andrews and Jonathan Colt's father had been partners with the Richmond Police department. Andrews had never married, seemed to have no family of his own. At least neither Jonathan nor Genna had ever heard him mention any. When Jonathan lost his father in his late teens, Andrews had stepped in to fill the role of father to Jonathan and his sister. And though Genna and Jonathan called him Uncle Kevin, he was in fact the father figure to them both.

Andrews' loose blue denim shirt sported a small piece of apple, and Genna wondered if he'd tried to share his snack with the fearful canine mother-to-be. A ready supply of food and drink was stashed on the end table within easy reach, but Genna was pleased to note that the food consisted of various pieces of fresh fruit and both bottles of liquid contained two flavors of Crystal Light drink.

A half-filled bottle of spring water stood beside a small dog bowl on the table also, mute testimony to the fact that Andrews had considered his tiny companion's needs before walling them both away from the rest of the house and mob.

Andrews' battle with excess weight was a constant and often unsuccessful trial. Sometimes amusing to others but never him. He'd recently joined

Beguiling Bundle: Death Takes Best of Breed

Weight Watchers, dropped thirty-seven pounds and was working hard to drop another thirty. Genna started to compliment him on keeping to his current eating regime, but decided that he didn't need to be reminded of any other stress in his life

"Any signs of labor yet?" Genna inquired of Andrews.

"No, thank God!" The strong face reflected Andrews' sincere relief at being spared dealing with that upcoming event in Genna's absence.

"Thanks for sitting with her. I'd never have been able to leave her alone," Genna hugged him gratefully. "She already had milk in her tits this morning, so she could deliver at any time."

"Glad I was here, now that nothing happened," Andrews admitted with a grin.

The three Papillons at Genna's feet danced and jumped around her in their determination to displace the little bundle she held in her arms. But the black Shepard mix was more interested in getting to Andrews and managed to tip the portable fence in her exuberance to reach him.

Genna and Andrews grabbed for the fence at the same time and managed to keep it from falling. "Guess my girl has had about enough of being walled away from me," Andrews observed. "Shall I fold this back up and put it away?"

"No. For now, let's just put Twinkle back inside so she won't be bothered by this energetic crew."

Andrews stepped over the panel to caress the black head of the larger dog that was pushing herself against him.

"Anything interesting happen while I was out?" Genna asked as she gently returned Twinkle to the sheltered area inside the fencing.

"Jonathan called," Andrews said. "He's having a very successful book tour, hasn't had much time for

15

anything else. The presentation at the Wickem Library, don't remember what town that was in, was very well attended, standing room only, and the crowd asked some very interesting questions."

"Interesting in what way?" Genna injected. She turned away to hide her grin from Andrews who was usually extremely puzzled and bored by Jonathan's science fiction plots. Try as the logical-minded detective might to understand the involved time-travel and otherworld scenarios that Jonathan wove into his stories, Andrews often yawned or dozed off in the middle of the descriptions.

"Beats me! Something to do with his plot! You know I never understand a thing he tries to explain about them," Andrews snorted. "He said he'd call back later tonight."

Genna's husband Jonathan had been torn about going on this book tour, since it conflicted with Andrews' two-week vacation and visit with the Colts at Heron's Rest. Genna and Andrews had convinced him that the tour was too important to his writing career to miss. His daily calls always included apologies for his absence, which were then followed by excited descriptions of the book-related events of his day.

"What's for dinner?" Andrews turned the subject away from Jonathan and his book doings to something closer to his understanding and heart.

"I thought I'd grill some shrimp in olive oil and seasoning, and have a little broccoli and rice," Genna responded. "Will you have enough points to cover that?" Andrews success at weight loss had come utilizing the idea of counting points of various foods, based on the calories, fat and fiber grams. He was allowed so much a day, and Genna was trying to reorient her thinking about food in terms of these three characteristics rather than just the calorie

16

count.

"I'll eat whatever you want to serve," Andrews said, "but go lightly on the broccoli. And I wouldn't say no to some dessert. I'm a bit hungry for something sweet."

Genna nodded but did not give away her plans to serve him fresh berries with yogurt. She'd secretly gotten one of the point counters from a friend who'd also utilized Weight Watchers to curb her weight. With the point counter she could evaluate the foods she gave him to insure that he continued on this latest successful effort to control his weight. According to Andrews' many dogmatic statements, HE DID NOT LIKE YOGURT!! But when he didn't know he was eating yogurt, he ate it with relish.

Sky, Rusty and Amber swirled around Genna's feet as she collected and put away her purse and case and hung the jacket to her pants suit in the closet. When she moved to the kitchen and opened the fridge to find the making for dinner, three little noses pushed their way into freezer and fridge sections to investigate her every movement. Andrews settled into a seat around the kitchen table. Blacky abandoned Andrews' side to join the smaller canines in supervising the meal preparations.

* * *

An hour later, Genna had managed a long conversation with Jonathan, numerous handouts to her four eager canine helpers in the kitchen, preparation of a warm and nourishing dish for Twinkle which the soon-to-be mother dog had refused to eat, and a tempting meal with dessert for herself and Andrews. Twinkle was settled quietly in her bed protected by the portable fence. Genna and Andrews elected to eat at the round kitchen table from which they could watch Twinkle and had more or less convinced the other four fur-people to settle at their feet. The two had just seated themselves in front of their dishes when the phone rang again.

Genna answered it without thinking, expecting it to be Jonathan calling back for a third time, and was annoyed to hear the voice of her boss on the line.

"I was just sitting down to dinner," she responded shortly. She silently mouthed an apology to Andrews for taking the phone call and waved encouragement to him to start eating without her.

"Oh, so Hunter called you, did he," she continued. "Now don't you start! You get the same answer I've given Hunter and Swinson. I am not working this weekend. In fact, you are disturbing my dinner with Uncle Kevin now."

She paused to listen to her caller and utilized the break to maneuver a fork full of shrimp to her mouth. "You're already on my shit list for sticking me with today's meeting anyway. I hope your implant was worth it, because I intend to extract many favors for having to deal with Hunter by myself. Including," she emphasized, "the understanding that the time off I'd requested and arranged for this weekend is not disturbed."

"Defensive!" she snorted after another pause and another mouthful of shrimp, "Hunter was positively accusatory! I was already steamed before he as much as called me a liar because he said you'd told him this Swinson fellow was not only a veteran but an Army Ranger and that I had to have known it too."

Andrews smiled at Genna's tough talk and continued to devour his meal, even the broccoli.

She managed another mouthful of shrimp and rice before continuing, "Well, he didn't say he'd told you about Swinson, he insisted you'd told him and therefore I had to have known."

18

Beguiling Bundle: Death Takes Best of Breed

"I know," she continued between chews, "I understand his brother was killed in Viet Nam, and he's highly defensive about presumed slights to military personnel, but Hunter is just plain nuts. Sky and I have a pen pal that is part of a K-9 unit in Iraq with whom we feel a special bond. Moreover, I really liked Swinson. But I did not appreciate Hunter trying to make out that I was a liar about knowing something about him, whether you told Hunter or Hunter told you."

Andrews had managed to consume the healthy offerings on his plate, but thanks to Genna's distraction with her phone conversation, her plate was still half full. He eyed an appealing blue, red and white concoction in a tall parfait glass beside his plate with interest, but seemed reluctant to start on his dessert while Genna was still trying to eat her own dinner.

Genna smiled in spite of her frustration with Carter for the interruption to her dinner. "I'm sorry but work on the prototypes is out of the question until Monday night. I've got to go. Hope your jaw doesn't give you any trouble tonight." *Though I may make it hurt for you when I see you if you don't leave me alone about these prototypes this weekend,* she thought to herself. Aloud she added, "I'll talk to you later."

"Sorry," she said to Andrews. "I should have checked caller ID before answering that, but I thought it was Jonathan calling back. He's so torn by missing this first part of your visit."

"Don't wait on me. Dig into your dessert and see how you like it," she continued.

"What is it?" Andrews was already picking at the whipped cream on top to get at the colorful mixture below.

"Strawberries, blueberries, artificial sweetener,

19

fat-free whip mostly," Genna hedged. She wasn't about to mention the strawberry yogurt in the mix."

She hid her smile at Andrews' rapid consumption of his dessert with an equally appreciative enjoyment of her own. Any further conversation was interrupted by the noise of frantic scratching and whining by Twinkle. Sky and Blackie managed to move from under the table to the edge of the portable fence in slightly more than a nanosecond, and only Andrews' equally quick response saved the portable fencing from being toppled by the excited canine duo.

"Is she alright?" Andrews asked.

"She's starting into labor," Genna explained, as her own chair fell backwards and hit the floor in her hurry to respond to the new crisis. "And I still have to give baths to Rusty and Sky for the show tomorrow."

If she'd known about the confusion and murder that would accompany tomorrow's show she might have considered abandoning the baths along with any idea of going to the show.

CHAPTER THREE

Genna was doing her best to keep her eyes open, but the tensions of the day and the frantic scrambling of the evening had taken their toll on even her adrenalin charged body.

Andrews and Blacky had finally retired to the guest room, accompanied by Sky in his role as host. With a great deal of help from Andrews and a minimal amount of interference from Blacky, the leftovers and dishes from dinner had gotten cleared away, and Rusty and Sky had gotten bathed, groomed, trimmed and readied for their appearance at the first of four local dog shows in which the two were entered.

Genna glanced at the clock mounted on a soft cream wall in front of her, mentally ticking off the seven short hours left before her other guests arrived and nine hours before she would need to get Sky and Rusty to the first of those shows.

The beautiful and colorful butterfly on the clock's face reminded her of the other dear face who

21

had gifted her with the clock on her last birthday and mounted it within easy sight on the wall of the room. She missed having Jonathan near to help with things, not the least of which were the stresses of work which still wrangled and the challenge of the litter of two puppies which Twinkle had presented her with shortly after midnight.

A slight sound of tiny nails clicking against the wood floor of the puppy nursery announced the return of Sky from his hosting and patrol duties. Genna had left the half door from the hallway into the nursery ajar knowing that Sky would make a big fuss if he could not join her at will.

"Hello, Love. Did you get Blacky and Uncle Kevin settled in for the night?" Genna whispered to the tiny busybody.

Black-accented ears flashed up and cupped forward as the tiny dog crossed to Genna's feet and licked her bare ankles in response. His newly washed and dried coat floated on the air stirred up by his movement. The pleasant scent of the conditioner she'd used muted the less pleasant smell of wipes used to clean one of the puppies' back end.

The room was too warm for Genna's tastes, but she was reluctant to move in order to adjust the temperature. Listed on the architect's drawings of Heron's Rest as an exercise room and located between the master suite and the large bonus room over the garage, it had an independent heating and cooling system to accommodate the needs of exercising humans. But the room was used exclusively as a nursery for the little dogs that Genna called her children, and was decorated in soft creams and restful blues with large oils and watercolors of the treasured canine members of the Colt/Kingsley clan on the walls.

Beguiling Bundle: Death Takes Best of Breed

Genna's eyes rested lovingly on the large oil painting on the wall above the table. The larger-than-life size picture of Sky returned her look, his long black and red fringes slightly flared, trailing from alert ears cupped forward on his beautifully tilted head. The brass plaque attached to the bottom of the frame read simply, Champion Wing's Red Sky at Morning, CDX. It needed polishing, she noted absently. It also brought a tired chuckle. Andrews was fond of saying that Sky lived up to the line of poetry for which he'd been named and that sailors and everyone else had best take warning when Sky came into the room.

The model for the painting busied himself with a patrol of the room, sniffing for any possible intruders who might have dared to invade his domain while he'd been occupied with helping Andrews and Blacky settle into the guest room.

Twinkle and her two puppies were resting comfortably on the table at which Genna was seated. Their soft bed was warmed by water bottles and within reach of Genna's hands. The high lip of the bed was easily crossed by Twinkle but too high to allow a puppy to bumble out of the bed.

Twinkle had produced the two puppies easily, but the little boy was the subject of deep concern to the new mother, and to the two humans who'd struggled to help. Born with a harelip and a tiny cleft palate, he was not able to get closure of his lips to produce suction. With Andrews' help, Genna had managed to milk colostrum into a syringe and drop it onto the back of the puppy's tongue, but the defect also meant he could not nurse and had to be hand fed every two hours. Andrews had set up a card table and two chairs in the puppy nursery to make it easier for Genna to work with the tiny puppy. He and Blacky, along with Sky, had hovered about offering help to the exasperation of Twinkle. Finally Genna had convinced her two guests to go to bed, indicating to Andrews that one of the two humans in the house had to be alert enough to fix coffee in the morning. The top of the table was crowded with the small bed, a tray of feeding and medical supplies and a small electrical heating unit. The harsh, green-plaid tablecloth that had been hastily thrown over the tabletop did nothing for the otherwise restful décor of the room, but at the moment Genna was too tired to care. At least it was clean. That was more than she could say for the lower sleeves of her robe and pajama top. Smears of yellow gunk, probably colostrum, and darker smears which she didn't care to identify ran a counterpoint to the soft blue and lavender plaid of the robe and stood out sharply against the pale blue cuff of her pajama top, but were of little concern to the weary puppy caretaker.

Rusty and Amber were hopefully asleep in their large wire enclosures in the dog room downstairs. Genna fleetingly worried that Rusty had not gotten completely dry from his bath, and that his hair would not be correct for tomorrow's show. Given the choice of where to allot her time, she reminded herself that his handler, Russell Harper, would deal with that in the morning hours, which were approaching all too rapidly.

Sky rose on his hind legs and put his front feet on Genna's right knee to ease his head under Genna's wrist in a bid for her attention. A soft grumble from Twinkle and an equally soft correction from Genna convinced him that he had gone too far. Thwarted, he wandered over to the couch and found a blue fleece throw to his liking. Even his seemingly inexhaustible energy had been severely challenged if not extinguished by the night's events. He settled for dragging the throw back to Genna's feet,

24

scrunching it into a bed which suited him, circling it enough times to lay an egg at least the size of a duck's, and flopping down on his prize, his head on the soft blue bedroom shoe covering Genna's foot. In a few minutes, the long silky hairs of his ear fringes tickled her bare ankles in time with his slow, even snores.

How am I going to handle this problem, she despaired. The weekend had been destined for enough stress with a normal delivery, Twinkles' due date having coincided with Andrews' planned visit, Jonathan's unexpected book tour, a four-day dog show and expected visits by two other doggie friends and their canine show dogs. Attempts to inject an accelerated evaluation of the prototypes for the Sirius mission had already sent her nerves into overdrive, and now this! The tiny bit of life, no more than four ounces of helpless puppy, was trying so desperately to survive and was missing the capability most essential for that survival.

"What was it Uncle Kevin called him?" she crooned to Twinkle. "A beguiling bundle who has no notion of the difficulties he's facing."

The tiny, black-and-white subject of Genna's monologue squirmed and twitched. He would soon be hungry again. In the dimmed light of the nursery, the now dry coat of his slightly larger sister showed a reddish hint of the clear red and white coat she would sport as an adult. Her stomach was better filled since she got most of her mother's milk, and she rolled away from her more fractious littermate and returned to a deeper sleep.

Sky moved his head from Genna's foot to rest it on a mound of his throw but did not get up when Genna quietly moved to the small fridge, which held the puppy formula. She warmed it and had it ready when the tiny puppy began to nose his dam and whimper for food. He was not happy when Genna picked him up in a small wrap warmed by a second heating pad and placed the long nipple attached to a syringe in the back of his mouth. He wanted his dam's milk and the formula was obviously a poor substitute in his opinion.

Twinkle deserted her remaining sleeping pup to come out of the bed and sit on the table beside Genna as the formula was slowly dripped onto the back of the puppy's tongue. The feeding complete, Genna held the tiny mite so that his dam could stimulate bowel and bladder eliminations, marveling that this once abused and neglected canine would accept so readily the human help and handling of her puppy.

"What shall we call him?" Genna whispered to the dedicated mother dog. "We could name him Beguiling Bundle and call him Guy or Bunny. I don't like Guy! It sounds too old and mature for such an adorable little fellow. Besides, we can't really validate his sire, and he'll never be registered with AKC. So we only need a call name for our little treasure. How about we call him Bunny!"

Twinkle's tongue was too busy with her cleanup to respond. It would seem that she didn't find the taste of the puppy formula bad at all. She was giving Bunny's face and neck a good wash to remove any dribbles that might have occurred during the feeding.

Now that the feeding was done, the exhaustion that Genna had kept at bay suddenly made her arms feel heavy. To keep herself awake while she waited for Twinkle to finish cleaning little Bunny to her exacting standards, she continued with her naming game.

"Now what shall we call your little girl? We have to have a name for her also. She'll be a red and white. If she were going to be registered, we could have named her Be Mine, Valentine and called her Tina. So how about we name her Tina. Tina and Bunny! Will that suit you, little mother?"

Twinkles gave no indication that she cared. Apparently satisfied with her cleaning chore, she returned to her bed, assured herself that her other puppy was still settled and looked expectantly at Genna.

"You don't need a spoken language, do you little one?" Genna whispered a tired laugh to her voice. "Yes, I'll put little Bunny back in bed with you."

Exhaustion deepened the laugh lines at Genna's mouth. She brushed an unruly strand of hair away from eyes that burned from weariness. The tired woman cleaned up the feeding equipment, and spoke softly to the dog curled at her feet.

"Come on, Sky. Let's see if we can get a little nap before we have to repeat this process in a couple of hours. We might as well crash right here instead of wasting time walking down the hall to the bedroom."

She set a small alarm for a two-hour interval, picked Sky's bed up from the floor and crashed on the sofa with Sky on her shoulder and the throw covering her feet, which always seemed to be cold even if the rest of her was overly warm. Twice more during the night, she answered the call of the alarm to repeat her feeding and cleaning of the tiny puppy that fought for life but could not nurse on his own.

"You'll be too tired to hold your tail up in the ring today," she croaked to the faithful companion who always rose when she did, to curl around her feet as she fed and cared for little Bunny.

27

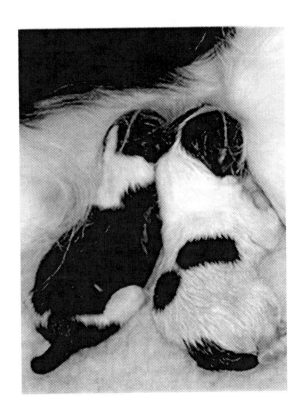

Twinkle's little darlings

CHAPTER FOUR

The ringing phone startled Andrews so badly that he sloshed the coffee in his overfilled cup on the way to a chair at the kitchen table. A glance at the caller identification assured him that it was Jonathan. He grabbed the receiver off the wall mount before it could ring a second time.

"Hi, old thing," he greeted his absent host in a tone more cheerful than he felt. "Yep! Your lovely wife is up and functioning already but dragging from very little sleep. She's upstairs in the nursery feeding the little male puppy again."

Andrews tried to get a sip of his too hot brew before continuing. "It might be a good idea if you waited a bit before trying to talk to her."

Andrews chuckled to himself at Jonathan's apology for calling so early. "Actually, you're the second caller of the morning. Your vet called about twenty minutes ago."

29

Jean C. Keating

He finally managed a mouthful of welcomed caffeine before continuing. "Well, you know that the little puppy has a hare lip and probably a cleft. He can't nurse and Genna has been feeding him with a long nipple attached to a syringe every two hours since his birth. And..."

Andrews paused briefly to listen to Jonathan's comment, and then continued. "That's exactly what I thought you'd say and why I think you'd better wait to talk to Genna later. The vet gently suggested that she bring the puppy over and have it put down and she exploded at the suggestion. She'll respond the same to you, so I'd recommend that you just keep such thoughts to yourself at the moment."

After another pause, Andrews continued. "I know you're thinking of her. But she's just thinking of the puppy, which isn't real to you, but is very much a live, needy baby to Genna. She had a bad day yesterday with too many crises pulling at her; she's slept very little, and right now she's wearing her emotions on her sleeve."

A long response from Jonathan gave Andrews a chance to gulp two swallows of his much needed coffee and burn his tongue in the bargain.

"You know I'm helping all I can. Don't laugh, but I was weaker in the knees after helping her deliver those two pups late last night than I ever was facing my first felon holding a gun! You know Genna is strung out when she hands the mother dog to me and tells me to take all the dogs out this morning. When have you ever known her to entrust Sky to anyone else? Or a mother dog for that matter?"

"I tell you what. Since you don't want to leave your cell phone on in the meeting there, how about calling back in an hour. Genna's two dog show buddies are scheduled to arrive here at any minute, and maybe they can help figure out how we're going to handle things today. Genna can't go to the show and be here to feed the puppy also. Something's got to give! Call her back in an hour and maybe she'll be in better shape to talk with you."

"Wait, before you hang up ... just remember when you call, do not suggest to her that she put this puppy down. She will explode in your face!"

The loud clicking of dog's nails on the brick floor of the entrance way heralded the arrival of an over-exuberant Blacky, as Andrews ended his phone conversation. "Good, talk to you later."

The sleek black body wiggled in counter-point with the flowing tail, as Blacky pranced to Andrews' side, nosing her head under his hand for attention.

"Oh, you're very pleased with yourself this morning, and now I suppose you expect breakfast," he said with a chuckle. "You desert me to keep Genna and Sky company even when you're not wanted in Twinkle's domain. Did they throw you out again?"

He gulped down the last of his coffee, which had fortunately had time to cool and buzzed about the kitchen getting breakfast for the canines and for Genna and himself. He closed the gate to the upstairs, opened the door to the dog room off the kitchen and quieted the resulting barks and yodels as Rusty and Amber joined Blacky in the kitchen. He patrolled the dog room, made certain the water containers in each dog's sleeping crate were clean and full, then set food down for Amber, Rusty and Blacky. They managed to inhale their portions with a minimal of squabbling.

Ten minutes later a bleary-eyed Genna staggered downstairs, Sky a constant shadow by her side. Andrews shooed the three other dogs back into the dog room and closed the door to keep them away from the food bowl he placed on the floor for Sky.

31

Blacky protested loudly at being separated from his side.

He set a cup of coffee at one of the places at the table and pulled out a chair for Genna. She weakly eased into the chair and had her nose buried in the coffee cup when he set two plates on the table and sat down with her.

"Eat," he said, keeping it simple.

"Thanks," she replied. She was partway through the plate before her mind caught up with the breakfast preparations sufficiently to ask, "Are you supposed to have fried eggs?"

"Cripes! Can't you forget about my diet for once?" Andrews fairly snorted. Then he softened and smiled. "Yes," he assured his sleep-deprived companion. "I scrambled them with olive oil which I'm supposed to have, and the toast is multigrain. You have bacon; I don't. So I'm legal and you're healthy."

"It tastes wonderful," Genna admitted, her throat a little raspy from too little sleep. Her rumpled bathrobe had a few more stains of one color or another, which she didn't care to identify or dwell upon. "You're dressed already," she observed, noting the comfortable jeans and snappy blue and white tee on Andrews' trimmer torso.

"You said the show would probably be hot and humid by the time Sky and Rusty showed, so I wanted to be comfortable," Andrews said.

Sky pushed his way to Genna's side, his now empty food dish in his mouth.

"No more for you just now, Little One, or you'll never bait for anyone at the show," Genna remarked to the insistent little dog, 'assuming you even get there with everything else that's going on today."

The sound of her voice set off a chorus of barks and yodels from the dog room beyond the kitchen. Andrews carried his plate to the sink, picking up Sky's empty dish from the floor on his way to acknowledge the insistent pleas of the other three canines to be allowed to join the humans. Blacky, Amber and Rusty rushed the door the minute Andrews turned the door knob, flowing like water around and over his feet on their way to greet Genna.

Andrews retrieved two glasses of juice from the refrigerator, and waded his way through the wiggling bodies of three Papillons and one black shepherd mix to put a glass of orange juice in front of Genna. He settled into his own chair to enjoy his V8 juice.

"Did I hear the phone?" Genna asked a faint orange mustache about her upper lip from the froth on her juice.

"Jonathan. He had to get back to a meeting with the publicist. He'll call later."

"Sorry I missed him." Genna sounded wistful as well as very, very tired.

"I told him you had your hands full just then with feeding the puppy and suggested he call back later," Andrews admitted that much. "He said to tell you he loved you."

He was rewarded with a tired smile that did not quite reach her red-rimmed eyes.

"This is good," Genna nodded at her glass. "Don't you like orange juice?"

"Too many points," Andrews responded cryptically. "Besides, having zero points, V8 helps me get my vegetable count in for the day."

"You're looking great," Genna observed trying to conceal a big yawn.

"And it puts you right to sleep," Andrews teased.

"No, really, you're looking very streamlined. And I know how hard you found dieting in the past. I'm just so proud of you for keeping to your diet plans. "

"Well, Blacky keeps me focused with her demands for two long walks a day, and I feel much

33

better without the extra thirty odd pounds around my middle."

At the sound of her name, the black dog rushed to put her head on Andrews' denim clad knee and push her head into the hand of the human with whom she now shared her life. Their past year together had been filled with changes, especially for Andrews.

Once he'd decided to take her to live with him, he'd been forced because of the no-pet clause to move from the apartment he'd called home for more years than he'd cared to count. He'd bought a tiny house with a large yard on a quiet street. It meant a longer commute to work for him but a better environment for Blacky. She'd become such an important focus of his life that in learning to feed her correctly, he'd moved on to finally cooking and eating correctly for himself. He'd joined Weight Watchers to learn more about the healthy way to diet and eat. The results were a slimmer, trimmer Andrews and a sleeker, healthier Blacky.

"How's the puppy?" Andrews voiced the concern the two had been avoiding.

"The little girl has gained a quarter ounce. The little boy may have lost a smidgen, but he tries so hard to eat." Genna's voice cracked from more than just exhaustion and the red-rimmed eyes brimmed with tears. "I just don't know what else to do that I'm not already doing."

"Just keep doing what you're doing," Andrews consoled. "You said it was a good sign that Twinkle does not push him away."

"I'm hoping that the hare lip and the slight break in the palate that I can see are his only problems. If there are internal problems, usually the dam will push the puppy away from her healthy ones. And Twinkle doesn't do that. She helps me clean him after each

34

feeding and wants him back nestled against her and Tina."

"Tina?" Andrews asked.

"I named the little girl Tina. And I'm going to call the little boy Bunny. You are the one who said he was a beguiling bundle, with his tiny pink nose and muzzle, and delicate little mouth despite the harelip. So I named him Bunny."

Andrews collected both of their coffee cups and carried them to the counter, turning his back to Genna as he poured coffee for himself. "Want another cup?" he asked. With his face hidden so Genna would not see his concern, he tried to hold his voice even and casual as he continued, "Do you think it's a good idea to name them so early? I mean, before you know if you can save the little fellow?"

"He wants to live, and we're going to make it happen!" Genna snapped back.

The big man turned back to the table, two cups of steaming coffee in his hands and a gentle expression on his face. Many a felon who'd encountered him in his role as homicide detective would have been astonished at the compassion he allowed to show through in the privacy of this, his second home. The dogs crowded around Genna, sensing the stress in her voice, they pushed against her legs offering their own sympathetic support. Sky rose on his hind legs to put both front paws on her leg and licked the left hand she trailed in her lap.

She reached ineffectively to pat the four heads crowding around her and nodded apologetically to Andrews. "Sorry. Didn't mean to take your head off! I'm just so tired and so frustrated and its only just beginning."

"I know. Have some more caffeine. Right now you need it." Andrews set the cup beside her empty orange juice glass and returned to his seat to join her at the table. Blacky discontinued her attempts to console Genna and returned to snuggle against Andrews' knee.

"I washed out the dog's water bowls in the back room and fed them before you and Sky came down to breakfast," Andrews said, steering the conversation to less stressful topics. "But I haven't seen Kit Kat."

"He's up on Jonathan's pillow in the master bedroom sulking because he had to sleep alone last night," Genna said. She brightened at the thought of the sleek, black shorthaired cat that had adopted Jonathan years before he and Genna met. Though cats generally hate changes of any king, Kit Kat had not only managed to endure the amalgamation of the two households but had also adjusted to sharing the bed with not just Genna but her ever-present shadow Sky.

"Now that he's gotten accustomed to a bed filled with two humans, and from one to three dogs to provide body warmth to his royal person, he sulks when Jonathan goes away on book tours. Some nights it's all I can do to get any bed space, especially if Amber and Rusty decide to sleep upstairs with the rest of us. Kat usually manages to push Amber and Rusty to the foot of the bed, but no amount of hissing or fussing has ever moved Sky from beside my pillow." Genna's tired chin managed a weak smile at the memory. "Last night was a shock to the poor old fellow; he had the bed all to himself. He subjected me to a lot of meowing and yowling this morning when I moved his litter box to the master bath and put his food and water in there for the weekend."

"I thought maybe he had forgotten Blacky once lived here and didn't want to come around her."

Blacky had entered Andrews' and Genna's lives more than a year ago when she'd been found at the scene of a murder of a prominent oncologist in Richmond. When numerous suspects sought to acquire his canine witness, supposedly to utilize her in on-going drug experiments, Andrews had arranged for Blacky to be housed and protected by Genna at Heron's Rest. He'd told himself it was just until he could solve the crime. Genna's sympathies were, of course, with the pathetic, fearful black shepherd. She'd taken an instant dislike to the victim and cared far less about Andrew's goal of finding the killer than about making certain Blacky was not returned to the research lab. She'd thwarted rather than helped Andrews to exploit Blacky's exposure to the murderer to find the killer. He wasn't too sure just how she'd managed to bring her substantial private income into play to protect the dog, but in the end, when he'd finally solved the murder, no thanks to Genna, the research center had all but paid him to keep Blacky.

"No, but he certainly won't want anything to do with Shirley's and Peggy's dogs when they arrive," she said, referring to the two dog show friends who would be her additional houseguests for the weekend. "Kat will be happier in the master suite for the duration of the weekend, but right now, he's not convinced of that at all."

The phone on the kitchen wall behind Andrews' head interrupted them. Andrews checked the caller ID before attempting to answer. "Do you want to talk to Russell Harper?"

The stress lines around Genna's eyes deepened even more. "No, but I guess I have to," she said, reaching her hand to take the handset which Andrews passed to her.

"Hi, Russell! Please don't tell me you have some problem with showing Rusty today!" Her head dropped into her left hand as she listened to the voice on the other end of the phone.

Jean C. Keating

"Well, that just about destroys any chance for today producing enough points for a major. Papillon people will be ready to tar and feather me. But it can't be helped. Originally, I could have tried to show Rusty myself along with Sky, though I'd not wanted to do that which is why I hired you. But now I've got a problem here with a newborn puppy that has to be hand fed every two hours, so I don't see how I can get to the show either."

Andrews edged her coffee cup against the elbow of her free hand, worried at her added stress, which showed in her eyes and face.

Genna's expression brightened slightly as she absently picked up the cup being urged upon her by Andrews and added, "If you can get Edward Spratt to fill in for you, I'd certainly appreciate that. It'd be wonderful if I don't have to pull Rusty. Two friends are dropping by on their way to the show, and are staying with me for the weekend. One of them or my Uncle Kevin can get Rusty to the show grounds and hand him off to Edward."

Rusty and Sky had gotten bored with Genna's lack of attention to them and were engaged in trying to draw and quarter a small orange bear which one of them had brought in from the toy box. Genna paused to shush the escalation of buzzing sounds coming from the two play-fighters and then added with another frown, "I suppose he'll be late showing up! He always is. Always makes me nervous, and it won't give Rusty the needed time to get accustomed to showing for Edward. But it's a darn sight better than having Rusty break the major when people may have traveled great distances just to have the chance to get one."

Genna absently sipped her coffee, nodding in agreement at whatever her caller was saying and then concluded, "Appreciate you taking care of this.

If I don't hear back from you, I'll know you talked with Edward and he'll show Rusty. Hope your back is better soon. Bye for now."

Returning her coffee cup to the table and the handset to Andrews, Genna dropped her head into both of her hands, her fingers raking the hair on both sides of her head upward in her continuing frustration. Her dark hair was already disheveled, a small piece of it standing straight out over her left ear. "What else can go wrong today?"

"Don't tempt fate by asking," Andrews responded, trying to keep it light.

"I can't help listening in on your conversations for all the good it does me when you're talking some kind of code," he teased.

"What code?" Genna asked. She sounded as dejected as ever, but her head came up and out of her hands and her face showed a small amount of interest as she focused on his challenge.

"Major? Breaking the major? You're as bad as Jonathan with his time travel plots," Andrews joked. Then he added on a more serious note, "Actually I can stay here and feed the puppy while you're at the show, so you can explain it all to me when you feel more rested."

"No," Genna countered. "One of the reasons for picking this time as your vacation was because I wanted you to share the fun of this dog show weekend so you understood a bit more about what your grand-dogs and I do for fun."

Her square chin lifted as Genna's stubborn look of determination replaced the dejected, defeated expression. "I'll get an experienced sitter for Bunny. We're going ahead with the plans for our day."

Andrews had given up on responses that he was not grandpa to dogs.

Sky interrupted the two humans to proudly thrust the almost-whole orange teddy against Genna's knee. She barely had time to give his head a pat before Rusty was grabbing at a dangling appendage in another attempt to wrestle the toy away from his sire.

"OK!" Genna straightened her spine and focused on trying to explain the involved American Kennel Club rules governing the acquisition of conformation championship status for dogs. "Majors! It works like this. A dog has to acquire a total of 15 points in competition to be named a champion. The number of dogs in competition in a show dictates the number of points awarded for a win, and the number in competition needed for each point count differs by breed, gender, region of the country and by year."

Andrews groaned! "Why do I think I'm going to be sorry I asked?"

"It just sounds complicated. Once you get the hang of it, it's easy."

"How come the announcers at Westminster never explained this while they were telling the TV audience about all the different breeds?"

"Because all the dogs that appear at Westminster are already champions. There isn't any competition for points toward championships at Westminster any more," Genna explained.

"Any more?" a confused Andrews injected.

"Forget Westminster. Do you want to understand a major or not?" she challenged.

At a nod from Andrews, she continued, a growing passion for her subject suppressing another tired yawn. "So, show points are based on the number of dogs competing for the win at a given show. Wins at large shows may bring an award of 3, 4 or 5 points. No show, regardless of the number of competitors entered, is worth more than 5 points. These points are added up to produce a championship, which takes

15 points. But, just winning a total of 15 points isn't enough to be named a champion. To qualify as a conformation champion with the AKC a canine must win at two shows of sufficient size within their breed and under two different judges to qualify as a major show [one that justifies an award of at least 3 points]. Show dogs pursue events in which they can acquire their major wins."

Andrews' face was about as clouded as when Jonathan explained his time travel plots. But he was a very good homicide detective, so he tried hard to put it all together.

"Understand now?" Genna queried.

"I think I understand. A major show is one with enough entries in a breed to produce at least a 3-point award to the winner."

"Right!" Genna beamed at him.

"And if Rusty isn't there, the number of entries will not be enough to produce a three point award!"

The topic of their discussion had finally gotten possession of the orange bear and was racing around Genna's chair in an attempt to evade Sky's pursuit. Amber and Blacky looked on from their aloof positions beneath the table.

"You got it in one."

Andrews muttered more to himself than to Genna: "Hence the expression that his absence would 'break the major'! Okay. But why would people be mad at you if he didn't show?"

"Because there are just enough but no entries to spare to make the major for Papillons. Many of the competitors may have decided to come to this show based on the chance of it being a major show. Their dogs may only need a major show. They're only able to justify the long drive to this show because of the chance of competing at a show, which will count as championship. For these four days of shows, there's supposed to be a major every day at least in dogs."

"Are they also showing cats?" Andrews decided to inject some foolishness into the conversation and was rewarded with a weak laugh from Genna.

"No, silly! Before a dog, well let's call it a canine, acquires its championship, they compete against their own sex for the points. Male canines are called dogs. Females are called bitches. So at this show today, there are just enough dogs or males to make a win worth 3 points or worth a major. But there aren't enough bitches or females entered to produce a major in Papillons on three of the four days of the show."

"Oh, my dear! Such language from a tired, old, Southern lady," Andrews teased.

"Now don't you start," Genna responded with spirit. "I just told you that it's just the show term for a female canine."

"I suppose I can look forward to a weekend of these colorful colloquial expressions from you and your two doggie friends who are due to stay with us?"

"Probably," Genna laughed. "Dog can mean both genders or just a male depending on whether we're speaking in general or about a specific one." And despite the smudges of gunk on the cuffs of her robe and pajama top and the stray pieces sticking out here and there from her rumpled hair, the mirth finally reached her eye.

"Shirley, Peggy and I will try to stick to plain English for your sake," she said. "I know you like them and I hope you enjoy dog showing and spending the weekend with them as much as the pack and I."

Beguiling Bundle: Death Takes Best of Breed

"Speaking of which," Andrews responded, as all four dogs around his feet exploded into motion and bounced into each other in their rush to be the first to one of the two major wins their dog needs for his get to the front door, "I believe the ladies are here now."

CHAPTER FIVE

Sylvia Spratt's thin fingers toyed with her limp bangs, pulling the ends of the left most fringes into her mouth and chewing on them in frustration. Her hair might have been a glorious red halo if she'd had time to shampoo it. Instead oil dulled the long flowing strands and her agitated state made her normally fair complexion look splotchy and washed out. The pale lashes and brows did nothing to help the green eyes which darted from coffee pot to fry pan as she attempted to adjust her plans for the day, fix breakfast for her sluggard of a husband, and struggle with the normal morning chore of getting Edward out of bed.

He'd been pleasant enough to Russell Harper. Harper had called just after 7:00 am to enlist Edward's aid in taking over handling duties on one of Harper's client's dogs. But then Edward had informed her he was going to get another hour of sleep and to call him at eight. Which she had! Five times! It was now 8:23 am, Edward was still in bed, and he would blame her for not keeping him to his schedule.

Beguiling Bundle: Death Takes Best of Breed

Sylvia twisted the strand of her bangs once more, and returned the ends to her mouth where she gnawed on them in time with the gurgles of the coffee pot. Heaven knows they needed the extra money the handling assignment would bring. And it was for the entire weekend, four shows. Russell had said he didn't want to tempt trouble with his back and would just like to have Edward take over for him for the weekend. The fees for four shows would really be a nice addition to their stretched budget. Edward was always reminding her of how tight their finances were, in spite of both of them holding jobs.

"*But did it have to be today?*" Sylvia fretted. She'd planned it so carefully. Edward worked the evening shift, didn't get home till 2:00 am, and generally slept till noon. He'd never have missed her. Friday was her normal day off so he would expect her to be doing chores. If she'd been delayed in returning, she'd have been able to cover her absence with a story of grocery shopping. In fact, she had a sack of non-perishables hidden in the kitchen, ready to transfer them to the trunk of their one car to cover that story.

But now!! He'd told Russell he'd be at the dog show site by 10:30 am. How was she going to get the car, or get to her appointment without him missing her? And asking questions she had no intentions of answering?

"Blast it, Sylvia!" Edward's accusatory voice snapped from the direction of the bedroom. "Can't you do one simple thing I ask?"

"I've called you five times already," Sylvia responded, trying to sound cool and nonchalant. The tension she already felt over the looming difficulties with concealing her plans caused her hand to shake and she spilled the coffee she tried to pour into his mug. "Your breakfast is on the table, all but your eggs. I'll fix them when you're ready."

"I'm ready now, woman! I'm already twenty-five minutes behind schedule thanks to you. Why didn't you get me up when I asked you to?" A medium everything figure followed the angry words into the kitchen. Edward Spratt was distinguishable by nothing: medium brown hair, eyes, height and build. The only thing remarkable at this point in time was the angry flush that gave some color to his otherwise bland complexion. He had not shaved, but even his day old beard was sparse and did little to add dimensions to the planes of his face.

"I take on extra work for the weekend to try and gain us a little extra money for all those things you're always wanting. All I asked of you was to wake me on time, and you can't even do that," the cranky man fumed as he stumbled to the table.

Sylvia considered challenging his unfair accusations, but decided it would just make her efforts to convince him to leave her with their only car that much more difficult. And she had to have that car. This morning of all mornings!

She slid a plate with eggs and bacon under his nose, repositioned the plate with toast and butter to within easy reach of his other hand, and tried to radiate a calm she did not feel!

Edward was fully involved with stuffing his mouth before Sylvia opened her campaign about the car.

"I suppose I can drop you and your gear off at the show and have plenty of time to do some chores before I need to pick you up again."

As she'd feared, he mumbled, "I need the car at the show. You'll have to do chores later."

"Well, that won't change for the rest of the weekend, and we'll run out of things to eat, before you run out of handling assignments," she countered. "I guess you can always take us out to eat." She tried to keep her voice light and teasing.

"There you go again," Edward responded, the disapproving frown he intended to display ruined by his non-stop chewing. "How many times must I stress we have to be very careful with our money!"

"Well, I'm off today but I have to work tomorrow. What do you want to do about groceries then? Do you want me to give you a list of groceries and have you get them tomorrow?" She knew he hated grocery shopping. He loved to instruct her in the judicious usage of coupons to conserve their meager income, over which he was always fretting. He hated to do it himself.

As expected, he responded, "You know I do not! I suppose I'll just have to make do at the show without a car, but you be sure you're through with everything and are back to get me by 3:00 pm. I've got to get back here and get ready to go to work by 6:00 pm."

Sylvia tried not to show the relief she felt.

"Well, do I have a dress-up outfit clean and pressed that I can wear at the dog show?" Edward growled by way of masking his concession regarding the car.

"I'll make sure," Sylvia said, swinging her long, red hair across her face as she gathered her plate and took it to the sink. The hair concealed any momentary satisfaction her facial expression might have shown at her successful manipulation of her husband over the car. *"Now,"* she thought, *"all I have to do is deal with the outcome of today's visit."*

CHAPTER SIX

Andrews smiled to himself, amused as always at the forcefulness exhibited by Genna's friend Peggy. Short in statue and tiny in build, Peggy Longbowker was a human whirlwind that impacted those around her out of all proportion to her physical size. She had been one of Andrews' favorite additions to his circle of friends since Jonathan had met and married Genna. He'd encountered Peggy on several occasions when Genna and her band of canines and cronies were on their way to or coming from a dog show. But today was his first time to be swept up into the swirling tides of activity created by her.

The diminutive dynamo had arrived before seven this morning in company with her more laid-back traveling companion Shirley Douglas. Peggy had assessed the situation with Twinkle's puppy, established a schedule that left Shirley at Heron's Rest to care for little Bunny since Shirley was not showing today, and had hustled Genna, Sky, Rusty

48

and himself off to the dog show with time to spare. And without increasing her breathing rate, to boot! As near as Andrews could tell, every hair of her frosted blond head was smoothly in place, and her sage green jacket and paisley printed skirt were flawlessly pressed and fashionably accented by matching green shoes. Even the lead on her little black and white Papillon was green. Only the soft, light brown of her eyes failed to adhere to her color scheme.

He was mildly surprised that Genna had allowed her houseguest to dictate the morning agenda, but delighted with the results. He'd even gotten into the spirit of things and meekly allowed himself to be ordered about in a final grooming of Sky and Rusty before the group had departed for the show.

Thanks to the human whirlwind, their party arrived at the show site and the correct ring with some time to spare before the beautifully groomed and highly excited butterflies held in the anxious hands of their party were due to compete.

Genna had exchanged her stained bathrobe and pjs for a medium blue, short-sleeved blazer over matching walking shorts. A matching flap concealed the legs of the shorts and was intended to make it resemble a short skirt. It didn't quite work that way, because Genna's foot tapped the grass with sufficient energy to keep the flap waving like a blue flag around her hips.

"Nervous?" Andrews sought to distract the dark haired woman. He'd managed five hours of uninterrupted sleep and was somewhat accustomed to having his sleep patterns interrupted by the demands of police work. He figured Genna had slept at most 90 minutes at a time, and had achieved only three of those sleep intervals.

"Grumpy," Genna admitted. "The coffee helped,

but sleep deprivation does not improve my disposition."

Early morning sunlight reflected off the light sprinkling of silver in Genna's dark hair and off the drops of moisture that dotted her forehead. Andrews could feel his lightweight tee shirt already sticking to his body in places, sweat showing as darkened splotches on the blue stripes, as the humidity made even the early morning temperatures uncomfortable.

"I can hold one of the boys," he offered.

Genna nodded her thanks. "They don't weigh twelve pounds between them, but they do get heavy," she added, handing Rusty to Andrews.

Sky took advantage of the handoff to snip at Rusty's ear and follow it up with a wet kiss on Genna's cheek at her soft reprimand. He was in his element. His large cupped ears trailed dark red and black fringes that tickled Genna's nose as they rotated like radar dishes to pick up the sounds carried on the humid morning air. His body seemed to absorb and reflect the suppressed excitement from the collected competitors and radiate back energy from every long, silky hair.

Peggy returned with a handful of rubber bands and long, white rectangles of stiff paper on which were printed large black numbers. "I picked up Sky's and Rusty's numbers. Shall I put Sky's on your arm for you?"

Genna obediently extended her left hand and wrist toward a stretched elastic band, which Peggy held open. Peggy's little bitch Muffin seemed unconcerned at being tucked under Peggy's arm like a purse. Peggy managed to slide a numbered piece of paper under the elastic and straighten it to face outward from Genna's left upper arm.

"Thanks," Genna acknowledged Peggy's help. "Now where is Spratt?"

50

Beguiling Bundle: Death Takes Best of Breed

"Well, if he didn't know about this handling assignment until this morning, probably rushing to get here," Peggy responded.

"If he doesn't hurry he won't have time to even gait Rusty before they have to go in the ring," Genna complained.

A large blue-and-white striped tent provided shade to a wide aisle between two rows of rings. The entrance to the rings and the judges' table in each ring were shaded from the sun, while the competitors and their dogs gaited out into the sunlight of the uncovered portion of the rings to show their stuff to the judges. Each of the ten rings was already in use with a different breed of dog being showcased.

Somewhere in the camping area behind the tents of vendors to Andrews' left, a lone dog's frustrated bark sounded. Under the tent, only the humans' voices compromised conversation. Although some 400 dogs representing about twenty different breeds were already concentrated around the ten exhibition rings at this beginning hour of the show, barking was rarely heard from these canine showmen. Further behind the vendors, grooming and official tents that surrounded the show rings, in campers and trailers around the site, dogs representing 143 breeds were gathered for this outdoor show at Jamestown Festival Park. Some 2000 dogs were entered, but the number in the campground probably amounted to more than double that count, as campers generally brought far more dogs than they entered, and spectators tended to bring their four-footed friends with them to watch the fun. The series of four outdoor shows drew competitors from all over the country to this flat, camping site on the banks of the James River.

Andrews was impressed with the restraint shown by the dogs. There was no lack of animation from the canine competitors; lots of tail wags, head motion, and butt sniffing if the handler allowed enough length of lead, but no barking. He wished he could say the same for all the human chatter!

"Rusty will do fine," Peggy responded. "Now, if you're okay for a bit, I want to talk to that woman with the Shih Tzu across the aisle and find out what she used for accenting that dog's coat. I've never seen such a bright contrast between black and white on a show coat. Muffin could sure use some of it. Hope she'll tell me!"

Andrews chuckled to himself at that thought. The woman with the Shih Tzu would tell or be smothered by the human cyclone until she did.

"I take it that this ring is where my granddogs will be shown," he said to Genna, nodding in the direction of the number 5 ring by which they were standing.

"Yes," Genna responded, "as soon as the Cavaliers are done."

"What time will that be?" Andrews was a bit leery of asking, given how agitated Genna was about the missing handler, but being a logical person he figured he needed facts in order to be of any help.

"Depends on when Cavaliers finish," Genna responded, her head swinging from side to side as she searched the surrounding aisles for some sign of the expected handler. "They just finished Winners Dog for Cavaliers. Papillons are up next. Rusty is entered in 12 to 18 month dogs and there aren't any younger puppy classes."

"Excuse me!" Andrews teased. "I thought you agreed to stick to English for the sake of this poor neophyte!" He was rewarded with a slight smile on Genna's face.

"Sorry," Genna said. "Time at dog shows is a bit difficult to correlate with your watch. Groups of breeds are listed in order of starting time. But after that, the judging proceeds in a set fashion of classes within each breed, and a judging of the second breed listed in a group doesn't begin until all the classes in the previous breed have been judged."

"And the significant of Winners Dog is..." Andrews prompted.

"*Winners Dog* signifies that a major segment of the judging of Cavaliers is done. Non-champions in all breeds are judged in a series of classes, and the order of the classes is a fixed sequence. First, *Puppy-dog* which may or may not be divided into 6-9 months, 9-12 months, 12-18 months classes; then, *Bred-by-Exhibitor* dog, then *American Bred dog* [if any dog], then *Open Dog,* then the first place winners of each of the classes [if all exist] compete for *Winners Dog.* You repeat the procedure all over again for the bitches."

In spite of exposure to Genna's doggie friends during previous visits, Andrews still experienced a slight shock when neatly attired ladies in smart suits and elegantly coffered hair ran around bragging loudly that they had 'taken Winners Bitch.'

"And then the champions go in for competition to determine the one who will represent the breed in the groups. Winners Dog and Winners Bitch also compete in the Breed ring," Genna continued, and "then it's Rusty's turn. Because there are no other puppies entered, his class of 12-18 month dog will be the first in the ring for Papillons. But that won't happen until the judge finishes with judging Cavaliers. And it's hard to put a clock time on exactly how long that will take."

Genna's attention returned to an anxious searching of the aisles and the tempo of her foot tapping increased in proportion to her frustration.

As the classes for Cavaliers were completed,

53

Jean C. Keating

other competitors, who held one or more of the tiny, long-coated and butterfly-eared Papillons, took the places around the ring. The Paps' humans greeted each other and engaged in light conversation, or ignored each other entirely, depending on past feelings of friendship or rivalry.

"Genna," a soft voice whispered from behind. Genna turned so abruptly that Sky's long coat caught briefly on Andrews' finger. The thin figure in a russet pants suit clutched another striking black-and-white Papillon against her chest with one hand and threw her other around Genna in an affectionate greeting. Marge Jenkins was a fellow competitor and Papillon friend of many years.

"Oh, hello Marge! And how is Mr. Pepper this morning?" Genna's voice was pitched slightly higher as she smiled broadly at Marge's dog; Mr. Pepper wagged his tail harder at the sound of his name.

"Pepper is fine, but I'm about as nervous as you look," Marge said. "What's up? You don't look very pleased this morning." Marge reached to scratch Sky lightly under his chin, a move that made the little dog wiggle with delight

"The rescue I'm fostering presented me with a puppy last night that can't nurse. He's got a hare lip and a slight break in the palate in the front, so he can't achieve suction. He's a little fighter, though, and I've been trying to feed him every two hours," Genna explained. "You don't get much sleep when you're feeding a little puppy every two hours."

"Don't I know it!" Marge said. "I struggled and failed to save the litter mate to Pepper. You don't often succeed in tubing a fading puppy either. I certainly know how that goes. And you're anxious to get home," Marge continued.

"Actually Shirley Douglas is at my house looking after things, so I'm not pushed to get home," Genna

54

replied.

"I thought Shirley was entered."

"Not today. She doesn't like this judge. He doesn't like solid headed Papillons according to Shirley," Genna explained. "No, it's not the puppy that has me climbing the walls right now. My frustration is with a missing handler. I wanted to enjoy showing Sky without the worry of switching off from one dog to the other, among other things. So I hired Russell Harper to show Rusty for the weekend."

"Oh, that's right! I saw in the program that he was showing Rusty," Marge acknowledged. "Harper does a great job with the young toys. He really seems to have a calming touch with them. Not even you will be able to find fault with his gentleness with Rusty."

"It would have been great," Genna said, "but Harper called early this morning, said he was having trouble standing — the old problem with his lower back. Anyway when he heard about the difficulty with Twinkle's puppy, he said he'd arrange for Edward Spratt to take over for him. Russell didn't call me back, so I assumed he'd made the arrangements. But now Spratt isn't here."

Marge nodded in sympathy, Pepper tried to lean over and give the anxious human a kiss, and Sky registered a jealous complaint at such an act of familiarity with his human.

Genna grumbled on as she continued to scan the increasing crowd of people gathering around the show rings. "They're judging winners bitch in Cavaliers now, and there are only four champions in breed so it won't take long. Papillons are next, and Rusty's in the first class. Drat the man! I wanted him to have time to at least gait Rusty outside the ring before they have to go in."

She bumped into Andrews as she fidgeted about, and only then seemed to remember her manners.

"Oh, Marge," Genna put one arm around the older man's shoulder, "excuse my manners. You remember my Uncle Kevin I'm sure. You met him at the Richmond show."

"'Course I do," Marge nodded and smiled at Andrews. "As I recall, you're a police detective. Hope this is pleasure and not business," she teased.

"Well," Andrews hedged. "I'm not certain how much pleasure I'm finding at being chief fluffer and dryer of these two little imps, but the day is young yet."

"Well, you've done a grand job of bathing assistant," Marge said. "Sky and Rusty look just beautiful, as usual."

The silky coat of red-and-white squirmed in Genna's arms at the sound of his name and Rusty did his best to squirm out of Andrews' grasp in a quickly aborted attempt to lick Marge's nose.

"I'd offer to show Rusty for you, but with Mr. Pepper entered..." Marge continued.

"Oh, I can show him myself if I have to," Genna injected, frustration evident in her tone. "I just didn't want to. I'd rather the judge see me for the first time when I go in the Breed ring with Sky, not feel that he's already given me something with Rusty and maybe not want to pick Sky."

Andrews was suddenly bumped aside by a stocky figure which pushed his way to Genna's side. Andrews first thought was that he looked like a high-class hood. His gray shirt over black slacks seemed to match his gray-streaked mustache and beard. Andrews was about to comment on his rudeness, when the man spoke to Genna.

"I was afraid I'd miss your show. Did I make it in time? Is this your dog?"

Andrews quickly decided against making any

56

comments to the man. The look of aggravation on Genna's face strongly suggested that she would take care of correcting his manners in her own way.

Genna managed to contain her aggravation. "Hello, Mr. Swinson. I didn't expect to see you before Tuesday."

Andrews chuckled to himself. If he was any good at reading emotions on people, and he thought he could read Genna fairly well after three years of knowing her, not only did she not expect to see Stinson, she didn't want to see him.

"Well, after I heard you mention yesterday that you'd be busy this weekend showing your dogs, I figured I might just come out and see the fun and cheer you on," the hairy faced man said. "Since I have to stay in town until Tuesday to conclude my business with NASA, I thought I'd check out this event. It seems to be the big news in these parts for the weekend. I've seen it advertised on the local TV and in the local paper."

"That's very nice of you." Genna's stern tone belied the statement as she turned Swinson's attention to Marge and Pepper. "This is my friend Marge Jenkins and her dog Pepper." She brushed Swinson's body back a step with her free hand to include Andrews in the grouping Swinson had disturbed before continuing. "And this is my uncle, Kevin Andrews. Uncle Kevin, Marge, this is Carlton Swinson, the president of CS Industries, the developers of the new tracking system under contract with NASA. He's just delivered the prototypes for testing."

Marge voiced an appropriate greeting. The two men shook hands. Swinson attempted to pat Sky, but the tiny bundle of fur in Genna's arms jerked his head out of the way.

Genna shifted a shoulder to move the tiny

57

champion out of the big man's reach. "I'm afraid Sky is very focused on his job right now, that of performing at his best in the ring. He's not much for visiting before a show."

Andrews hoped Genna's nose didn't grow longer for the lie. And he hoped that Swinson had not witnessed Sky's warm response to Marge earlier. In truth, Sky could probably care less. Genna didn't appreciate strangers messing up Sky's ears and coat before a show, but Swinson was too unaware of proper show etiquette to know that his behavior was rude.

Now Andrews remembered. Genna had described this man as a human Schnauzer. He hoped the man had better sense than to have come to the show to continue his campaign to have Genna work on the prototypes he'd delivered. Hopefully his brain wasn't as rock-solid as the muscles that stretched his gray tee.

"I also wondered if I could be of any help with your validating the performance stats on the star tracker. I know you'll be rushed with these little contests. I know dealing with definitions of quadrants in the analysis is tricky and I'll be glad to furnish you with our analysis to help shorten your effort. You know, leave you more time for the little doggies."

Andrews almost felt sorry for the stupid fool. Almost! The man had pushed his way into their midst. And was now figuratively digging a very large hole for himself.

"Your executive summary is all you're allowed to submit with the prototype," Genna's tone was cold, professional, cutting. Andrews figured the 'little doggies' comment alone was going to cost this man at least the entire time she'd given herself to respond on his project. Any pity she might have had for his financial troubles had just been erased.

"I utilize haversines to evaluate astronomical orientation anyway, so quadrants aren't an issue. I'm not likely to have difficulty in knowing up from down."

Swinson looked puzzled by that statement. Genna ignored him.

"Ah," Genna alerted to a rapidly moving figure headed in her direction. A young man, dressed neatly in a navy blazer over tan pants said something to Peggy, followed the direction of Peggy's finger pointed at Genna, and walked rapidly toward them.

"You'll have to excuse me. I have to talk with Rusty's handler."

CHAPTER SEVEN

"I'm so sorry to be late," the young man said to Genna as he closed the remaining gap between them. Anxiety made his voice raspy as he continued. "Russell Harper only called me this morning. He said he had a conflict and asked me to help. He said he'd talked with you and explained."

Andrews briefly considered what a group of witnesses would articulate if called upon to describe the figure. Except for the traditional navy and tan casual-business attire, the young man was remarkable for having nothing remarkable as to height, build, coloring, except perhaps for the level of anxiety he was showing.

Finally realizing that he had started in the middle of a conversation, the figure continued, "Oh, I'm Edward Spratt. I guess I should have introduced myself first. Is this your puppy?" He looked appreciatively at the dog Genna held in her arms.

"No." Genna responded gruffly in the midst of a

60

long exhale. Some of her tensions seemed to ease with the arrival of Edward. "This is my champion, Sky." Turning slightly to make it easier for Edward to see Andrews and the dog he held, she added, "This is little Rusty."

"Do you know his number?" Edward asked as he reached to take the squirming tri-colored bundle from Andrews.

Peggy came up behind him and answered before Andrews or Genna could. "I've picked it up already," she said, pulling another large printed square of cardboard from her pocket and waving it at Edward. "Stick your arm out."

Peggy quickly slipped the entry number and rubber band over Edward's navy blazer sleeve, securing it in place on Edward's left upper arm as Genna introduced him to Peggy, Marge, Andrews and with less enthusiasm, to Swinson.

"The breed class for Cavaliers is in the ring now. There are only four specials. Paps are next and Rusty's class is first," Genna chided.

"Okay. Let me just see how he gaits for me down the side of the aisle here. We'll be right back."

Swinson looked totally confused, and glanced at Andrews for help.

"Don't ask me what they just said," Andrews responded to his unspoken question. "They speak in code!"

Genna glared at them both. Taking pity on the unwelcome one in their midst, Andrews continued in a whisper, "Somehow that means something to these dog people about the time remaining before Rusty has to go in the ring."

Rusty seemed confused at first on whether to obey the signals of the lead from this strange man who'd so abruptly taken him from Andrews and set him on the ground. He balked and fought to stay

61

near Genna. He made several half-circles before finally walking on four legs beside the young handler. Edward pulled a small piece of something from his pocket and waved it in front of Rusty's nose, encouraging him to walk in the direction Edward wanted to go. The two completed a jerky walk-away, a coordinated turn, and a smooth return. Edward praised the little dog before lifting his head to smile at Genna.

"Rusty doesn't much care for liver, but he's a sucker for a little piece of hot dog." Genna's voice was decidedly friendlier as she pulled some small red pieces from a bait bag inside her own pocket and handed them to Edward.

All four of the little butterfly dogs responded to the smell emanating from Genna's treasure. Mr. Pepper and Muffin went into hyper alert mode, ears up and cupped forward and tails beating a faster tattoo. Sky tried to snag a piece as it passed by his nose. Rusty lunged on two legs in his attempt to follow the hot dog pieces being transferred between the humans.

"Thanks." Edward nodded, returning the liver treat to his pocket and reaching for the offered hot dog pieces. "We'll get along just fine, I think."

In the ring beside them, the judge made his picks of the Cavaliers, and was passing out the ribbons, purple to the tri-colored dog picked for Breed and a blue-and-white and a red-and-white to the ruby winners bitch.

The Cavalier handlers and their dogs exited the ring, two with happy faces and four more with the fixed smiles of determined sportsmen.

"Papillon, 12-18 month puppy dog." a second man inside the ring with the judge consulted his program and announced in a booming voice.

"That's us," Edward said and walked hurriedly

toward the entrance to ring #5. He and Rusty were second in line as three pairs of competitors took their places inside the show ring.

Genna turned her back on Swinson and Andrews and moved adjacent to the entrance to the ring to get a clear view of the competitors.

"Excuse me," Marge said to the two men and to Peggy. "I'd better join Genna. Pepper and I are in bred-by."

Swinson's puzzled look intensified. It brought a soft laugh from Andrews. "As I was saying, they have a language of their own. They understand what they mean, and I just nod and try not to look as uninformed as I feel."

"So, you live here in Williamsburg, also?" Swinson seemed determined to carry on a conversation instead of watching the dogs in the ring and received a wilting look from Peggy.

"No," Andrews whispered. "In Richmond! I work for the city." He downplayed his occupation. Genna's agitation over this man's intrusion with his personal agenda at ring side was already excessive. Andrews didn't want the usual questions at the mention of his profession. Before Peggy could favor them both with a blistering comment about inattention to Rusty's performance, he continued in a whisper, "I came down to spend the holiday weekend with my family and see my granddogs perform."

He leaned over to distract Peggy with a dog-related query. "All those Cavaliers have hairy feet. Why did I have to clip Rusty's and Sky's this morning?"

"Different breeds, different standards," Peggy responded. "Furnishings are considered very important in Cavaliers, but are unacceptable on a Pap."

Swinson kept his eyes on Genna, who was

63

focused on the action taking place in the ring. But he could not keep his mouth shut or his focus on the dogs and the show.

"I didn't mean to anger her," Swinson babbled. "The infrared scanner was made by another contractor. My company was responsible for the star tracker and for assembling the two instruments into the complete payload. And I've had no end of trouble with the people who worked putting them together I might add."

The hefty company president paid no attention to the dirty looks he was getting from Peggy or to the pained expression on Andrews' face.

He continued to jabber nervously as he stared at Genna who gave no indication that she knew he was alive. "Despite instructions to the contrary, one heavy smoker kept puffing away on a cigarette around the infrared seeker, and I didn't know he was there until he focused his light into the viewer and it worked in spite of all that smoke. No thanks to the fool."

Peggy bumped against the talkative intruder and interrupted Swinson's line of conversation with a side comment to Andrews. "Rusty should have this class, unless the judge is blind to the bad rear on the first dog and the awful top line on the lat one."

"The words are English; it's the way they're used that doesn't make sense," he teased. His joke drew the hint of a smile from Peggy, but Swinson didn't appear to notice.

When Swinson opened his mouth to continue his non-dog related monologue, Andrews tried to stop his line of conversation. "Don't worry about your deadlines," Andrews added, "Genna will review your summary and provide the needed evaluations by the time she promised. I may not get my dinner with everything that is going on, but you'll get your evaluation summary."

Beguiling Bundle: Death Takes Best of Breed

Swinson continued to focus only on Genna, who now began to smile broadly, as the judge moved Rusty and his handler to the front of the line of the three pairs in the ring. Marge reached over to pat Genna on the shoulder. The judge sent the competitors around the ring again, before pointing his finger at Rusty signifying the awarding of first place to him in 12 to 18 month puppy class.

"Yes," Peggy cheered and reached over to squeeze Andrews' arm.

Marge gave Genna a quick hug while the judge's choices lined up in front of markers at the side of the ring signifying their ranking, and Edward accepted the blue ribbon handed him by the judge. "He's on his way. Let's hope Pepper does as well."

She put her beautiful black-and-white dog on the ground and adjusted the length of the lead in her left hand in preparation for entry into the ring for the next class as Rusty and the other two puppies and their handlers exited.

Swinson fidgeted. "Do you know where I can get a cup of coffee? It seems like breakfast was a long time ago."

"Tell me about it!" Andrews pointed in the direction of several stands to their left. "I think several of the vendors over there would have some."

After asking Andrews if he'd like anything and receiving a negative reply, the snubbed man took one last glance in Genna's direction before wandering off toward the food booths."

For a brief interval Andrews considered following him. Coffee helped suppress his hunger. It had been a long time since breakfast. He was beginning to feel a bit empty. He reined himself in sharply, reminding himself of how hard it had been to lose the thirty odd pounds. He certainly didn't want to gain it back. "Should have brought a snack," he mumbled.

The master organizer and human dynamo beside him quickly pulled a plastic bag out of her purse, which didn't look large enough to carry her keys. Passing it to Andrews, she said, "Here's the apple you're supposed to have this morning. You stay away from those vendors!"

He didn't know whether to be annoyed at her bossiness or grateful for her forethought. He settled for a chuckle and a simple thank you.

Marge came out of the ring with a blue ribbon for her efforts and a larger group of six Papillons took their place in the ring. The areas around the rings were filling rapidly with noisy humans and beautiful dogs of many breeds. Peggy and Andrews moved up to stand directly behind Marge and Genna near the entrance to the Papillon ring. The two discussed the six dogs now exhibiting in the ring; each picked a different winner of this open dog class from the one actually awarded the blue ribbon by the judge. Then it was time for the three class winners to reenter the ring for competition for Winners dog and the points, or so Peggy explained.

Marge and Genna exchanged wishes for good luck, and Marge with Pepper and Edward with Rusty joined the judge's pick for open dog in the ring to compete for Winners dog.

Andrews stepped into the space left by Marge, taking advantage of Swinson's departure to satisfy his curiosity. Sky fretted in Genna's arms and had to be quieted.

"Has he gone?" Genna snipped.

"Maybe only to get coffee," Andrews replied. "What is a haversine? Something you dreamed up on the spot to make him more nervous than he was already?"

"No. Ordinary trig functions focus on quadrants. Haversines focus on hemispheres. Makes the job half as difficult, you might say and is useful in dealing with special orientation. It's my ace in the hole for evaluating his prototype and getting a report back to NASA by Tuesday, in spite of Bunny's problems, four dog shows, and enjoying my guests."

"I get the feeling you don't like this fellow."

"I thought he was a bit pushy at the NASA meeting, but not nearly as maddening as John Hunter who I detest. Mostly I felt sorry for him for getting his company into such a mess with cash flow. I wanted to help and it annoyed me at the same time that he was making me feel guilty. But he really pushed my button when he showed up here to intrude on my time with friends and dogs at this show."

Genna kept her voice low while she struggled with an increasingly excitable Sky. The small furball twisted in her arms, trying to get down, trying to lick Andrews' face, most of all trying to join the fun in the ring.

The judge focused his attention on Edward and Rusty as they gaited once more around the ring.

Genna turned her full attention to Rusty. She held her breath, clenched her teeth, and muttered softly, "Oh, stop pulling back, Baby. You've got a beautiful front. Reach for it."

The monologue meant about as much to Andrews as had Genna's explanation of haversines. "Attending dog shows with you is an exercise in frustration. Half the time I don't know whether you're speaking English or some crazy mumbo jumbo."

He thought Genna wasn't listening, but she smiled at him and countered, "Serves you right. I feel the same when you start talking about law enforcement rules and restrictions. Somehow I think justice for the victims and innocents gets trampled in an obsession to protect the guilty."

Suddenly, Genna squeezed Sky so tightly he

uttered a small squeal.

"Now what?"

"The handler on the open dog is crowding Rusty to make him spook."

Andrews focused sharply on the figures in the ring close to Rusty in time to see Edward step smoothly between Rusty and a bigger dog behind him. The other dog was attempting to sniff Rusty's butt.

"Ha!" Genna chirped, probably loud enough to be heard by the people inside the ring. She continued in a whisper to Andrews, "Russell was right. Young Edward knows his stuff. He's positioned himself to protect Rusty."

"I thought this was supposed to be fun and good sportsmanship," Andrews said.

"There's a three-point major at stake here." Genna's square jaw stuck out so far that Sky's upwardly moving head collided with it, as the excited little bundle of red and white fur picked up his human's agitation. "Focused, furious, and frustrating, but not always fun! That dratted man does it all the time."

"Ha! The judge caught him at it." Genna's face went from tense and frowning to a glowing smile, as the judge pointed to little Rusty. Edward scooped up his young charge, praised him as the two moved to the side of the ring in front of a sign that was lettered WINNERS.

A young woman in an orange pantsuit pushed by Andrews with a hurried apology and rushed into the ring to take her place in line with Marge and the handler that had been the focus of Genna's frustration.

"Sorry," Andrews muttered as the orange streak went by. Then to Genna he continued, "wasn't she in the ring before?"

"She came in second in puppy class so now she's eligible to compete for Reserve."

Andrews shook his head. "I'm sorry I asked." It was all too confusing for him. "I'm getting hungry. When is this finished?"

"Oh, you are not hungry. Peggy brought a snack for you. Rusty just took his first major. Your grandson is major pointed! This is fun."

"Oh, now it's fun," Andrews mocked. "A few seconds ago you were ready to stomp that fellow in the blue suit."

"The judge did it for me." Genna balanced Sky in one hand, whispered to him that his son was now major-pointed, and reached to squeeze Andrews' upper arm with her other hand.

In the ring, the judge pointed to Marge who moved off with Pepper to stand beside Rusty and Edward. Blue suit and orange blur exited the ring with their dogs. Genna smiled sweetly at blue suit's sour frown.

"Is it Sky's turn yet?" Andrews certainly hoped so. Thoughts of food were gaining in importance.

"No. First the girls are judged."

Andrews reluctantly opened the plastic bag Peggy had given him, removed a piece of apple, and bit down on this less than satisfactory substitute for the hamburger he was beginning to crave.

Edward exited the ring with a purple ribbon in his hand, an excited Rusty in his arms, and a smile of wattage sufficient to have illuminated Andrews' entire house.

"I thought we'd blown it on the far turn," he said. "Rusty was holding back, threatening to pull sideways. But we made it."

All signs of tension between the young man and Genna were gone. They chatted away with all the comfort and mutual understanding of long-time

69

friends. Andrews drolly smirked to himself, *"It is truly amazing what one little strip of purple ribbon can do."*

"That handler on the open dog was crowding you, and I was afraid Rusty would spook at the strange dog sniffing his rump," Genna admitted.

"Oh, he's always doing that. I don't know his name, but he's got a nasty reputation of always trying something. I just turned Rusty the other way and got between them until they stopped and set up and then I moved Rusty away from them."

The three stood for more long minutes discussing the Papillons being paraded in the ring, or rather Andrews listened while Genna and Edward did the discussing. Somewhere in all the swirling of human and canine bodies in and out of the ring, Peggy and Muffin took their turn, but were disappointed to receive only a yellow ribbon. Finally another purple ribbon was awarded to a dainty woman dressed in a lavender suit. Her black, tan and white dog sported a purple lead, and Andrews wondered briefly if females bought their outfits to match the dog's lead color or found leads to match their outfits.

The woman smiled sweetly at the judge, and stashed the ribbon in her pocket.

"This judge is lining up the champions in numerical order of their entry number. Sorry, but it looks like Sky and I will be directly in front of you and Rusty," Genna whispered at Edward, who nodded his understanding.

At least, Andrews hoped it meant something to Edward, because it meant nothing to him. What did pique his interest was another spectator who wandered by with a fully loaded hamburger in his hand. The tantalizing smell of caramelized onions heavy in the wind sent all sorts of diet-destructive messages to his brain. But Sky and Genna at last

70

moved to enter the ring and he knew he couldn't immediately pursue his interest in food.

Three other Papillons with their handlers joined Marge, Genna and Edward in the ring. The three finally got themselves sorted out in ascending order of their show numbers directly in front of Genna. Edward and Rusty lined up behind Genna and the lady in purple positioned herself at the end of the line. At the judge's signal, the six canine-human pairs began a group walk around the ring.

Peggy and Muffin were crowded against Andrews as more and more spectators collected at ring side, many with little black and white dogs with pushed in noses. Andrews was surprised to see that Genna was having trouble getting Sky to walk a straight line. Rusty was giving Edward an equal amount of trouble as he rushed ahead trying to get closer to Genna and Sky.

Sky suddenly darted in front of Genna, causing her to stumble over her feet or him and nearly fall. Rusty jerked forward and Edward crumpled face down on the grass of the ring. Genna's attempts to right herself and Sky were complicated by Rusty's appearance at her knee, his lead dangling loose, his front paws frantically digging at her leg.

The crowd around the ring gave a collective gasp of surprise as they suddenly realized Edward was not moving.

CHAPTER EIGHT

Genna sat on a wooden bench between two of the food vendors' tents, her elbows on the rough picnic table in front of her and her head in her hands. She was thankful for the clouds, which provided an overcast to block the strong spring sunlight, but she shivered despite the heat.

"I can't believe he's dead!" she repeated for about the sixth time.

Sky and Rusty snuggled close to her on one side, calm now and for once not playing a one-upmanship game with each other. Sky's tiny body was warm and comforting pressed against Genna's hip on the seat of the picnic table. But it was Andrews' steady shoulder on her other side that kept her more or less upright.

Lack of sleep and shock dulled her memory of the last forty minutes, but the appalling sequence of events was still overwhelming. She'd been confused and trying to deal with Rusty as well as a very fractious Sky, not realizing why Edward was face-down in the grass of the show ring. She dimly remembered sharp and confusing instructions from the steward and the judge, and Andrews in the ring, flashing his badge, taking charge and shouting the judge, steward and the AKC representative into submission. Disjoined snapshots of scenes remained: Andrews checking Edward's neck for any sign of what? Life? Andrews voice carrying over all the din, ordering everyone back, calling for police back-up, marshalling the existing kennel club help to chores they'd never expected to deal with, ordering the roads out of the show site closed, banning anyone leaving the site.

Now yellow tape blocked off show ring #5, and a mob of men and women in uniforms swarmed the site where Edward and Genna had paraded their dogs and where Edward had fallen a short while before. Around them, in other rings, a very subdued crowd of people and nervous dogs tried to carry on as though everything was normal. The scarcity of excited human voices as well as the heightened activity around ring #5 belied the attempt.

"Why would anyone want to kill Edward?" Genna's voice cracked. "I mean the man was always late. Frustrating! Hardly a reason to kill him!"

Andrews put his arms around her shoulders. Sky's attempt to plant a sloppy kiss on Genna's cheek missed and wet Andrews' hand instead.

"I suppose it was deliberate," she added.

"Do people usually bring high powered rifles with silencers to the dog shows you frequent?" Andrews replied reasonably.

Genna tried to focus, to force her mind to make some sense out of the unthinkable! Her head came up as some disturbing ideas began to stir in her sleepy, stressed-out brain.

"Well, someone had to plan for this then. But how would anyone have known he'd be here?

Edward, I mean! I might have told a few people that Russell would be handling for me today, and anyone could have found that out by reading the show catalog or checking the web site, but that wouldn't have been available until an hour before this show started. And only a handful of people could have known that Edward Spratt was replacing Russell, so how could anyone have planned ahead and brought a rifle to the show."

Genna babbled on without noting the tense look on Andrews' face, which her ramblings had generated.

Andrews tried to keep his voice calm. "What catalog and what web site?"

"Oh, these little orange booklets that a lot of people of carrying around." Genna waved a hand at a passing woman who was consulting a thin paperbound book as she walked. "That's a show catalogue for today's show. It describes the entire list of entries. It gives the ring times and ring locations for each entry, but also the dog's name, parents, age, owner, breeder, and who is showing the dog. Rusty's name is in there and the number that Rusty's handler was . . . will be . . . whatever . . . wearing, but it shows Russell's name as his agent or handler. Except for Russell, you, me, I guess Jonathan, Peggy, Shirley, and Marge no one knew Edward would be handling Rusty in that ring. And his wife, of course! But none of us knew before early this morning. Unless you could say that Russell knew he was going to ask him. So how could someone have planned to kill Edward here?"

Peggy approached the picnic table in time to hear her name being used. Muffin, for once, was using her dainty little legs to walk at Peggy's side. The human whirlwind's hands were full with a boxed carryall piled high with three drink containers and numerous wrapped parcels of food from which enticing odors were apparent as were the greasy spots already showing through the paper.

"And just what have I done now?" the tiny woman asked.

"You have just been put on Genna's list of murder suspects," Andrews tried to keep it light. His eyes were bright with interest in the food being placed under his nose. The keenness of his gaze was akin to that of a whippet's focus on the lure on a tracking course.

"I did not," Genna responded. "And I hope you didn't get a burger for Uncle Kevin. It's the worst thing he can eat with his diet."

Andrews tried to indicate his agreement with making an exception, but Peggy and Genna went right on dictating his menu without allowing him any input.

"I got him crab cakes and had them hold the bun. He's cool!"

Two little Papillon heads appeared at the edge of the table as Sky and Rusty rushed to offer their assistance with any morsel of fast food that Andrews or anyone else didn't want. Muffin was trying her best to jump up on the seat of the table to get in on the fun.

"Great," Genna said, "since we can't get home any time soon, that will at least keep Uncle Kevin from getting too hungry and eating the wrong things."

"And just how did my name get linked with what happened to Edward?" Peggy asked.

"I was just saying to Uncle Kevin that very few people even knew Edward would be showing Rusty today. Only a few of us knew he'd be here and not Russell. And we only knew early this morning. I was explaining that the catalog and the web site maintained by the show superintendent would show

Russell as the handler." Genna succumbed to the smell of a warm, greasy hamburger in front of her, opened the paper, and took a big bite. She mumbled on with her mouth full. "So how would anyone have time to plan ahead, to bring a rifle and silencer with them to the show? It doesn't make sense!"

"Diet coke?" Andrews asked, as he pulled the nearest drink container toward him. At Peggy's affirmative nod, he jabbed a straw through the opening in the lid. Opening the package Peggy handed him, he was rewarded with two plump looking crab cakes, which he speedily proceeded to consume.

"What web site?" Andrews returned to the conversation he and Genna had been sharing before Peggy's reappearance.

Genna took a moment to refocus her attention from her savory hamburger, which she was trying to eat in spite of two intrusive Papillon noses jostling her wrists for handouts.

"Oh, the show program! Well, the show superintendent maintains a web site on which the show entries with all the information I described is posted. Just before the show started this morning, the web site was open to anyone who wished to view it. So anyone could have read that Russell was going to be showing Rusty in ring #5 at such and such approximate time on this date."

"But there'd be no mention of Edward?" Andrews probed. "Or would the web site have been amended this morning to reflect the change?"

"No. Neither the web site nor the catalogue would have been available until about an hour before the show. And both would show Russell Harper as the handler. Neither would have ever mentioned Edward Spratt's name. That's why it doesn't make sense anyone would have known Edward would be here except for the few of us really."

Andrews' attention to details did not diminish his enjoyment of his meal. He mumbled his queries as he finished the last scrap of his second crab cake.

"But someone had to produce the catalogue and upload the web site. So someone had to know that Harper would be showing Rusty today. But few people, mostly the handful of people connected with Heron's Rest, knew that Spratt would be involved. I need to relay this information to Lt. Red who's in charge of this investigation. You ladies sit tight. I'll be back shortly."

He took a long pull on his diet drink, before prying himself off the bench and heading off in the direction of the cluster of uniformed figures swarming around ring #5.

Peggy gave up trying to keep Muffin's tiny muzzle out of her food and gave her the last scraps of her burger. "I'll be sorry for that tonight. I'll be doing a butt bath by dark."

Genna nodded in agreement. Greasy people food led to loose stools which messed up flowing white feathering down the back of Papillon's legs which led to, at the least, a bath to the dog's back end.

"We need to call Shirley ..." Genna began, but was interrupted by Peggy's nod.

"Already did! Tina is doing fine and has gained a tiny bit. Bunny isn't losing any, is still fussing about wanting his mom but drinking the formula fine. Jonathan called again and said he'd call you back tonight."

"I already called him while you were getting food. If I interrupted him at a bad time, he didn't say so. He asked if I wanted him to come right home, and I told him Uncle Kevin and I, along with Shirley and you, could handle things. I just needed to hear his

77

voice." Genna reached to pull Sky and Rusty into a loose embrace, shivering with disbelief at the events of the day.

The crowd had kept their distance while Andrews sat at Genna's side, perhaps fearing to get drawn into the official investigations. People and dogs were clustered tightly around but at a distance, close enough to hear, curious as a hunting pack to know what was being said. But the group kept a safe distance so as to beat a hasty retreat at the first sign that any official might want to question them. With Andrews' departure, the caution seemed to vanish, and many of the show people came over to hug Peggy or Genna and to say a few words of comfort or sympathy.

One asked if Genna would try to finish showing Rusty and Sky when the hastily rescheduled breed judging for Paps took place in a substitute ring. Genna's reaction was part horror at anything remotely resembling a retake of the events of the last hour and partly frustration as she spotted Carlton Swinson pushing his way through the crowds surrounding her and heading in her direction.

"Oh, God! I can't," she responded.

Peggy glanced quickly in the direction of Genna's line of sight and noted Swinson's imminent reappearance. She had half risen from her seat to head Swinson off, when another man separated himself from a large mastiff that was doing his best to macramé his lead around the man's boots, and called to Genna in a cheerful voice. His tight fitting jeans were nearly new and carefully pressed. A brief encounter of fabric with the inside of the mastiff's drooling jaw left a dark stain on the outer knee of one leg.

"Hi, Partner. I've been looking all over for you."

Genna turned toward the newest claim on her

attention. "Oh, for goodness sakes. Paul, what are you doing here?"

A bright smile softened the rugged face of the newcomer. Laugh lines at the eyes and mouth indicated that he might be a bit older than the boyish, solid body straining the seams of his red-plaid shirt would have otherwise suggested.

"Trying to find you," he replied as his long stride brought him to the side of the table where Genna and Peggy were packing away the paper and cups from their lunch. "You sounded a bit put out with me last night, so I thought I'd come by and see how you and the dogs were getting on, and apologize for not being there to handle things with Hunter yesterday."

"Did you see Swinson?" Genna asked. She turned her head to check the spot where she'd just seen Swinson but found he was no longer in sight.

"The head of CS? What's he doing here?"

"Probably the same as you're considering! Trying to push me about validating the star tracker and scanner. He was headed this way just as you arrived. And before you say anything else, let me warn you ..." Genna began huffily.

As though responding to Genna's frustration, Sky had gone into defense mode, placing his front feet and upper body on the table and growling softly at the new arrival. Rusty was vacillating between backing his sire up in his defense posture and curling against Genna for reassurance.

"Not I." The grin on the man's face widened, accentuating a dimple in his square chin. "I know better! Besides, I wouldn't want to challenge your defenders there," he continued, nodding at Sky and Rusty.

Genna drew Sky closer to her, tightened her hold on Rusty, and belatedly remembered her manners.

"I'm sorry. Things seem to be coming at me too

79

fast this morning."

"Peggy, this is my boss Paul Carter."

"Paul, this is my friend Peggy Longbowker and her little Papillon Muffin."

The two exchanged the normal social pleasantries while Genna continued to make soothing noises to her two dogs.

"This show seems to be the big area event for the weekend, and I just thought I'd swing by, say hello, tell you thanks for handling things yesterday, and maybe learn a little bit of what fascinates you so about dog shows," Paul explained. He included the two women and three dogs in his bright smile.

Andrews reappeared, a thin man in a dark gray suit by his side. The younger man's long oval face was far less lined than Andrews' but tightness around his warm, brown eyes already showed the stress of dealing with this recent violence. Andrews introduced him all around as Lt. Charles Red of the James City County Police Department. Genna, in turn, introduced Paul Carter to Andrews and his companion.

Carter seemed a bit uneasy around the two homicide officers. "I suppose you have things to discuss without an audience, so I'd best make myself scarce," he commented. Getting no disagreement from Andrews and Lt. Red, he concluded, "I'll see you later, Genna."

"Don't worry about the work on the Sirius payloads. I'll get them validated somehow before Tuesday," she reassured him, taking pity on his discomfort.

"Why don't we sit down," Red suggested and eased his long frame on to the bench beside Genna. Sky immediately decided to investigate the man's pockets, finding a thin thread, which provided the design stitching around the edging and getting it

80

caught in a front claw.

"Oh, I'm sorry," Genna hastily separated Sky from Red's jacket before the little dog could do any damage. "I don't know what is wrong with Sky today. He doesn't seem to be acting at all normal."

"I'm afraid that goes for most of us," Red responded pleasantly. "We've had troubles before at this campground but nothing as blatant as this killing."

Genna flinched at the reminder.

Red continued, "Lt. Andrews has apprised me of the issues you've raised about the printed program for this show and about the information available on the Internet about the event and the substitution of the victim as handler. It will take us some time to sort everything out. Right now, we need to try to notify the victim's next of kin. So far, we're getting no answer at his home phone and have sent an officer to his home address to follow up on that task."

"It's Friday," Genna injected. "His wife works, but I'm afraid I don't know where. I could give you Russell Harper's number. Russell is the one who was supposed to be handling Rusty today, the one who called Edward to substitute for him. He might know more about Edward's wife's schedule."

At an affirmative nod from Red, Genna released her tight hold on Sky and Rusty to fish in her purse. Sky promptly returned to his interest in the cuff of Red's jacket, which was enticingly near.

"Oh, Sky. Will you please behave," Genna admonished, handing her address book to Lt. Red so he could copy Russell's number into his notepad and retrieving her overactive canine. Rusty seemed happy just to look on from her other side.

"He smells my dog," Red said with a laugh. "Junket always rubs against my sleeve just before I leave to mark me as his I think."

81

Jean C. Keating

"Thanks," he continued, returning her address book to her.

"Now, Lt. Andrews has explained that you have one guest at your home and a newborn puppy in need of your care. I don't want to keep you longer than necessary. But I do need to ask if you observed anything just before or after the shooting that might have been odd. Even if you don't think it is connected to this killing, please share it with me."

"I don't remember anything as odd, except that Sky seemed fractious at having Rusty just behind him, and breaking stride in front of me. I stumbled over him and almost fell. I was concentrating very hard on recovering and getting Sky under control. Then Rusty came up beside me and jumped up on my leg. I was about ready to snap at Edward for letting Rusty come up too close behind me. And then I realized that Rusty's lead was dragging in the grass, and when I glanced back to find Edward, he was lying on the ground."

"Did you observe the crowd standing outside the ring?"

"No. Once I realized Edward wasn't in control of Rusty, I leaned over to get his lead. I didn't want him loose and running out of the ring or something."

"What did you notice next?"

Genna looked at Andrews, the strain of panic in her eyes. "I don't really know. It was all a blur. I think I noticed a dark spot on the back of his coat, but it was hot. The jacket was navy. A lot of people's jackets have wet spots in this heat. And the next few minutes seemed to flash by like a sped-up movie. Uncle Kevin was in the ring, and he was ordering the different representatives connected with the show to stand back, and then Peggy and Muffin were beside me and leading me out of the ring."

"And you didn't notice anything out of the

82

ordinary about the people around the ring?" Red prodded.

"Well, they were screaming and then hushed. But that wouldn't be unexpected given the scene in the ring."

Andrews had remained standing during Red's conversation. Now he moved up beside Genna and put his arm around her, getting a wet lick on his hand from Sky for his trouble.

Red nodded to his professional colleague and closed his notebook.

"Suppose I issue a pass to you and Ms. Longbowker so you can get on home. I'll come by your house later this afternoon and go over your information. Maybe by then we'll have made contact with the victim's wife and will have some further ideas to pursue."

Genna nodded, still numb from shock and sleep withdrawal. "I just can't believe he's dead," she mumbled. "Who'd want to kill Edward?"

"I don't know but we certainly have a wealth of possibilities of those with the opportunity. Between the show people and those who just came here to camp for the weekend, and those who made the wrong turn but were trying to get on the ferry to Surry, and those in the boy scout camp which adjoins this property, and . . ." Red looked very frustrated at the list of people to be considered, screened and released. "Right now, I'd sure like to trade this investigation for a clean, locked room scenario.

83

CHAPTER NINE

Sylvia stared at the pair of officials seated on her sofa. The gray eyes of the uniformed female focused squarely on her. Compassion was equally mixed with sharp interest in Sylvia's anticipated response to Lt. Charles Red's questions.

The handsome male figure in the blue suit waited expectantly for her answer.

But what should she say? Fear predominated over grief at the moment. The thin young woman struggled to deal with the shock of hearing her husband had been killed and silently weighed what she could or should tell them about her afternoon's activities. She couldn't tell them where she'd been this afternoon! Could she? Wouldn't it be the ruin of her life if she did?

"I don't understand," she voiced. "Who'd want to kill Eddie?"

Red's hand pushed into the seat of the sofa on which he sat, straining the fabric of the old green and orange print covering it. A small thread of Sylvia's

Beguiling Bundle: Death Takes Best of Breed

thoughts briefly crowded out her bigger worries with an irrelevant hope that the man's squirming wouldn't tear the thinning cover.

"That's what we need to determine," Red responded softly. "Has he been threatened or had a fight with anyone lately?"

"*Only with me,*" she thought.

She'd been so sure her parents and friends were wrong, so sure that she and Eddie could make a decent life for themselves, so sure that neither needed to try for a college education. They both worked hard. It had seemed so right, being independent, holding full time jobs. But their combined income never seemed to be enough to cover their needs. God knows Eddie was always careful, even tight, with their money. The house was small and rented, the furniture second hand pieces from her parents or his.

And now, Eddie was gone! And the full impact of this afternoon's venture was her responsibility alone.

Her parents and his had made their objections regarding the foolishness of their marrying so young very clear. And they'd been very emphatic that they would not be available to help if she and Eddie went through with "their crazy plans" and couldn't make it on their own. Of course, they may not have meant it. She hoped they didn't. At least she hoped her parents didn't. But her dad had been awfully mad about her marriage.

"Mrs. Spratt, anything you can recall, however insignificant it might seem to you, might be of help to us now." Red's compelling tone brought Sylvia back to the immediate dilemma facing her.

"I can't think of anyone who'd want to hurt Eddie," Sylvia said. "I dropped him off at the show grounds around 9:30 am. I kept our car to run errands.

We both work. Friday is a big day for chores, at least for me."

"*There! That sounded fine,*" she thought to herself. "*Hopefully they won't expect me to give them an exact itinerary of where I went and when.*"

"Did he seem worried or nervous about going to the show?" Red queried.

"No. Well, a bit frustrated that he was running late. He worked his regular shift last night, and was asleep when Russell Harper called early this morning to ask him to handle a dog today and the other three days of this show weekend."

"I understand that before this morning, your husband was not expected to handle Mrs. Colt's dog. What about attending the show? Did your husband intend to be at the show today before the phone call from Russell Harper asking him to handle the Colt dog?

"Not to my knowledge. He'd planned to sleep all day, get up late, maybe get his own breakfast, because I'd have been out running errands."

"Who else did you tell about his altered plans for the day?" Red inquired.

"No one. I just dropped him off at the show site and went about my chores."

"Are you sure you didn't speak to friends or family about it?"

"I didn't have time," Sylvia insisted. "I got the groceries, stopped by the Good Will store to see if I could find a pair of used jeans." She gestured feebly toward a bag of groceries that she'd deposited absent mindedly on the dining table as the three of them had come into the house earlier. She'd pulled the bag out of the car and started toward her front door before being interrupted by the pair of officers who'd been waiting at the curb for her to return home. Even in her present state of defensive agitation coupled with the shock of learning of Eddie's death, she utilized the bag of groceries as tangible proof of her excuse regarding grocery shopping. It had been intended to cover today's venture to Eddie. It must now serve to cover that venture from the police.

"Did you meet anyone you knew in these places and mention where your husband had gone?"

Sylvia tensed. It wouldn't do to have Red ask her which grocery store. It wouldn't do at all to be asked to produce the name of the grocery store, the one she'd gone to on her lunch hour yesterday but had not been anywhere near today!

"No, I spoke to no one about my business or Eddie's. I haven't talked to my family today. I dropped Eddie off, did chores, came home to put the groceries away before picking him up at the show, and found you two at my curb."

Red queried her for awhile longer, seeking her input regarding the listing of Russell Harper's name in the show program and on the web site. But she knew very little of the technicalities of show competition.

Tears came unbidden to Sylvia's eyes and spilled down her cheeks and into the side of her face, salting the long, side fringes of bangs. Despite her attempts to remain calm and in control, she found herself pulling the longest of the fringes into her mouth and chewing nervously on her hair. "Do you need us to notify someone in your family to come and stay with you?" the uniformed officer asked.

"Thank you, but no. I'll call my dad soon, but right now I just need to be alone." Sylvia couldn't remember the name of the woman. The officer's wise and gentle eyes made her want to throw herself in the older woman's arms and scream for help. But she couldn't. It might ruin everything. She needed to get the officer and the handsome detective out of her house so she could think what to do next.

87

CHAPTER TEN

Andrews sat quietly on the floor of the whelping room. Blacky's head rested possessively on his right knee as his right hand gently caressed her head and ears. Her fluffy tail waved slowly back and forth, displacing the corner of the soft blue rug beneath them with each swing. She didn't seem to mind that Sky squirmed and fretted but was held tightly against her master's left thigh.

One of the payoffs for dropping nearly forty pounds was Andrews' new found freedom to get up and down easier from a position on the floor. For now, he preferred to show off this new ability rather than sitting on the old sofa in the room.

The three were enthralled at the show being put on at the nearby table. Genna was attempting to feed a fussing Bunny while Twinkle sat on the table beside her puppy and supervised the proceedings. The wide sleeves of a butterfly print smock she'd thrown over her blue skort outfit kept covering the target of her attention. Genna struggled to keep the puppy's mouth still with two fingers and hold him with the same hand. Bunny did his best to twist his head and shake lose the long nozzle of a formula loaded syringe with which Genna was attempting to feed him. Twinkle alternated between licking the puppy's backside and tummy, which made holding him more of a challenge, and licking at his mouth to sample the formula which made Genna's application of dispenser to tiny mouth all the more difficult.

"Twinkle, you are not helping," Genna said.

"I could help," Andrews responded.

"I already have way too many hands in play with this tiny little body. I'd end up getting the milk under your nails instead of down his throat," she replied. "It would help if Twinkle would stay with Tina and let me do this feeding, but she's hell bent on playing Mommie."

Sky squirmed harder with each word from Genna, but Andrews held him firmly in his big hand. "Want me to hold Twinkle?"

"No. I should be glad she doesn't reject him. At least she's willing to do the job of stimulating him and keeping his backside clean. I shouldn't complain, but there's just been a bit more coming at me the past two days than I can handle."

"You're dealing with everything just fine," Andrews said, "but you need sleep. Why don't you try to rest and let Peggy or Shirley deal with Bunny?"

"You said Red wanted to come over soon, so I'm trying to stay awake to talk with him."

"Well, he is, but you could nap till he arrived."

"Not really. Once my head hits a pillow, I'm going to be down for a while. Besides, Peggy, Shirley, and I have it all worked out. Peggy has already gone to bed. Shirley will finish fixing dinner, and then keep the watch and feedings till midnight. Peggy will take over at midnight. They both insist I need a full night's sleep tonight, so I can function tomorrow. I can't argue with them, since my arms feel like lead weights already. I've decided not to try to show the rest of the weekend. I just couldn't face seeing that show site again. All I'd be able to think of would be Edward's body face down in that ring."

"Sounds like a good plan," Andrews responded agreeably.

"Well, you might not think so when I tell you you've gotten tapped for kitchen clean-up to help Shirley."

"Oh, I think I can manage that. Blacky will be delighted to assist with plate cleaning, won't you girl?"

The sleek body at his side wiggled in counter-motion to her happily waving tail. She might not have understood what was being said, but, as always, she reacted with delight at the sound of her name on her human's lips."

"Well, we do have a dishwasher, you know," Genna teased back.

The tiny bundle in Genna's hands squirmed and kicked out of all proportion to his tiny size. Weighing slightly more than four ounces, with ears and eyes sealed shut, Bunny still managed to make his wishes about the formula very well know: he didn't like it. He wanted his dam's milk. His tiny, overactive front paws pulled and pushed to get the long, floppy nozzle of the feeding apparatus out of his mouth.

"Don't I wish I had your energy, you little rascal," Genna cooed at him. "A lot of good it does me to keep a heated pad for you to rest your little rump on while we're doing this. You wiggle so much the only thing that stays on the pad is my hand."

Sky responded to the affection in his mistress' voice with renewed attempts to be free of Andrews' hand.

Beguiling Bundle: Death Takes Best of Breed

The soft slap of sandals against the hall floor foretold the arrival of Genna's friend, Shirley Douglas, a few seconds before a head of long, tightly waved hair appeared in the door opening. A bright smile illuminated Shirley's slightly flushed face. A huge butterfly clamp in bright pinks and greens did its best to keep back the mass of curly hair, but had already lost the battle to six or seven loose strands.

"Lt. Red is here. I parked him in the kitchen with a cup of coffee. Do you want me to take over feeding Bunny?"

"Please," Genna responded. "I hope I'll be of more use to Lt. Red than I seem to be with feeding Bunny."

Shirley moved to Genna's side, as Genna rose from the table and relinquished puppy and syringe to Shirley. Twinkle bristled a bit, trying to put her body between her puppy and Shirley's hands at first, but quickly subsiding to the role she'd exhibited with Genna, that of helper to the human's feeding of her baby.

Shirley's deep pink pants suit was decorated with bright butterflies separated by green bamboo stalks and leaves. A few tell-tale spots here and there on one of her sleeves suggested that some of Bunny's earlier feedings might have landed among the butterflies.

"I just weighed him, and he's lost a quarter ounce. But I can't seem to get him to take any more formula." Genna's voice was strained from more than sleep loss.

"Well, even puppies that are perfectly healthy sometimes lose a bit the first day. Don't buy trouble yet. We'll just keep on keeping on," Shirley said serenely.

Andrew's tried to hold on to Sky and heave himself up from the floor at the same time. It was a losing battle. The little dog wrenched himself free of Andrews' hold and flung himself against Genna's leg begging for attention. She picked him up with one hand and offered the other to Andrews who responded, "What's the matter! Don't think a fat old man can get up by himself?"

Genna's laugh was forced and her eyes looked dull and haunted. "Just didn't want you falling on Blacky. One canine in need of nursing is enough! Let's go see what we can do to help Lt. Red."

"Dinner will be ready in about twenty minutes. You two decide whether I need to set a fourth plate for your guest. Peggy grabbed a sandwich before she went up to nap and said not to call her till midnight," Shirley mumbled. She had finally gotten the correct grip on little Bunny to hold him steady while holding his little mouth open and was attempting to transfer more formula to his mouth without Twinkle getting to it first.

Andrews managed not to laugh when he looked back at Shirley – but only just. The tip of Shirley's tongue was showing just past her lip as she focused intently on the struggle with puppy, syringe, floppy nipple, and Twinkle's unhelpful tongue.

He and Genna, accompanied by Blacky and Sky, were just outside the puppy nursery when Shirley's voice stopped them. "Oh, Genna! I've just had Rusty, Muffin, Jessie and Amber out for a potty break. I put Amber in your bedroom to keep Kit Kat company. He was meowing enough to shake the roof about being left alone. Besides, Amber seemed to think Twinkle and I needed help with this feeding effort earlier and Twinkle wasn't buying it. The other three are in the dog room in their crates with treats. Our two girls are exhausted from the heat and the excitement of the show today, and I thought you'd like to keep Rusty's ear fringes away from Sky's mouth

92

in case you decide you want Peggy or me to show him tomorrow."

Genna blew a soft thanks at her, but shook her head at Andrews.

* * *

A good half hour later, Genna, Andrews and Charlie Red had exhausted the subject of the afternoon's homicide. Andrews' lengthy statement had already been filed away. Genna's contributions had been less clean and direct, and her eyes were glazed with the memory of death that touched so closely. Thanks in great part to Red's comfort at being around a fellow colleague, the younger detective had shed his coat and sat at the table in his shirtsleeves, enjoying his third cup of coffee. His coat had to be thrown over the end of the countertop in the kitchen, the only place high enough to keep it safe from Sky's continuing fascination with the decorative stitching detailing the collar and front.

"I hope I've given you everything I can remember," Genna said. "You do understand about the printed program and the web site information."

"Your uncle had explained it earlier today and you've been very clear about that," Red assured her. "Anyone could have known Harper would be using that numbered arm band at the show, but they would have had access to that information only about an hour before the show began. A select group would have known from the time of your registration that Harper would be using that armband number. Only a very small group could have known that Spratt would have replaced Harper. I agree with you that it limits who could have expected either Harper, much less Spratt, to be at the show."

Red shook his head in frustration. "It certainly

93

doesn't make things any simpler. What about Russell Harper? Could the killer have thought he was killing Harper and killed Spratt by mistake?"

Both men looked sharply at Genna for her response. It came swiftly with a negative shake of her head.

"Not if he or she knew Harper. Russell has flaming and unruly red hair. Bareheaded in the ring, it always looks like a blazing sunset. Spratt's hair is non-descript brown. I really can't see how anyone could have mistaken Edward for Russell."

"Unless the killer didn't know his victim," Red added.

"A contract killing? I don't see how either man could have generated enough enmity to have drawn that kind of attention. Have you found anything in Spratt's background that would indicate he was other than a young man struggling to work a regular job and earn a bit extra by showing dogs?" Genna shook her head in denial.

"No, not a thing! Our team will continue to look at bank records and retrace his routine over the past few days, but so far nothing seems out of place. Except the young man is dead! Shot while walking around in a dog show ring with about 350 spectators looking on. There must have been easier places to kill him if that were the object. Why was it so important to kill him then that one would take the chance of being observed by so many people?"

Shirley breezed in and interrupted them briefly, but finally succeeded in extracting Blacky and Sky from their places under the table and shepherding them outside for a potty break. Neither dog was happy about being separated from their favorite human but they went. Andrews was amused to see that, when necessary, Shirley was as bossy as the human dynamo currently asleep upstairs despite the

94

calmer, laid back impression she gave at other times.

Genna's mouth was tensed in a frown. She seemed distracted as she urged Sky to follow Shirley outside. "It seems like there was something else I needed to tell you, but I can't seem to remember what."

"Now don't keep things to yourself," Andrews urged. He still remembered the last time she was supposed to help with a homicide investigation and had deliberately avoided alerting him to important implications she'd unearthed. "We don't need a repeat of the Porter case."

"Oh, I don't know," Genna said. "You got a beautiful companion out of that one." Any possibility of lightening the mood of either herself or Andrews was lost in their depression over the current killing.

Red looked from one to the other for enlightenment. "Am I supposed to understand what the two of you are saying?"

"No. You're better off not knowing," Andrews assured him with a grimace.

Two energetic bundles of flying hair barreled back into the kitchen ahead of Shirley. Sky jumped up on Genna's lap for a quick check to be certain he'd missed nothing during his less than seven minute absence and Blacky conducted a more leisurely inspection of Andrews' shoes and pants legs.

Red laughed, "Reminds me of Junket."

"Hope you three are about done," Shirley heralded as she dusted the imprint of a paw off her pants. "Dinner is ready to come out of the oven, and you three look like you could use a break."

"I'd best be getting back to the office and leave you folks to your dinner," Red said, pushing away from the table and his coffee.

"And get a hamburger on the way?" Genna injected. "No way! You said you'd arranged for someone to feed Junket, so you just keep your seat and eat with us."

Red looked at her sharply. But then his nose got a whiff of the dish Shirley was removing from the oven.

Andrews just chuckled. If he had to *watch his food intake*, nothing was more appealing to *watch* than his favorite dish of barbecued salmon with ginger. He'd pointed out the recipe to Shirley earlier in the day, before leaving with Genna for the show this morning. And Shirley had turned his unspoken request into a delicious and tempting entrée.

Red's nose picked up the mingled scent of fresh lemon and orange zest, mixed with ketchup, soy sauce, and ground ginger and came to the conclusion that it wouldn't be bending too many rules to have dinner with a fellow homicide detective before returning to his investigation.

Andrews read his thoughts perfectly and gave him the final excuse for joining them for dinner. "Besides, Genna might just remember what is so all fired important to have you add to your notes once she settles down to eat."

Thirty minutes later the four humans were pleasantly full. Even the two canines had managed a taste of the salmon and the curried sweet potato wedges, although both Sky and Blacky had drawn the line at sampling the roasted asparagus.

Shirley finally returned their conversation indirectly to the homicide under investigation. "Will the police have Ring #5 taped off again tomorrow do you think? I believe Papillons are supposed to show in that ring again."

"Our crime scene people should be through by tomorrow," Red responded. "Will all of you be at the show?"

"I won't," Genna was quick to reply. "I just can't

face being there. I'd just keep seeing Edward lying there in the grass. Besides, someone has to stay here and feed a little newborn puppy every two hours. I plan to stay home with little Bunny if you need me for anything."

"Well, you know Sky won't show for anyone else, but I can take Rusty in for you. There'd only be a conflict if he took Winner's Dog and my little Jessie took Winner's Bitch. Then I would have a problem on who to show in Breed."

"That's it! That's what I was trying to remember," Genna shouted at Red. "Timing is very important in a murder investigation. And really, there was so very little time for anyone to have known that either handler would have been in that Breed ring." She looked expectantly at Andrews for support but he looked as confused as Charlie Red. Genna tried once more to make them understand. "Unless Rusty won Winner's Dog, neither handler – Edward or Russell – would have been present in the Breed ring. And no one could have known that it would happen or that it did happen until the judging yesterday was completed and Rusty was named Winner's Dog. If the killer was going after either man, why wait for the Breed competition. Why not shoot him while they competed in the class in which Rusty was entered? It doesn't make sense!"

CHAPTER ELEVEN

Genna's bombshell had caused a flurry of conversation between Andrews and Red, much consulting of Red's notes, and endless repetition of questions from Red about who was standing around the ring when Rusty won the right to move up to the Breed competition. She remembered little of what was going on around the ring, or who might have been there. She explained with growing weariness that her focus had been on Edward, on Rusty, and on insuring that Sky was ready for his own appearance.

She'd finally left the two men sitting at the kitchen table and checked in on Bunny. In spite of constant attention from Shirley throughout the day, he was losing ground. The puppy seemed weaker at days end as he approached his one day birthday. Shirley hugged Genna and reminded her that she could do nothing that Shirley was not already doing except make herself sick and limit her ability to care for the puppy the following day.

Reluctantly, Genna had taken Shirley's advice.

Beguiling Bundle: Death Takes Best of Breed

She and Sky had joined Amber and Kit Kat in the master bedroom. A long, consoling phone conversation with Jonathan had brought a little solace, and her sleep-starved body had done the rest. In spite of her depressed mood, she had slept deep and hard. When Peggy's pounding on her bedroom door failed to rouse her in the morning, Sky and Amber had brought her around with their doggie kisses. Kit Kat contributed to the morning by looking exceedingly annoyed at being awakened by all the noise and activity.

Genna had managed to shower and dress casually in jeans and a lavender tee. She pulled a pair of lace tennis slippers out of her closet, and then decided she could not face trying to keep them tied all day, so she substituted a bedraggled pair of denim tennis slip-ons instead. The grungy look was more than compensated by the ease of wear and not having to worry about this little Papillon or that one that would pull and untie her laces.

She did feel a bit frumpy when she joined Shirley and Peggy at the breakfast table for a brief visit over a bracing cup of coffee. Peggy looked even more petite in a smart navy blazer and camel pleated skirt and blouse. The bold, brightly colored butterfly pin on her left lapel echoed a brightly printed butterfly skirt worn by Shirley. The two briefed her on Bunny's progress during the night – all negative. She'd decided to send Rusty with them to the dog show, since it would have broken the major to pull him.

Andrews and Blacky seemed to be oblivious to the early morning activity. Genna was glad that Andrews was getting some rest. This was supposed to be his vacation after all. Shirley had indicated that Red had stayed late into the evening, the two homicide detectives dissecting the various issues of

99

the case. Genna was glad she'd left them to it. She could not see how going over and over the same ground again and again would gain anything.

It was still more than an hour until Bunny's next feeding when Shirley, Peggy, their two dogs and Rusty left for the show site. Genna decided to take Amber and Sky on a brisk walk around the grounds of Heron's Rest, which occupied them for some twenty minutes. They returned to find Kit Kat in the kitchen demanding food, water and attention in that order. Sky attempted to steal a bite of cat food and got a pop on his ear from a little cat paw for his trouble. He returned to Genna's chair, managed to jump into her lap despite the lack of room between her legs and the underside of the table. He combined silent pleas for consolation with a little begging for a sip of her second cup of coffee.

"I do not think you need any more energizing than you already have this morning," Genna told the little troublemaker, but she put her cup down to Sky's level for him to sample anyway.

He didn't like it. It was too hot for his taste. So he got back down on the floor again and waltzed over to pester Kit Kat for another sample of cat food.

Amber seemed to regard Sky's rejection of the coffee as an invitation to her. She crawled up in Genna's lap to exercise her own coffee begging talents. Genna finally gave up trying to enjoy her second cup of coffee, and poured the last half of the cup down the sink.

"Come on you two. Let's go see if we can interest Bunny in some more formula." Genna led the way from the kitchen to the entrance hall, but Sky and Amber both pushed ahead of her on the stairs, their four legs and tinier bodies proving a lot faster as a means of gaining the puppy room on the second floor. Twinkle issued a low, cautionary growl to

100

Beguiling Bundle: Death Takes Best of Breed

Amber as the two dogs turned the corner into the whelping room while Genna was still shuffling down the hall.

A long thirty minutes later, Twinkle and Genna were bent over the bundle in Genna's hand. Bunny had been fed as much of the warmed formula as he would take and Twinkle had performed her clean up duties diligently. Amber and Sky were curled on the old sofa, having been ordered to stay there by Genna.

Blacky's nails clicked on the floor of the hallway, announcing her arrival along with a freshly shaved and dressed Andrews. Genna turned red-rimmed eyes toward them in greeting, the tracks of tears fresh on her cheeks. Andrews crossed the room to put a strong arm around her shoulders and administer a supportive hug. Twinkle growled a warning at Blacky not to come too close.

"He's weaker," Genna whispered.

"But still fighting," Andrews countered. "How's the little girl?

"She's gained a half-ounce since birth. She's getting all of Twinkle's milk."

Amber apparently decided that Blacky's presence in the puppy room meant that she was not bound by Genna's command to stay on the sofa, and jumped down to touch noses with her larger canine visitor. Twinkle's unrest turned to loud rumbles of dissatisfaction at the growing number of bodies near her fragile puppy.

"Can you do anything else for Bunny at the moment?" Andrews asked gently before Genna could correct Amber or send Blacky out of the room.

"No." Genna reached one hand to console Twinkle while she returned the puppy to the dog bed at the end of the table. Twinkle followed the puppy into the sleeping box, and curled around him,

101

nudging his much larger sister against the warmth of her belly.

"Then leave him to his mother, let him sleep and make use of the food you've just given him. You come downstairs and have breakfast with me. He'll rest better without all of this activity around him."

Genna nodded submissively. She cleaned away the formula and feeding instruments, stored the remaining formula in the small fridge under the table, and dimmed the lights in the nursery. Sky was still sitting on the sofa, but wiggling in frustration to be allowed to join Amber, Blacky, and Genna. She called him softly and he exploded off the sofa to reach her side in less than a nanosecond.

The two Papillons and one larger black shepherd treated the stairs like a raceway but arrived downstairs in a dead heat. Genna and Andrews were slower to descend, having only two feet each with which to negotiate the stairs. Sky refused to leave Genna, but Amber continued on out into the yard with Andrews and Blacky for Blacky's morning attention to business.

Genna, with Sky's help, had concocted a plate of eggs scrambled in olive oil and wheat toast along with a steaming cup of coffee and had set them at Andrews' place by the time the three returned from outdoors. To Sky's disgust, Genna had removed Kit Kat's food bowl, and made certain the bowls were filled with water and dry dog kibble. She joined Andrews at the table with yet another cup of coffee. Blacky busied herself with sampling the dry kibble, but returned very quickly to claim a place at Andrews' knee, just in case some of his food might fall and require her clean-up.

"This is delicious. Thanks." Andrews made short work of the food on his plate and turned to his coffee. "Now, it seems to me that the first thing we need to do is make up a schedule of who's feeding that little fellow and when."

"Well, I should be doing that. Peggy, Shirley and you are here on vacation and to participate in the show."

Andrews shook his head gently. "You've got three helpers who love dogs as much as you. You need to utilize us all so that you're as fresh and alert as possible at all times. Sleep-deprivation on your part translates to inferior care for Bunny."

Genna could only nod in agreement, knowing he was right. She also wanted to hug him for knowing just how to appeal to her best instincts to get her to focus on positive things. Crying over the helpless little puppy would accomplish nothing. Planning would provide him with the best chance of survival.

She pushed Sky and Amber out of the way with her feet as she rose and retrieved a pad of paper and pen from the holder on the front of her fridge. For the next twenty minutes she and Andrews roughed out a schedule of feedings, naps, sleep periods, show attendances, and a cooking schedule.

"Next, you need to include time in your schedule to work on those prototypes I know are worrying you," Andrews cautioned.

That produced a stubborn set to Genna's chin. But she quickly subsided with the acknowledgment that he was right on target. "First, I'd like to hear what, if anything, Red has discovered about Edward's murder."

"Fair enough! Can I have a fresh coffee first?" Andrews requested.

Sky, Amber and Blacky all had to reshuffle their positions under the table as Genna retrieved the coffee pot from the countertop and filled Andrews' cup.

"Red hasn't found a great deal of positive things,

103

but he has ruled out a lot of possibilities."

"He thinks Edward's wife is hiding something, but it doesn't seem to be possible for her to have killed her husband. The people at the Good Will identified her as being in the store at the time of his death. Their finances are shaky, stretched, and leave no room for her to have hired someone to kill her husband. Neighbors and their families regard them as a too-young, too-immature-to-be-married couple of lovebirds that scrap a lot over money but are still in the honeymoon stage of their love story. All bank deposits are easily identifiable as coming from their salaries or small amounts that would be consistent with odd jobs like handling dogs on weekends. There's no hint either are involved in anything illegal."

He sipped his coffee appreciatively before continuing. "Russell Harper was home at the time of Edwards' murder. In addition to his wife's statement, another visitor was at the Harper home picking up a client's dog from Russell. He'd apparently asked another handler to deal with a whippet champion that was at his house and the man had dropped by to get the dog before an afternoon show time."

"No suspicious money trails or hint of activities that would provide a motive for murder have been found. No reason to doubt that Harper's last minute withdrawal from showing little Rusty was anything but the reason he gave you. Harper's neighbors and friends all seem to know he suffers periodically with a bad back. He injured it in a motorcycle accident many years ago."

"So obviously Harper wasn't the shooter. Is there any reason Red can figure for someone wanting to kill Harper and not knowing it was Spratt on the other end of Rusty's lead?"

"Nothing that Red has turned up so far gives any

clue in that direction." Andrews's paused to enjoy a big gulp of his coffee.

"Too bad we don't know who all was at the show yesterday," Genna said.

"Well, we won't ever be sure, since that campground butts up against woods, the boy scout camp, and a long road on the east side, but we do have long lists of people who were camped there or who attended the show for the day and had to be listed before being allowed to leave last night."

"You mean, Red accomplished all that and still had time to eat with us and talk the night away." Genna's face expressed great surprise at the Herculean efforts Andrews was describing.

"You forget that around here when extra manpower is needed, that William and Mary, Busch Gardens, and Colonial Williamsburg all have excellent security forces who respond with trained help. They were all working together like a well-oiled team. I should be so lucky with my cases as to have that much help."

"So where does that leave us?" Genna shook her head in confusion.

"We're back to the unanswered question of who knew Rusty won yesterday. It had to be someone standing around the ring. But what made that individual decide to kill Edward just then? Or Harper if he was their target?"

"I thought you said that Red found no reason to kill either man!"

"No reason that he's found, yet!" Andrews stressed. "He'll have to keep looking at both their lives. We've got a corpse. We, or rather Red, since you and I are just bystanders in this one, don't really know which man was the intended victim. A nut taking a pot shot for no reason is a lot less likely than someone having a very strong reason to want one of

105

those two men dead!"

"It's too much for me. I'm going to call the vet and see if he has any suggestions on anything else to do about Bunny. And then I'll see if John Hunter has gotten the data runs on the prototypes done and forwarded the results to my computer."

Genna lifted her eyes upward and finished her conversation with a quick prayer. "With everything else going on, please don't make it necessary for me to have to talk to Hunter today."

Genna pushed away from the table and started to collect the dishes but Andrews waved her away. "I'm very good at loading dishwashers. You go make that call and check your computer mail."

Blacky jumped up expectantly, followed quickly by Sky and Amber.

Genna managed a weak laugh. "Well, okay, but no utilizing these three to do any pre-washing!"

Need anymore help loading this thing?

CHAPTER TWELVE

Andrews busied himself with lunch. He had bragged to Genna that he was acquiring some proficiency in cooking for himself (and Blacky) in a manner that was both tasty and healthy. Leave it to Genna to maneuver him into proving it!

Deciding that simplicity was the best bet, he had raided the vegetable bin for fresh veggies. He'd produced one of the staples of his cooking, a large pot of vegetable soup that was easy to make. Blacky would not be agreeable with the tasty part.

The mellow, black shepherd mix had shadowed every step he'd taken between fridge, cabinet, and stove. At their home in Richmond, Blacky would have found a comfortable spot under the table and waited 'to be served.' Here at Heron's Rest, she seemed more concerned with making certain his feet did not travel anywhere without her. In deference to Blacky, and because he liked it too, he'd added toast smeared with peanut butter as a side dish.

Beguiling Bundle: Death Takes Best of Breed

An excited Genna, followed by her two shadows, Amber and Sky, breezed into the kitchen before he had time to put bread in the toaster. "Guess what! Bunny has gained a quarter ounce!"

Amber, Sky, and Blacky all had to do a mutual butt sniff before jockeying for room under the table. Genna plopped herself down in one of the chairs facing Andrews, finally acknowledging his cooking efforts. "That smells delicious. What is it?"

"Never mind! You'll like it!" Andrews was not about to admit that seasoning, water, and veggies were the sole contents of the soup. Genna would just say she didn't like vegetables.

"Did you call your vet?" He added two slices of wheat bread to the toaster.

"Yes. He said if Twinkle was still cleaning her puppy, and Bunny was still eating, that I should just keep on with what I'm doing. Thank God, he's as much of a softie as I am, so he didn't suggest I put the puppy down. Probably knows I wouldn't listen anyway. He said that I could add a little honey to the formula and maybe that would appeal more to Bunny as well as help with weight gain. But he's already gained a little, so maybe he's going to make it."

"Not able to nurse, however?"

"He'll never be able to nurse on his own, until he has surgery to correct that hare lip. By then he'll be on solid food.

"Could he have surgery now? Feeding the little fellow every two hours is doable now, with me and Peggy and Shirley around to help. But can you and I handle it alone when the ladies go home? And can you and Jonathan handle it when I go home?"

"Well, Bunny could have the surgery now, but it wouldn't be nearly as effective, and he'd need more surgery later on as he grew. And it would be more dangerous to him. Better to wait until he's older if we can just get him through these first three weeks and on to solid food. It'll be rough. But it's doable." Genna's stubborn jaw and determined frown said it had better be doable or he and Jonathan would never hear the end of it.

"Soup's ready!"

Genna jumped up to get small plates, as Andrews spread peanut butter over two hot slices of toast. The three dogs churned and swirled under the table in anticipation of sharing in the humans' food. Andrews added two glasses of lemonade to the table along with the toast and the steaming bowls of soup, before joining Genna. He managed to consume most of his soup and half the toast before yielding to Blacky's persistent begging by passing the remaining piece of toast to her under the table. That set off a clamor from Sky and Amber for their share, and Genna chuckled as she obliged with a small piece to each of the little dogs.

"You're a bad example, you know. My father tried and tried to teach me without success not to feed the dogs under the table."

"And the dogs always won!"

The phone interrupted their funning. Genna checked the Caller ID before muttering, "Now what does Paul Carter want?"

She took a sip of her lemonade and gargled into the phone, "Hi, Paul."

Andrews hoped the frown on Genna's face and her puckered lips were from the tartness of the lemonade and not from the caller's response. Otherwise Paul Carter was in big trouble.

He quietly collected the dirty plates and soup bowls and moved to the sink with them, escorted by all three canines.

"No. I guess we've been too busy to read the Gazette today. So the story of yesterday's homicide has drawn a huge crowd of spectators to the show site. Well, too bad the kennel club didn't charge admission to the show. They can always use the revenue. But maybe the larger than normal crowds will benefit the vendors."

Sky decided that Andrews was not going to provide any handouts, and bounced back across the kitchen to put his front two feet on Genna's leg demanding attention. She put her lemonade glass down and scooped the little fur ball on to her lap. "My friend Peggy who you met yesterday and another friend Shirley are at the show with little Rusty. But I just couldn't face the sight of that ring after what happened yesterday."

Sky tried to put his nose into the phone and got pushed away. "Oh. So you saw them there today. I hope they won."

Genna tossed her head from side to side and smirked at Andrews as she and her caller engaged in a bit more small talk. Then she seemed to take pity on Carter and brought the conversation around to what had probably been his reason for calling, a topic he seemed to be having so much trouble broaching.

"Well, enough small talk. I suppose you're wondering how the homicide will impact the validation of the prototypes." Genna nodded knowingly to Andrews. "Well, in a word, it won't. I've already checked my computer and the raw data from the validation runs I requested on Thursday are here. I'm planning on doing some work on them this afternoon. Thanks to my guests, the little puppy is well cared for, everyone is taking turns with the cooking, and I've caught up on my sleep. So I'll start work on the data this afternoon."

She smiled and pushed Sky's nose out of the phone again before continuing, "Don't worry. I'm not neglecting anything at home, and I'm not mad at you for calling."

A slight chuckle accompanied another brief pause before she added, "Hunter, I'm always annoyed with. Enjoy the rest of the show."

Genna scrunched her mouth and rolled her hazel eyes in exasperation, as she shared the news garnered in her phone call with Andrews. "The local paper ran big headlines about the homicide at the show yesterday. So today, the place is packed with morbid spectators who could care less about the dog show but just can't wait to view at close hand the site of the murder. How awful!"

"And one of these morbid spectators just happened to be your boss, I take it."

"Well, yes. Paul never could stand to miss a news event."

* * *

Andrews offered to handle the 2:00 PM feeding for Bunny, saying he'd like to get his experience now while things were on the upswing.

"Just remember that Twinkle isn't thrilled with Blacky being too close to her puppy. You might want to close the door between the hallway and the puppy nursery with her outside," Genna said.

"Oh, having her scratch and jump on the door will make Twinkle more comfortable," Andrews countered with a smirk. "You go take care of those haversines or whatever you need to do to that data from the prototypes."

"Suit yourself. If you're sure you'll be comfortable by yourself for a bit, I'll go do some serious number crunching."

Sky and Amber twirled and jumped around Genna's legs as the three of them disappeared in the direction of Genna's study.

Blacky followed the tinier dogs for a few paces, but quickly returned to Andrews' side when she realized he did not intend to follow Genna.

"Now, girl, let's you and me see what is on the TV around here. Too bad there's no football this time of year."

It would not have mattered, because the two of them were soon asleep, some mindless sitcom providing a soft background to their peaceful snoring. The small alarm Andrews had carried with him from the kitchen awakened them a good five minutes before Bunny's next scheduled feeding.

Andrews' attempt to sneak away upstairs and leave the sleepy black shepherd worked only as long as it took him to reach the room's door. So Blacky accompanied him upstairs to feed Bunny. Twinkle expressed a mild complaint at Blacky's arrival, but soon accepted Andrews' offered bribe of the formula newly augmented with honey and forgot all about the large, black body curled around Andrews' feet.

He was thankful that little Bunny seemed more eager to slurp down the offered concoction which had been thoroughly 'mother tested and approved." Holding the diminutive puppy, holding his mouth open, slowly pushing the formula into the back of his mouth at a rate that kept him swallowing without choking him looked a lot easier when Genna was doing it. Especially with the eager tongue of Twinkle added to the mix.

He felt a bit stressed by the time he and Blacky retreated to the TV room and returned to their lengthy afternoon rest. It didn't seem possible that only fifteen minutes had elapsed. He felt his efforts warranted an ice cream. But he might just as well forget that, he cautioned himself, because Genna had made sure there were no sweets in the house.

Sometimes his family could be just a little too helpful.

A few minutes of channel surfing convinced him that there was really nothing on the TV of interest. He reset the small alarm by his chair for 4:00 pm, turned the volume down on the least obnoxious channel offering, and he and Blacky resumed their slow breathing. Despite everything else that was going on, the two were taking their vacation seriously and enjoying the luxury of afternoon cat naps.

What awakened him this time was not the alarm. Amber and Sky exploded down the stairs from the second floor barking and yodeling, to be joined at the back door by Blacky. The three crowded around the door, raising a chorus of warnings, Amber's higher pitched squeals in counterpoint to Blacky's rapid barking and Sky's piercing mixture of barks and yodels.

"What's going on down there?" Genna yelled from upstairs.

Thanks to years of training as a cop, Andrews was moving toward the door before he even knew he was awake. But his more or less unrestricted view of the backyard and property could find no reason for the three-alarm commotion provided by the dogs crowding around the back door.

"Don't know. I don't see a thing," he called back to Genna. "Maybe they just need to go out for a break. How about I take them out and you go back to doing what you need to do."

"Well, alright. But they don't usually act this way unless something unusual is in the backyard. Just be certain no raccoon or other animal with claws is inside the fence before you let them out."

Andrews scanned the secured area beyond the door, but could detect nothing unusual within the yard. The three at his feet were still milling and

114

fussing to get out, so he opened the door. An explosion of three hairy bodies dashed through, bumping each other in their haste. The dogs cleared the small deck and raced across the yard to the back gate leading into the wooded expanse of property toward the James River.

Andrews followed at a much slower pace. The three canines were disappointed when he would not allow them to follow him through the back gate into the open woodland area. They crowded against the gate which confined them to the fenced yard, complaining loudly with yodels and yips at being barred from following him.

"Now let's see how good a tracker I am," Andrews muttered.

He walked carefully around the area near the gate but could see nothing out of the ordinary. The last remnants of white dogwood blossoms dotted the lush spring green of the grass here and there, but he could see no indication of a disturbance to the expanse of white and green. Going back to the gate, he opened it to the three fussing dogs. They rushed past him, noses to the ground, milling around but finally circling a large ironwood tree about 200 yards from the back gate. Andrews wondered if a possum might have been the source of the alert. Did raccoons climb trees, he wondered. He did not expect to find any tracks to solve his question, but he circled the tree to examine it more closely just the same. What he found raised the short hairs on the back of his neck.

A large scrape on the side of the tree away from the house indicated contact with something a lot larger than a raccoon or possum. And the footprint in the dirt around the tree was man made, not animal. He'd missed it when he'd examined the area before turning the dogs out the back gate. He hurriedly tried to shield the print from the twelve eager dog paws that sought to investigate it now.

"Some professional I am." His grumbling was audible only to the three canines that eagerly tried to get to the footprint he struggled to shield from their disruptive paws.

Calling them sharply to him, he was pleasantly surprised to have Sky obey him for once. He led the reluctant mob back into the house, where he secured a plastic garbage bag, split it to form a plastic sheet, and managed another exit without canine escort to the yard. There he spread the sheet over the footprint and secured the sheet with bricks stolen from the edging of the nearby azalea beds.

When he returned to the house, only Blacky awaited him at the door. Sky and Amber had apparently lost interest and returned to Genna's study upstairs.

Using the kitchen phone, he put in a call for Charlie Red. As expected the busy detective was not at his desk, but Andrews left word for him to call as soon as he could be reached.

Andrews and Blacky quietly returned to his bedroom upstairs where he removed his service revolver from a locked case in the closet, secured it to his belt, and pulled the tail of the tee shirt he was wearing from the confines of his belt to cover the weapon and holster.

* * *

Andrews drew a deep breath and tried to relax before walking the few steps to the open doorway of Genna's small study at the end of the second floor hallway.

"Sorry to disturb you," he said as he tapped lightly on the doorframe, "but we have to talk. Now!"

Beguiling Bundle: Death Takes Best of Breed

Sky and Amber looked up with interest as Blacky's head appeared beside Andrew's leg but did not get up from their position under the well of Genna's desk.

Genna swung her chair toward the doorway at his entrance. Frustration was plain to read in the frown lines between her eyebrows and a stubborn set to her jaw. Then her eyes widened with surprise, as she noted the loose drape of his shirt and the bulge at his left waist line.

"Okay! Have a seat." Genna's hand shook slightly as she gestured toward one of two chairs against the wall opposite the doorway.

Andrews was very familiar with Jonathan's study on the first floor, but this was the first time he had ever intruded on the much smaller space that Genna claimed for her professional work. Jonathan's study was surrounded on three sides by large windows, which provided sunlight and a near endless panorama of woods and gardens, no doubt the expansive source of the highly imaginative worlds he created in his science fiction novels. Genna's study was small, closed in, and self-contained.

The chair to which Genna gestured was trim, modern, and well padded. Covered in soft blue velvet, a pair of the chairs dominated the wall opposite the doorway. The tiny, blue lamp, which rested on a small, white table between the blue chairs was not meant for illumination, Andrews decided, but it provided a nice accent to the room. The blue fabric of the chairs blended quietly with the blue walls and blue woodwork. A print of lavender, blue, and multi-color flowers, which Andrews recognized as a copy of Monet's *Water Lilies,* appeared on accent pillows and curtains on the one large window behind the chairs and the tiny window above the desk and computer. The result was a serene and peaceful backdrop for the pile of printouts

117

scattered over the table against the right wall and a sharp contrast to the frantic peaks and valleys of the line graphic which filled the screen of Genna's computer.

Andrews eased his rear into the chair, reaching with his left hand to shift the shirt-covered gun and its holster forward a bit so that his bulk fit.

"Whatever is wrong? You're wearing your gun in the house?" There was a slight quiver to Genna's voice but she managed to keep the tone and volume near normal. Sky and Amber shifted their positions as she turned further to face Andrews. The two little fur people apparently decided that the other blue chair was a better position from which to view the interchange between the humans. The two dogs crossed to the vacant twin to the chair chosen by Andrews and executed dual jumps onto its seat.

"It's necessary. I've put in a call for Lt. Red. We have to talk."

"I'm listening," Genna responded.

"First, I need you to be coldly logical about this."

"I'm always logical," Genna said.

"Not always," Andrews countered. "You've been anything but logical these last few days about Bunny."

Genna started to protest, but subsided when Andrews held up his hand. Blacky had squirmed and circled the room in frustration at the tension she sensed between her two favorite humans. She finally settled with a loud sigh on the rug at Andrews' feet.

"Okay. I can accept that."

""Can you talk logically about Bunny?"

"What does that have to do with your wearing a gun in the house?"

"If you can adjust your thinking to at least discuss his situation logically, I would feel more confident that you can handle this new problem in the same way."

"That's fair enough." Genna nodded, indicating her willingness to accept Andrews' challenge, though her face clearly bespoke her puzzlement as to where the conversation was leading.

"Why did you respond with such an emotional outburst over your vet's suggestion that it might be best to put Bunny down?"

The green lights in Genna's hazel eyes flashed with anger and pain. She opened her mouth on a sharp response, but chocked off her reply. Drawing a deep breath, she finally said, "Logically! All right, logically."

It grieved Andrews that he had to make her go down this road. But he needed to prime her thinking to deal with another very painful problem. To accomplish that, he felt she must draw on her logic rather than her compassion.

As though they sensed the tension for their beloved mistress, Sky and Amber deserted the blue chair to go to Genna's side once more. She put a hand on each, unconsciously petting them as she formed the words to respond to Andrews' question.

"There may be other medical issues with little Bunny that can't be seen. It is a good sign that Twinkle doesn't sense them and reject him. But that isn't conclusive evidence that they aren't there. He will eventually require very expensive surgery to correct his harelip if he is to have any chance at a normal life. Even with corrective surgery, he will have a harder time than a healthy, normal puppy in finding a loving family to adopt him. There are always more dogs needing homes than there are homes for them."

"So why do you ...?"

Genna interrupted him sharply. "He wants to live. He's trying so hard to nurse and survive. And I will not

119

rob him of that. I will fight as long as he fights to live. I will do all in my power to save him."

Andrews raised his hand to stop her commenting. "I'm not trying to debate what you're doing for Bunny. I only want to demonstrate the difference in approaching a problem from a purely logical side and one colored by compassion, respect, and emotion."

Genna exhaled loudly, the sound ragged and choppy. "To what end?" Genna challenged. Her eyes dared him to dispute her decision to fight for this puppy's life.

"Keeping that distinction in mind, can you think of anyone who might have wanted to kill you yesterday?"

Genna's lips drew together in a small circle that resembled the pulsing mouth of a fish out of water. "What! Whatever gave you such an idea?"

"We've already established that few people even knew Spratt would be at the show yesterday. Those that did, except for Harper and Spratt's wife, I had in my sights. While the entire list of attendees at the show could have known that Harper would be showing Rusty, they didn't know until shortly before the show opened. The same goes for the internet community. It just wasn't known until the last minute. And while the creators of the internet site, the catalogue and the printers could have known sooner, you said yourself, no one could have known either man would be in the Breed ring until minutes before when the judge tapped Rusty with the win for Winners Dog."

Genna nodded in agreement to Andrews' word but did not interrupt him.

He continued. "And those that did don't seem to have been in a position to have killed him. Russell was listed as Rusty's handler in the catalog that people got the morning of the show, but until Rusty won the points yesterday, it was not known that he would be competing for Best of Breed, not known that he and whichever handler was with him would be in that ring. But you and Sky were listed. So anyone with access to that printed program would have known you would be in that ring yesterday."

Blacky had picked up on the tension in the room, and came first to lick Andrews' hand and then to push Amber away from Genna's hand and push her head against Genna begging for attention. Genna obliged by scratching the ears of the larger dog without taking her eyes off Andrews' face.

"But I wasn't hurt. Spratt was killed," Genna said. Dark eyebrows were flexed together, separated by a deep frown line. Her fixed expression clearly reflected her shock and disbelief at Andrews' words.

"Because Sky was cutting a rip in the ring. He was jerking his lead. He cut in front of you and tripped you just as the shot was fired. He probably saved your life, and the bullet that was meant for you hit Spratt instead."

Genna stared at Andrews. "Oh, how awful! How can that be possible?" she stammered.

"Logically, it's very possible. The shot came from a rifle a good distance away. The shooter was positioned in a tree at the fringe of the show site. By the time the police arrived and traced the vector of the bullet backward to the weapon's location, the shooter was long gone of course. They found the weapon, but have not been able to trace it. There's a side road that runs along that tree line, winds back to several housing areas and a Boy Scout campground, and then back onto Jamestown Road."

Amber tried to jump into Genna's lap, and was rewarded by a command to all three dogs to lie down. Genna brought her hands together in front of her face, index fingers touching her lower lip in concentration.

"What has made you focus on such an idea? Does this have something to do with your suddenly deciding to wear your gun in the house?"

"The alert from the dogs may have been, probably was, in response to a human's presence in the back of the house. I found a scrape mark made by something heavier than a human's clothing or body on the trunk of that tree outside the den window. It could have resulted from someone trying to drag a rifle up behind them after they'd climbed the tree. It would be consistent with the pattern of the shooting yesterday. And I found the print of a heavy boot in the soft bedding around the tree. Unfortunately, I let the dogs get to it before I realized what I was dealing with. But I've preserved it as best I can until Red can get here and check it out."

Genna shook her head in puzzlement. "Red is coming over?"

"Well, he will be, as soon as I can talk to him. As I told you earlier, I called him from the kitchen before I came upstairs and left a message for him to call me pronto."

Andrews paused briefly to let the urgency expressed in his words to sink in and then continued. "Now, who would have wanted to prevent you and Sky taking the breed badly enough to resort to murder?"

"No one." Genna's denial was swift and uncompromising.

"Logically now. Not emotionally!"

"I am being logical. Several people in Papillons might have liked to win, but it is a sport, not a money event. People don't bet on dog shows. People don't kill to win with their dogs."

"So everyone is a good sport and never tries to knock out a competitor?"

Beguiling Bundle: Death Takes Best of Breed

"I didn't say that! Unfortunately, it brings out the worst in a lot of people. They say nasty things to hurt a competitor – about the person, about the dog -- usually behind their backs. They do things in the ring to disrupt their competition, like one of the handlers did to Spratt in trying to run his dog up behind Rusty to spook Rusty and make him break his smooth gait. Some will accidentally on purpose put their dogs and themselves between the judge's line of sight and another dog. Poor sportsmanship! But not homicide! The worst to me is when someone gets angry at ringside because the judge doesn't pick them and takes it out by fussing at their dog. Those people bring out the worst in me, because I want to slap them. But they wouldn't actually kill someone to win a dog show."

"You! Want to physically abuse someone?"

"All right! Check and mate!" Genna nodded reluctantly. "Dogs stir raw emotions: sympathy, tenderness, love, protectiveness, anger, frustration! The competitiveness of dog shows is often less than sportsmanlike. People get their own egos tied up in winning, and it becomes a personal loss or defeat when their dogs fail to win, especially when the winner is a dog belonging to someone they don't like. It doesn't drive them to climbing trees and shooting people!"

"And the range of emotions you've just described characterizes most homicides. About all you've excluded is money! And show awards might be loosely characterized as gain! How sure can you be about someone else's responses?" Andrews persisted. "What about the next level up? You said, I think, that the winner of Breed in Papillons would go on to the Toy Group ring competition. Could someone have wanted to prevent you from competing in Toy Group?"

123

Genna shook her head in frustration at Andrews' questions. "Of course not. We're no competition for some of the top ranked dogs in the other breeds represented in the Toy Group that would have been, were, at the show yesterday."

"Then it has to be related to something else about you. Maybe the work you're doing this weekend. Though I can't figure why someone would pick a public place to try to harm you," Andrews sank back in his cozy, blue velvet chair, stress lines of concentration pulling his eyebrows closer together, shifting awkwardly when the arm hit against the holstered gun at his waist.

"Are you sure it's me?" Genna asked. Her eyes widened in a wistful, pleading look that begged him to deny his assertions.

"Yes. Maybe I wouldn't have been before someone climbed that tree in the back yard and then departed hurriedly when the dogs raised the alarm. But the two events taken together don't add up to anything else."

"I just can't believe it." Shock and puzzlement drew Genna's eyes into a squint. The tight pull of her lips gave her a harsh, frozen look. The three dogs reacted to the tension with further milling around between the two humans.

"You don't want to believe it," Andrews countered. "But you must, and you must consider what about the project on which you're currently working would warrant someone attacking you in full view of more than two hundred witnesses."

The ringing of the phone on the desk beside her interrupted the pained and frozen look on Genna's face. She turned woodenly to check the Caller ID, turned back toward Andrews to say, "It's Jonathan. Please don't mention any of this to him!"

Beguiling Bundle: Death Takes Best of Breed

* * *

Red paid more attention to the face of one of his visitors than to the flow of small talk that characterized the conversation. When Sylvia Spratt had appeared in his office accompanied by a lean, stick of a man she introduced as her father, Graham Moseley, he had immediately noted a change to her demeanor and appearance. Her green eyes were red rimmed from crying but somehow she seemed less strained than she had when he'd talked with her the day before. Her glorious red hair was freshly washed and shining with fiery lights. Sadness and grief were plain to read in her face, but the face was more open and at peace than when he'd last talked with her.

The thin man who'd accompanied her resembled her around the eyes and mouth and his hair, while liberally sprinkled with gray, might once have been the same brilliant red. Deep lines down his face from the corners of his eyes gave mute testimony to a life of struggles, but suggested strength and humor in dealing with those difficulties.

Sylvia reached to secure a broad, strong hand before continuing with her conversation, ". . . and so my Dad said I should come and explain it all to you. I can't really see that it matters, but you did say to tell you everything, even if it didn't seem important to Eddie's death."

The green eyes filled with tears at the mention of the victim's name, but a little sniff and a set mouth retarded any spillage of moisture.

"I didn't go grocery shopping yesterday. I had a doctor's appointment. I suspected that Eddie and I were going to have a baby." The pale face slightly colored in an appealing blush, but Sylvia's voice steadied and continued. "I didn't tell Eddie that I was going. I was afraid he'd be upset. Money was very

125

tight and he said we shouldn't start a family until we were better fixed financially."

The red-rimmed eyes appealed to Red to understand. When he nodded encouragingly, she continued on, her voice almost a whisper. "I never told him. He died without knowing that I'm going to have a baby. And then when you told me and wanted to know about yesterday, well ..." She looked toward her father for encouragement before continuing, "I was afraid to tell you about the baby. Our only insurance is in Eddie's name, and I was afraid if it got out about the baby, that his insurance coverage would get cancelled. My parents were upset with me about marrying in the first place and I didn't know where I could turn. But when I told my Dad last night, he said we'd work that out and I should just clear things with you so you don't go wasting time checking on stories that aren't true, or thinking I had something to do with Eddie's death when you found I wasn't telling you the whole truth."

Red restrained a smile with difficulty. The young woman seemed to relax now that she'd finished admitting to her subterfuge of yesterday. She looked like the young woman she was, too young to be taking on a baby alone. But from the slightly smug look on the older man's face at the mention of a baby, he didn't think Sylvia would be facing life alone. Proud grandfather would be there for the baby and Sylvia.

"I appreciate you correcting the record, Mrs. Spratt. Are you sure there isn't anything more you can tell me about yesterday, or about your husband's affairs?"

"Oh, no. Everything else I told you was the truth."

Her open face and shining eyes said clearly that it was, at least as far as she knew.

"Do you know anything more about who could

have done this?" Graham Moseley's voice, like his large, rough hands, was substantial.

Red shook his head. "At this time, all we can say is that there is no reason we have found for either Mr. Spratt being killed or for anyone to have wanted to kill Mr. Harper who was originally scheduled to be showing yesterday.

Father and daughter thanked him and rose to take their leave. A uniformed officer rushed over as Red and Moseley were shaking hands with a note marked 'urgent' to call a Kevin Andrews.

CHAPTER THIRTEEN

Shirley's hands fondled a strip of purple ribbon and pressed it against her skirt. Brightly colored butterflies on the black background of the light cotton fabric stood out sharply and all but overwhelmed the eight-by-two-inch treasure she held so lovingly. She could neither suppress the grin of joy that repeatedly erupted on her face or totally avoid the worried look that shadowed her eyes.

"You don't suppose Genna will be upset with me for not getting points on Rusty, do you?" She cast a worried look sideways at her friend. Peggy was relaxed in the driver's seat, one hand on the steering wheel as she smoothly negotiated the long drive into Heron's Rest.

"No, I think Genna will be pleased that Jessie won Winner's Bitch. Besides, I think she has faith that you did a great job with showing Rusty. He just didn't come up with the win today." Peggy's brisk reply held a bit of sharpness. Her little bitch Muffin had come in

Beguiling Bundle: Death Takes Best of Breed

second to Shirley's Jessie.

"I just hope she doesn't think that I was so intent on showing my own dog that I neglected to do a good job with Rusty."

"She won't and you know it!"

Shirley fiddled with her purple ribbon, smoothing it with her hand against the butterfly print of her skirt again. She'd removed her long-sleeved, soft pink jacket and welcomed the relief from the high mandarin-collar. The scooped neck, matching pink shell made her porcelain skin glow and accentuated the bright pink in the butterflies on her skirt. But she had eyes for only the strip of cheap, purple cloth in her lap. "I know you're right, but I still worry a bit!"

"And your point for worrying is?"

"I told her I'd show Rusty and he won yesterday and I just feel like I should have won with him today. I promised her I'd show him in Breed, and . . ."

"You did not. As I recall you said you'd only have a conflict with handling efforts if Jessie won Winner's Bitch and Rusty won Winner's Dog. And that little statement reminded Genna that no one could have known yesterday that Edward would even be in that Breed ring with Rusty. And that little bit of information sent Andrews and that detective in charge of the case into a tailspin of discussions. And that was the end of any promises about today."

"Oh, I guess you're right. I just feel so happy about Jessie finally getting a major in spite of her not having a white blaze. I guess I just have to feel guilty about something."

"Oh, right! You're making no sense you know. But you can feel guilty about me if that will help." The frosted blond head turned slightly toward her companion with a smirk. "Muffin and I are still pointless this weekend. So tomorrow is my turn!"

Peggy swung her focus back to negotiating the

drive just in time to avoid a black van coming out of the property. The driveway was well kept but never intended for two-way traffic. "What the heck is a police van doing here now?"

The abrupt swerve caused two of the dog crates to shift sharply in the rear of the SUV, and Rusty added some sharp barks and yodels to the confusion.

"Golly. Do you suppose something else has happened?"

"I guess we'll soon find out," Peggy responded.

* * *

The five human faces seated around the table in the kitchen at Heron's Rest were varying portraits of frustration and exhaustion. The technicians that Charlie Red had brought along with him to the house had come and gone in the black van that had almost collided with Peggy's SUV in the drive. Along with them went whatever recordings of the footprint discovered by Andrews they'd managed to collect. It hadn't amounted to much.

Genna had brought her two friends up to date on the presumed evidence of a human intruder in the backyard that afternoon. Red had strained their energies further by going over and over the show events of the previous day in an attempt to make any sense out of why Genna might have been the target in such a public manner.

Shirley was the first to put her foot down about the incessant dialogue. "I cannot contribute anything to this conversation. I was not at the dog show yesterday," she said finally. "I am going upstairs and change into something cool, check on Bunny and Twinkle and see to his royal something, the cat. I leave this detecting to you four."

"I managed his 4:00 pm feeding, but Twinkle

probably needs to go out in the yard. She wasn't much interested in an outing as long as all those strange people were milling around the outer part of the property." Genna put her hand out to touch Shirley's briefly in silent thanks for her help.

"Will do," Shirley reassured her with a smile.

"Do you three mind if I also excuse myself? I need to change into something a bit less formal and sweaty. It was more muggy than really hot out there today, but I should have known better than to wear a navy blazer to attract the sun's rays." Peggy didn't wait from their agreement.

Contrary to her words, she did not move immediately toward the stairs to follow Shirley. Instead, she headed for the rear door to the backyard. The dark spot of moisture between the shoulders of her navy blazer had dried while she'd been sitting around the kitchen table, leaving a noticeable water ring to accent her back.

She'd put the Papillons, including Sky and Amber out in the exercise yard when she and Shirley had returned to Genna's to join the confab going on among Red, Andrews and Genna. Blacky had refused to leave Andrews' side and was making herself into the smallest ball possible while remaining under the table with her head on Andrews' foot. The smaller canines in the backyard were voicing loud complaints about being left out of things.

Peggy looked back over her right shoulder as she reached for the door to the deck outside. "Shall I put Rusty and Amber in the dog room with Jessie and Muffin, or do you want them running loose with Sky?"

Andrews jumped up from the table and came up behind her before she could open the door. "Let's make certain all these clamors from the dogs are just demands to come inside. I don't want to be surprised by any more unknown visitors."

131

Peggy glanced at the outline of a holster at his waist, reminded again that he had shown enough concern for the situation to be wearing his gun. She failed to keep all of the alarm she felt out of her voice. Her response was at least three notes higher than her normal speaking tone as she responded. "They're all crowded at the door here begging to come in and join in the fun."

Andrews nodded his agreement after a brief look at the group of furry bodies milling around the door outside and stood back to allow Peggy to open the door. He walked back into the kitchen and resumed his seat with Genna and Red.

A blast of stuffy, moisture-ladened air came in with the dogs. Rusty bumped shoulders with his sire as the two played one-upmanship on getting through the door first. Sky responded with a growl and a nip that resulted in a sharp squawk from Rusty.

"Oh please, put all of them but Sky in their crates with a treat. Sky and Blacky are about all the distraction I can handle at the moment," Genna said.

"You've got it," Peggy responded with a bit more confidence than was justified by her abilities to convince Rusty, Amber, Muffin, and Jessie to cooperate. But with some help from Genna, four of the canines were finally bribed into the dog room and their crates.

Blacky resumed her role as invisible foot-warmer, reattaching herself to Andrews' right shoe the minute he returned to his seat. Sky oozed into the impossibly tight space in Genna's lap between her knees and the underside of the table.

Her assigned chore with the dogs completed, Peggy moved toward the stairs. "See you guys later," she said softly.

Genna, Andrews, and Charlie Red barely noticed. The three made a mismatched picture around the white tabletop. Red's dark gray suit jacket fit his athletic frame to perfection and the soft lavender shirt made his face look even younger than his years. His nervous habit of raking his fingers through his hair in front had the left side sticking straight up. It was somehow appealing and impish, but at odds with the formality of his dress.

He had not felt sufficiently relaxed to remove his jacket this time, and his professional attire contrasted sharply with Genna's and Andrews' casual jeans and tees. Genna's shirt was a slightly darker hue of lavender, which echoed Red's dress shirt. Both blended nicely with the soft blues, pinks and camel accents to the white counters and walnut cabinets of the kitchen. Andrews' darker green polo shirt did nothing for the décor, and nothing to hide the pouch that overflowed his belt line, even without the holstered gun it struggled to conceal.

Their only matching points were the strain showing on all three faces.

"Where were we?" Andrews asked.

"Still in shock that you think someone might have been threatening me," Genna replied, a mixture of disbelief and argument in her tone. The face she turned toward Andrews was lined with strain, frown lines rising sharply between her brows, which were drawn upward in peaks. One pesky strand of hair kept falling over her eyes. She wrinkled her mouth and blew it away from her face before continuing. "Murder was far more interesting when it didn't concern me directly. It just doesn't make sense! I didn't see anything! I didn't hear anything that would be of the slightest danger to anyone, much less some deranged nut who goes around shooting people in clear sight of two hundred or so spectators and exhibitors."

"Denial is a natural response to shock," Red said.

"But the partial footprint in the backyard was fresh. The departure was hurried. It could be nothing but a curious trespasser. But coming on the heels of the homicide, we can't take any chances."

"And my instincts say the threat is real," Andrews injected. Worry for Genna and aggravation with himself over allowing the dogs to spoil the footprint contributed to his strain. Age lines around his eyes and mouth bespoke the strain of every one of his fifty-nine years, especially the last few hours. "At some point, you learn to rely on your gut feelings. And I'm convinced we need to go over the events of yesterday very carefully until we find the reason for what happened."

Genna's voice quivered, but she nodded in agreement.

"All right! You've ruled Harper out of the picture." She nodded at Red.

"Yes. As the shooter, but not as the intended victim! He's alibied by his wife, which might not mean too much. But also by a second handler who was at their home to pick up another dog that Russell couldn't show. Russell was at home at the time of the shooting." Red removed a small pad from his pocket. The pencil that accompanied it turned out to have a broken point and he exchanged it for a pen while he continued. "And Spratt's wife is probably in the clear also. We'll check her latest story, but I'm sure she's telling us the truth now and that she was keeping a doctor's appointment at the time of her husband's murder." Tiny scrawls covered a thick number of the pages, mute testimony to the many notes Red had devoted to the case.

"You're sure that the motive could not have been to prevent you and Sky winning?" Andrews was still following the logic that the timing of the murder and the startling public place chosen for it seemed to coincide too close to the show events to be coincidental.

Genna was having none of it. "No. You'll just have to trust me on that. It could not have been a reason."

Andrews didn't argue with Genna's assessment further. "Then we're left with not only who but why."

His frustration translated into an urge to put something in his mouth. He pushed his white chair away from the table and headed toward the refrigerator. Blacky scrambled from beneath the table to follow him across the kitchen. "Would anyone besides me like something to drink?"

"A glass of water would be nice," Red admitted.

"If there are no cold *diet* sodas in the fridge," Genna stressed the adjective, "there's more in the cabinet under the burner top. I'll take some water also."

"Then the only thing left is that the why could be connected with your work or the shooter was after Harper. Red's checking further into Harper's background I take it." He nodded at Red and got an answering affirmative nod in return.

"Could someone have wanted to prevent you evaluating those prototypes?" Andrews managed to step over Blacky and juggle two glasses of water back to the table along with a can of diet Pepsi with only two drops and a long streak of moisture on the front of his dark green polo shirt to show for his efforts.

"You need napkins." Genna jumped up to get paper ones to keep the moisture from the glasses and the soda can from running on the white Formica table top, holding Sky in one hand while she fumbled to open a drawer, remove the paper napkins, and transfer them to the table one-handed. It gave her a slight break in which to formulate her answer.

She settled back into her white molded modern

chair with obvious reluctance, restored Sky to her lap, and adjusted the placement of her left foot to avoid the large black dog that was turning around three times before settling again with her head on Andrews' foot. Genna finally responded with a reluctance that was obvious to both men.

"John Hunter was angry with me for not acquiescing to his schedule. But shooting me wouldn't get him what he wanted." She appeared to view the idea as ridiculous. Her face showed a half-smile, the first sign of humor to surface since a gun-packing Andrews had intruded on her workroom earlier in the afternoon. "Besides, he's the one person connected to the project that I didn't see at the show."

"Swinson was there," Andrews said.

"And my boss, Paul Carter," Genna conceded. "But then this particular outdoor show is a big event for Williamsburg, and half the people in the area are likely to drop by at one time or another. Dogs attract a lot of interest. Since it's an outdoor show with plenty of food vendors, people can bring their own pets and their children, sit on the grass, eat, socialize, and have fun watching the dogs. It's like a big outdoor picnic with entertainment."

Red was not to be distracted. "Would Swinson have had any reason to want to prevent your completing the evaluations of the prototypes this weekend?" His question was logical. It produced a stunned expression on Genna's face.

"He certainly gave no indication of that. In fact, in my meeting with him on Thursday, he was pushing hard for me to finish it rapidly. And he seemed to have come to the show on Friday in the hopes of continuing his campaign to get me to work on the evaluations."

"Brer Rabbit, maybe? Please, Mr. Fox, don't

136

throw me in the briar patch?" Andrews' illusion to the old folk tale brought a sour look from Red, but a soft chuckle from Genna.

"No, I don't think he was trying reverse psychology. Okay, I was pretty keyed up about being treated with disrespect by Hunter and maybe taking it out on Swinson, but I don't think he was kidding about wanting to hurry me through the evaluations. If he was, he's a better psychologist than I give him credit for. I really felt like he was rudely trying to maneuver me into rushing through the evaluations. That's why I snubbed him and left him to talk to you."

"I remember it well," Andrews acknowledged and turned to Red, whose pen was poised but whose face revealed his confusion. "When Swinson referred to Genna's precious Sky and Rusty as 'little doggies' I knew he'd lost the battle of ever getting her to change her mind about his schedule."

"So, Swinson talked to you both, and then you moved away and left him to talk to the lieutenant here." Red flipped back through the pages of his small notebook before continuing. "Then, he made some excuse of getting something to drink and wandered away from ringside. How long was this before Spratt was shot?"

"About ten minutes was the guess I gave you before, I think." Andrews raised an eyebrow at Genna, silently inviting her input. She nodded in agreement.

Red had found the entry in his notes and responded, "Yes, you said you didn't remember exactly but you figured it was no more than ten minutes."

"Could he have been concealing a weapon while he was standing with you at ringside?"

Genna and Andrews gave a negative response in unison. "He was wearing a tight fitting gray polo shirt and slacks," Genna elaborated. "There's no way he

137

could have concealed any weapon on his body"

"Then he'd have had to secure the weapon from somewhere, climb a tree, set up and fire within that short span of time," Red went on thinking aloud.

"Oh, for heaven sakes! The man was an irritant, but why would he want to prevent me doing the very evaluation he was pushing for in the first place?"

"Maybe there's something wrong with the instruments," Red said.

"Then he'd hardly be pushing me to complete the evaluations, unless..." Genna's trail of words slowed to a stop like a wind-up toy with an unwound spring.

"...unless he hoped to hurry you into missing something!" Andrews finished for her. "Were you able to get any fix on the performance of the instruments or whatever you call them this afternoon? I know you didn't have a lot of time to work on your evaluations before I interrupted you with my concerns over the intruder."

Red looked from one to the other, his pen poised above his notepad.

"I finished validating the prototype of the star tracker. Like I told Swinson at the show, I use haversines. The mathematical correlations of the orbital motions of the star tracker and the sky background aren't that difficult to compute. The prototype appears to work within design specifications. And it appears to respond to light frequencies even fainter than the 2.0 magnitude."

Red put his notepad on the table. The fingers of his left hand pulled unconsciously at his hair. "Have a what? Would someone please explain to me what you just said?"

"She doesn't always speak a language I understand either," Andrews said with a snort in which frustration and humor were equally mixed.

Beguiling Bundle: Death Takes Best of Breed

"Sorry," Genna said. "I'm not sure you need to write this down," she continued as Red hastily retrieved his notepad and sat poised with his pen at the ready to record her response.

"You've studied trigonometry in school. So you know that when you're dealing with a full circle, there are all sorts of hoops you have to jump through with calculations because the trig tables only display information from zero through 90 degrees."

She looked at Red for reassurance that he followed her to that point.

Red nodded only slightly. Math had not been his favorite subject. In fact, one might say that it was his worst subject. He might have flunked algebra if his father had not thought to equate angles to the trajectory of the football he was so interested in throwing rather than doing his homework.

"Well, math wasn't my favorite subject in school," he finally admitted aloud.

"Mine either," Andrews chimed in. "But I doubt that will save either of us from getting lessons in it from my hostess here."

"Oh, hush, the two of you. Do you want to understand this or not." Genna ignored the frustrated look on the faces for her two listeners and continued with the explanation that was as confusing as the original statement.

"Anyway, with trig you constantly try to determine if you're adding a figure to 90 degrees or subtracting it from 180 degrees. Since navigational astronomy must always deal with a complete 360 degrees of freedom, there's a specialized form of computation, which I use. It operates on a hemisphere or 180 degrees of rotation rather than on a quadrant or 90 degrees of rotation. It's much easier and faster to use. The equations are called haversines. I could write the formula for you, but I can't see that it would help

139

you in any way. All you need to understand is that I can do the validations of the star tracker's performance with a great deal more speed using this specialized mathematical procedure than anyone could with normal trig."

Red looked at Andrews, hope and hopelessness equally mixed in his expression. His reward was a shrug of Andrews' shoulders. Finally deciding that looking foolish was better than missing a clue, he said, "And this has something to do with this have-a-what?"

Genna had managed to take a large swallow of water from her glass. The absurdity of her explanations finally penetrated, and her involuntary laugh produced a spill of water down her shirt. Now she and Andrews looked equally sloppy. "Haversines are a specialized form of math that makes evaluating the star tracker's performance much, much easier and quicker than ordinary trig would. That's really all you need to know about it."

Red's pen scrawled an entry in his notebook that read, "*Have-a-sign: easier, quicker, leave it at that!*"

"The important point here is that anyone not familiar with this specialized form of mathematics might have assumed that it would take a lot longer to validate the performance of the prototype than it has."

That point Red could understand and he scribbled rapidly in his notebook.

"So someone – say Swinson – could have assumed it would take you longer to do the task than it has." Andrews struggled with the relational aspects of what Genna was trying to tell them. "But that means he'd have even less reason to act hastily to prevent you doing the evaluation."

"I mentioned using haversines."

"But Swinson didn't have a clue what you

140

meant," Andrews cut her off.

"So..." Red prompted.

"So, it would seem that Swinson had every reason to suspect it would have taken me some time to do an evaluation of the star tracker. And he would have had little reason to act hastily to prevent me from getting to the evaluation, even if you can convince me he wanted to."

"What do light frequencies of – what was it? – 2.0 have to do with anything?" Red's pen again halted, waiting for clarification.

Andrews chocked off his gulp from his Pepsi long enough to inject, "And make this in English two poor detectives can understand, please!"

That brought a laugh from Genna as she set her water glass down on the table. "Okay. The simple explanation is that the lower the number given for a star's apparent brightness, meaning how it would be seen here on earth, the brighter its appearance. But, the brighter the apparent magnitude, the smaller the actual number of stars which appear to us on earth at that magnitude."

Red's and Andrews' expressions showed plainly that the conversation was giving them headaches, but Red bravely soldiered on with his note taking.

"If the star tracker is to perform correctly at most any orientation during flight, a minimum of three stars must be visible as it rotates and scans a 360 sweep of the sky. Don't ask how I know, or you'll need six of those notebooks. Just take my word for it that if the instrument is going to work successfully, it must be able to record the positions of stars down to the 2.0 magnitude. And it does. In fact it picks up even dimmer magnitudes, so it shows even more starts than necessary to perform satisfactorily," Genna said.

"And that's what you want?" Andrews asked.

"Yes. It means any orientation should produce

141

three or more stars in a rotational sweep."

"Well," Andrews nodded in Red's direction. "At least we've got that straight." The puzzlement registered on both men's faces lent doubt to his statement, however. "I guess Swinson didn't have to worry about the smoker mucking up the star whatever."

"Now you're the one talking in code," Genna chided. "To what smoker are you referring?"

"Oh, something Swinson said after you abandoned him and me to step closer to the ring yesterday. He said something about a guy smoking around the other payload and him not realizing he was even there."

Genna's face froze. She slowly lowered the glass she'd been preparing to put to her lips and set it very deliberately on the table. "Do you remember exactly what he said?"

"What's wrong? You said the star tracker was working fine! And Swinson said the light registered on the scanner just fine in spite of the smoke!" Andrews tensed at the change in Genna's attitude.

Genna's voice was flat, each word enunciated with care. "It's an infrared scanner!"

Andrews' eyebrow went up on one side, twisting his face into a funny expression. "I don't understand why you're alerting like a fox hound on a new scent."

"Infrared scanners respond to heat. What's a necessary and certain consequence of smoking a cigarette?"

Andrews opened his mouth wide with first surprise and finally understanding. "Heat?" he responded.

"Yes!"

Red seemed a tad slower to connect the dots with regard to the meaning of the dialogue.

Genna continued in a flat voice. "The

instrument should have registered the heat from a cigarette long before it responded to any light source."

"But Swinson said ..." Andrews began.

"I know what you said he said. It didn't sound like he knew what a slip his comment was. If the instrument didn't respond to someone smoking around it, then there's got to be a flaw in the instrument. I need to check the other instrument." She jumped up so swiftly that a startled Sky was dumped rudely in the floor, landing on Blacky's back. Both dogs came boiling out of the space beneath the table, getting in the way of Genna's scrambling feet as she headed swiftly toward the stairs to the second floor and her study. Sky recovered from his surprise and ran after his rapidly disappearing human. Four dainty white feet fought for space on the camel carpeting of the stairs as the little red and white blur did his best to pass his mistress and beat her to the second floor.

"But wait...." Red injected to her retreating back.

"Don't bother," Andrews said, his hand trying to sooth the black head of the larger dog who was frantically trying to decide whether to follow her buddy or stay with her human. "You'll not be able to get anything more out of her 'til she's checked out that scanner."

"But what should I do about Swinson?" Red stammered. "I don't really see that I have enough on him to bring him in for questioning. I sure don't understand all this techno-talk well enough to conduct an intelligent query of the guy. You both admit he wasn't carrying a weapon when he talked with you at ringside. And there wasn't time to get one and shoot Spratt." Red scratched his head with his pen, causing the hair in the short-cut center of his scalp to stand up at attention.

Jean C. Keating

In the sole company of another professional, Red allowed the frustration and confusion of the moment to show in his face. "And why would he shoot Spratt anyway?"

"Maybe he was shooting at Genna," Andrews replied. He suppressed a chuckle in spite of the seriousness of the topic. Red's unruly hair sticking out in front and up on top reminded him briefly of some old black and white showing of the Our Gang children's comedy. "*Long before he was born!*" Andrews thought to himself.

"So you think it is credible that Spratt was killed by accident and that Swinson or someone connected with him might have been trying to kill your hostess?"

"I think it is something we have to seriously consider. I don't think you should rule out that someone might have been after Harper. I'm assuming your investigations will need to continue on that front. But despite what Genna wants to believe, there was an intruder in the backyard."

"There are a number of explanations as to who that could be, however," Red said.

"Yes. But apparently no question now that there is something wrong with one of the prototypes Genna is supposed to be validating this weekend. So we – or rather you -- have two possible intended targets to worry about."

"So I'm back to square one. What do I do about Swinson?"

Andrews nodded in sympathy. "It's probably too early to reel the guy in. But can you at least keep a close eye on him for the present, just until Genna can do some checking on this instrument?"

The beginnings of an evil grin brightened Red's face. "Sure. I've got just the eager young man in my department who'll be perfect for the job."

CHAPTER FOURTEEN

Shirley's voice was soft and soothing as she crooned to the puppy she held in both hands against her lips. "You are just so precious, little one. And everyone is trying so hard to help you thrive."

Twinkle stretched her head as far as she could extend it without moving her back legs away from the sleeping box. The second puppy squirmed for a warmer position since her mother had displaced her from a nipple. The little rescue's tail was down and her ears indicated her continued anxiety with close proximity to Shirley, but her determination to protect her newborn overrode her fear. She stretched to lick Bunny from nose to backside and Shirley quickly lowered the puppy and extended her hands to allow Twinkle better access.

Soft flopping sounds in the hallway drew a fearful growl from Twinkle and Shirley responded by returning the puppy to the sleeping box as Peggy joined them.

Twinkle curled cautiously around the puppies and quickly nosed both of them against her underside, covering them with her tail and lowering her head and neck to cover them from the other direction. Then she sneezed loudly.

"Well, I guess you know what Twinkle thinks of your hair spray," Shirley quibbled.

Peggy had changed and washed her hair, shaping the short frosted strands with her hands and hair gel. The smell was not unpleasant, but it was strong, and apparently very annoying to Twinkle.

"I felt sweaty all over, so I thought I'd grab a quick shower and change, before anything else happens tonight. Do you think this will be suitable for entertaining unwelcome visitors, should we have any tonight?"

Peggy did a quick pirouette to show off her trim light coral knit top and matching pants. The coral color brought out the light blond strands in her hair. Deeper coral accent tape outlined the circular yoke of the top. The darker shade of coral was repeated in the flowers that decorated the olive leaves and vines, which circled the yoke. As usual Peggy had a pair of shoes that matched the outfit to perfection, and her woven leather mules sported alternating straps of olive, light and deep coral.

Shirley couldn't help herself. She just had to dig at her fashionably dressed friend. "Would have been better with a few butterflies on the shirt, but I guess it'll do!"

"Oh, you! Fine one you are to talk about butterflies. Looks like a few of yours have been fluttering through some muck!" Shirley had changed back into the hot pink knit pants suit she'd worn the previous day. The splatter of butterflies on bamboo shoots across the legs of the pants and across the top

146

piece was bright and beautiful. The embellishments looked hand painted but the top had acquired numerous drops of Bunny's formula in the succession of feedings, which Shirley had handled. Peggy's finger traced one of the larger blobs for emphasis.

"Well, I might just have come with a lot fewer clothes than the Queen of Style," Shirley retorted. "I only brought two pairs of shoes, and I'm tired of both." She held up one of her feet, clad only in a white sock, for emphasis.

"But you didn't leave any of your butterflies at home," Peggy teased, taking the large butterfly clip that held most of her friends curly locks away from her face.

Twinkle's eyes watched the exchange warily as she sank lower into the bedding of the sleeping box.

"Now look what we've done with our carping," Shirley acknowledged, lowering her voice and remembering to put a smile into her tone. "Poor little thing thinks we're really cross with each other."

Peggy turned her full attention to the fearful mother dog. "Oh, Little One. Shirley and I just like to tease each other." She extended a hand to gently touch the top of Twinkle's head. "I feel like such a jerk when I forget to go quietly around her. She's had so much fear and grief in her life, and she's taking all this commotion so much better than anyone has a right to expect of her."

"She's certainly taking things a lot better than I am," Shirley admitted. She too reached to pet the mother and reassure her that her world was safe and calm, even if it wasn't.

"Lt. Andrews is wearing a gun under that floppy shirt tail, isn't he?"

"Yes. Scares the hell out of me, too," Peggy said.

"Do you think we should just go home and forget

about the shows and the rest of the weekend?"

"And leave Genna to deal with Bunny, with her work problems, with this latest threat! Are you crazy?" Peggy's voice went up several notes of the scale, and Twinkle responded with a fearful roll of her eyes.

"Oh, sorry Little One." Peggy lowered her tone and volume but repeated, "Are you crazy? Genna needs us badly and we aren't going to fail her."

Shirley's response was a whisper for Twinkle's sake, but a knowing evaluation of her friend's thought processes. "And you wouldn't miss the excitement for the world."

Rapid nail taps on the hardwood floor of the hallway provided only a split-second warning of the arrival of a little red and white ball of energy, but Twinkle was ready with a low growl of warning as Sky erupted through the doorway of the nursery. Shirley's and Peggy's hands bumped into each other as both sought to reassure the anxious mother that all was well with a gentle pat to her head.

Sky rushed over to greet the two women with a happy sniff around each of their ankles before returning to the doorway in time to welcome the arrival of his beloved Genna.

One look at the pulled down lips and strained face of her friend brought an immediate imperative from Peggy. "Come sit a minute and let Shirley bring you up to date on Bunny. You need to catch your breath!"

Genna hesitated a moment, but then slowly crossed to the side of the table holding Twinkle and the puppies, sank to the floor with crossed legs and drew Sky into the shelter of her arms. "I am so sorry..." she began.

"For what? We're having the time of our lives!" Shirley reassured.

"I invited you for a weekend of dog shows and

fun. So far, you've been roped into caring for a struggling puppy, cooking for yourselves and for my other guests, being the chief witnesses to a homicide, and now being caught up in what may be a stalking and potentially physical danger!"

"Like Shirley said, we're having the time of our lives!" Peggy reiterated.

Taking note of the perfectly matched attire of her friend for the first time, Genna smiled. At least her mouth did, though the humor did not reach her tired eyes. "Well, I can see that none of these stressful events has interfered with your eye-catching dress. You really make me feel frumpy," she said, pulling the front of her lavender tee out by the front hem and emphasizing the still wet streak of water or whatever which darkened the front of her shirt.

"How's Bunny doing?" Genna injected without allowing any further comments about her appearance.

"I weighed him before giving him his 6:00 PM feeding. He weighs the same as he did this morning, but he doesn't seem to be any weaker. He hasn't gained any more weight, but he is taking all of his formula, even if it is a chore to keep Twinkle from sampling just a bit more than one would like. She really goes for the honey in his formula."

"Why don't we add a little to her kibble? God knows she's had enough stress in her life to need a good sugar lift. As long as it is honey on her dry food, it shouldn't cause digestive upset. All this stress makes me sorry I got all the sweets out of the house so Uncle Kevin wouldn't be tempted. I could sure use a good jolt of chocolate about now," Genna admitted.

"Wait right there!" Peggy said. She wheeled and headed for the door so rapidly Sky was beside himself trying to decide whether to follow and snoop or

149

remain in Genna's lap.

"I can't. I have to do some rush calculations to see if there might be something wrong with the second of the two prototypes," Genna said, but Peggy was already out the door.

Genna turned to her remaining guest. "I'm a terrible hostess. Did you two get lunch at the show?"

"Of course," Shirley laughed. "And those dratted hamburgers are still sitting right here in my stomach. How can anything smell so wonderful and taste so terrible the second and third belch around?"

"Oh, I'm so sorry! I really stopped in to ask if you two could deal with a late dinner. It's hard to make dinner with Uncle Kevin and Red at the table in the kitchen and in the middle of things. They should be finished in another thirty minutes or less. I thought I'd use that time to work on my computer and look at some of the performance stats for the infrared scanner. We've now got some questions as to whether it is really working right, and suppositions that if it isn't, maybe preventing my finding that out is behind all this violence." Genna's voice wound down into a soft mumble, tiredness and frustration equally mixed in the tone. Her left hand went up to her scalp in an unconscious gesture that raked her hair out at an angle that matched the little red ear on the head in her lap.

"I can start preparing dinner for us all as soon as I get my kitchen back – if you don't mind having dinner with a frumpy old bag lady in a stained tee and ratty sneakers."

"Absolutely not!" The chic coral figure reentered the nursery, a bag of Almond Joys in her hand. "You need reviving from all this stress. You will take two candies, retire to your bath for some necessary repairs to your soul, put on something beautiful, spray on your favorite perfume, and come down in about an hour to a dinner that has been prepared by Shirley and me." Peggy continued in her best take-charge tone. "And Shirley and I will prepare dinner for you to enjoy after you've properly pampered yourself."

She chuckled at the hungry look on Genna's face at the sight of the chocolates. "I knew you'd strip the house of one of the essentials to good living in your zeal of keeping Lt. Andrews on his diet. But I knew sooner or later this weekend the three of us would have to have a chocolate fix."

"But I can't let you two continue to carry the load of cooking and Bunny and everything else. You're my guests, or you're supposed to be."

"And murder is supposed to happen to someone else, and not us." Shirley joined Peggy in pledging support to her hostess. "Besides, it is rather fun to try to concoct dishes that your Uncle Kevin finds enjoyable now that he understands the four essential condiments!"

"Four?" Genna was too tired and depressed to pick up on Shirley's joke. "Yes, silly," Peggy responded. "Salt, pepper, lemon, and dog hair!"

Shirley continued with a laugh, "Yes, he's miles more fun now that he's a doggie person like the rest of us. Now go take a little time for yourself, forget work for a few hours, and give that poor cat some attention. He's been shut away in the master suite again and doesn't appreciate the solitude one little bit."

Before Genna could make any other protests, Peggy put two chocolates in her hand, and pulled her up from the floor. Sky wasn't at all distressed to be displaced from Genna's lap, since he had his eyes on the chocolates in Peggy's other hand. "None for you, little man," Peggy said, "chocolates aren't good for dogs."

"But he likes coconut also," Genna teased.

151

"Well, you keep those for yourself," Peggy responded. "Now go make yourself beautiful, enjoy a chocolate fix, pamper your body and your soul, and don't worry about cooking, Bunny, or that scanner-whatsit! It can wait till after dinner."

"You're the one who's been up since midnight. You need to rest, particularly if you're going to try to make the show tomorrow." Genna protested weakly but allowed herself to be pushed out the door of the nursery and aimed toward her bedroom. Sky had to turn around twice before he could tear his eyes away from the bag of candy in Peggy's hand and follow his mistress.

"And I'm going to have a wonderful dinner, leave Bunny's care to someone else tonight, and retire early myself," Peggy called to Genna's retreating figure. "Tomorrow is Muffin's turn for points! Now go and get revived!"

The dynamo was at her best when taking charge of everyone else's routine!

Twinkle raised her head by a minuscule amount, her nose pointed in the direction of the bag of chocolates.

"And you can't have chocolates either. Go back to sleep and keep those babies warm," Peggy whispered to the mother.

CHAPTER FIFTEEN

By the time Genna had managed to choose the scent of candles she wanted and light three groups of them around the tub, the inviting bath was five inches deep in fragrant bubbles.

"Peggy has the most delightful ideas," she commented to Sky. The snoop had already pushed his nose into the bubbles and sneezed -- loudly.

The face that peered back at Genna from a mirror rapidly vanishing in steam was scary. Red-rimmed eyes shone dully, tuffs of dark hair stuck out at odd angles here and there on her head; jowls sagged on either side of a face to match the bags under the eyes.

"You do not deal well with sleep deprivation," she accused her image. She stopped short of admitting that she also was not dealing well with being the possible target of a killer.

She eased her tired body into the soothing heat of the tub and pulled a dish containing two pieces of chocolate toward her. If she'd hoped the scented bubble bath and candles would mask her actions from Sky's sharp sense of smell, she'd forgotten about his keen sense of hearing that appeared to be able to distinguish the sound of candy wrappers tearing in the next county. Red ears flashed on a tiny head that proceeded two dainty white feet at the edge of the tub. Warm, pleading liquid eyes gazed wistfully at the chocolate covered mound of coconut which was now melting all over her fingers and then transferred their gaze to her face, trusting, pleading, silently projecting Sky's need for a share of her treat.

"You little schemer! You know you can't have chocolate!" Her laughter intensified his flickering glances from her face to the candy in her fingers and back again. She licked the chocolate coating off fingers and coconut, and then pinched off a small bit of the sugar saturated filling and put it into the waiting mouth of the eager dog.

The head bobbed up and down in happiness as Sky bounced on his hind legs, always returning his front feet to the side of the tub and his eyes to the block of candy still in Genna's hand. She broke off another chocolate-free piece of coconut and put the second piece in the eager dog's mouth before cramming the remainder into her own.

"All gone, now. Go away and let me relax!" Sky looked at her with a smirk and then looked toward the dish in which the second piece of candy lay.

"Oh, great! I have to get stuck with a dog that can count!" Genna chuckled, then gave in to the inevitable, removed paper from the second piece of candy, ate the chocolate from the filling and shared half the filling with the eager pest at tub-side.

"Now scram! Go bother Kit Kat, while I try to unwind." The head and chin of the little dog dropped to rest between his paws on the side of the tub, but he kept the empty candy wrappers in sight for a minute or two just in case more goodies should materialize. When Genna finally flicked some water at him, he withdrew to join Kit Kat on the bed.

She relaxed in the bubble infused bath until the water lost most of its heat, during which time a few yodels and hisses had accompanied the usual negotiations between Sky and Kit Kat on the distribution of pillow space on the bed. A blissfully relaxing half hour later she had quietly climbed out of the tub and managed to wrap a fluffy, white towel around her without interrupting Sky's soft snores. She was debating whether to try and remove the empty candy wrappers to a trash can and risk awakening Sky when the phone rang.

She glanced at the caller ID before answering it on the second ring. "Hi, Hon. I was hoping you'd call soon."

She shifted the phone to her other hand and attempted to calm an overly excited little Pap who'd been jerked awake from his sleep. "No, I'm not fixing dinner. As a matter of fact, I've just finished a relaxing bath, and my wonderful guests are manning the kitchen and the dinner preparations."

She paused and then chuckled at Jonathan's expression of concern that their Uncle Kevin might be concocting the wrong things in the kitchen. "Peggy and Shirley have been great about keeping the food preparations within the limits of his new healthy eating. And he's been very good. I'm the one who is suffering from sugar withdrawal. Peggy smuggled in some Almond Joys that I've been secretly enjoying with my bath."

She laughed aloud at Jonathan's response. "Of course, shared with Sky! You don't think he'd have it any other way, do you?" Stress lines in her face and around her eyes eased as she shared the humor of the little dog's habits with the man who'd been able to fit himself into both of their lives so smoothly.

Even though her mate was thousands of miles away, for this brief moment in time she felt wrapped in his caring embrace and sheltered from the world that was rapidly becoming more confused than she could deal with. She wanted to tell him about the latest problems, about the possibility of an intruder in the backyard, about Andrews' assessment of danger that had prompted the unusual response of wearing his gun around the house. *Didn't honesty and trust between them mean Jonathan had a right to expect the complete story?*

No, she decided, it would mean further conflicts for Jonathan. He was already stressed, pulled in two directions between the vacation and visit with Andrews he'd planned and the book tour, which was essential to his career as a writer. She was not, she reminded herself, going to make it any worse by whining to him for emotional support.

They chatted on for some time, and she told him about her worries with possible problems with the scanner but not the full story. Attuned as they were to the nuances in each other's voice and tone, Jonathan asked several times if she was alright, if she was sure he didn't need to pack things in and come straight home. She always managed to convince him that the stress with Bunny's precarious hold on life and the sleep deprivation caused by his need for constant care was the basis for her stress. Genna finally realized that between her soothing bath and equally soothing phone visit with Jonathan that almost an hour had passed.

"I suppose I have to get going, get dressed unless I intend to entertain my guests in my bathrobe, and put in an appearance in my own dining room in time to enjoy a dinner being prepared by my guests. Some hostess I am!"

Beguiling Bundle: Death Takes Best of Breed

Jonathan admitted to the need to scramble to a late afternoon session where he was, and the two said a loving goodbye.

Genna finished cleaning up the bathroom. An ever-hopeful little Papillon sat for a long time outside the cabinet door, which barred his access to the trash bin, into which the empty candy wrappers had been thrown.

Genna chuckled at the little dog while she bustled about the bedroom. She sprayed on her favorite perfume, feeling a sense of warmth from the memory of Jonathan's smile when he'd given it to her on her birthday, wrapped in gold paper with a beautiful card. She applied make-up carefully and succeeded in masking some of the redness around her eyes, though the bags underneath still looked like what they were. A brushing and spraying brought more success with taming her wayward hair. She chose white knit, flared leg pants and decided to dig a new pair of white flip-flops out of her closet to wear with them. Sky finally abandoned his vigil near the candy wrappers to follow her into the closet to offer his help with the digging.

She pulled out another tee with a butterfly on the front, but exchanged it for a dressier, paprika colored top with longer sleeves that had eyelet embellishments with circles that matched the geometric cutwork on her shoes.

Feeling almost human, she held the door open for her ever-present shadow, Sky to precede her into the hallway and downstairs to rejoin her guests. Kit Kat repositioned himself on the bed, turning his back to them both in a mute expression of aggravation at being abandoned once again.

* * *

157

Jean C. Keating

Amber and Rusty met Genna and Sky on the stairs. Their descent to the lower floor was slowed by the need to dodge the two other dancing and twirling dogs. Blacky, Muffin, and Jessie were waiting at the bottom of the stairs, so that Genna was royally welcomed into her kitchen by the troupe of six milling, canine bodies.

"Well, aren't you important," Peggy teased. "The entire pack has turned out to welcome you to dinner."

"Well, not quite all. Twinkle is busy elsewhere, I hope." Genna's smile was accompanied by an appreciative sniff at the delightful smells that pervaded the room. "And what smells so great?"

"Well, first we have some raw baby carrots with salsa for you to try." Andrews' smirk at the food offering was accompanied by a nod in appreciation at Genna's fresh attire. "Just don't drop the salsa on that pretty new top."

The five Papillons were running an extensive sniffing test on Genna's new flip-flops and the ankles of her white slacks. Blacky was utilizing her greater height to sniff the backs of Genna's knees where she had dabbed a splash of perfume. The resulting exam brought a loud sneeze from the gentle black shepherd and amused laughter from the humans.

"You smell nice too," Andrews added with a laugh, "even if Blacky doesn't seem to appreciate it. What's the perfume called?"

"Ever the data-gathering detective," Shirley injected before Genna could respond. "It's called *Joy* and you don't even want to know what it costs."

"Oh stop, you tease! It was a present from Jonathan," Genna said, but the appreciative responses to her beauty hour pleased her greatly. "What can I do to help, now that I've finally decided to join your party?"

"Sit and try the carrots and salsa!" Andrews

pulled out a chair for her.

"But..."

"No buts! Everything is almost ready. We were just going to call you when Amber and Rusty heard the door open and took off to escort you to dinner."

The table was set informally. Shirley pulled an appealingly arranged platter of sweet potato halves topped with a filling that exuded the sweet and tangy smells of cilantro, cayenne, mangos, and yogurt from the side counter. Peggy removed a flat oval tray from the oven heaped with grilled pork chops surrounded by green beans, halved cherry tomatoes, and almonds. Genna forgot all thoughts of being a bad hostess, remembering only that it had been a long and eventful afternoon and that she was very hungry.

Her three guests were quick to settle into the other three seats around the table. The six dogs picked their favorite person and settled at their feet to await any possible bits of food that might just happen to fall from the table in their direction.

Andrews tried a forkful of the sweet potato and its savory, sweet topping and managed to spill a dollop of it on his already spotted green shirt. "I really feel out of place in my stained shirt with three lovely ladies in fresh outfits joining me for dinner. Guess you'll evict me from the table next."

"You obviously have not noted the many additions to my butterfly shirt contributed by Bunny's attempt to reject his formula!" Shirley bit down on some beans and pork, before continuing. "Boy, this is really good! And I don't like veggies usually!"

"Speaking of Bunny, I have a suggestion on how to handle his feedings for the night, so we can all get our other work accomplished." Peggy didn't let her enjoyment of the food slow her efforts at keeping the group organized. "Instead of one of us taking a chunk of the night, I've made up a schedule that will give

159

each of us an assigned time for his feeding during the night, allow no less than four hour sleep intervals, and hopefully leave us all able to function tomorrow without feeling like sleep-deprived slugs!"

"Sounds fine," Genna said, "as long as you're not a part of any feedings tonight. You've been up since midnight and tonight you need to chill out."

She shook her head when Peggy opened her mouth to disagree. "I'm taking the evening till midnight anyway," Genna insisted. "I can alternate Bunny feedings with time on my computer. Not that I've figured out how to overlay a heat signature from a burning cigarette with the scanner requirements yet. But I've got to focus and try, and interspersing it with feedings every two hours isn't going to interrupt anything for me. Besides, thanks to some very kind friends, I got a good sleep last night."

"This conversation has gotten a little deep for my understanding," Shirley mumbled around a mouth full of food.

Genna had forgotten that Peggy and Shirley had excused themselves earlier before her conversation with Red and Andrews. "Sorry, Red, Uncle Kevin and I determined something interesting after the two of you took off upstairs earlier this evening. Swinson mentioned that a burning cigarette hadn't been noticed by the infrared scanner, which suggested that there was a flaw in the instrument. Now I've got to figure out how to prove it."

"Don't know what the cigarette and that *whatyoucallit* have to do with anything," Peggy admitted quickly, "but all of us will have plenty of time to get other things done and still provide Bunny with the supportive feedings and care he needs."

"I'm assuming that Rusty is going with Peggy and me to the show tomorrow." Shirley looked hesitantly at Genna.

Beguiling Bundle: Death Takes Best of Breed

When Genna nodded affirmatively, Shirley looked toward Andrews and continued. "Don't you want to go back to the show, Lt. Andrews?"

"If Genna wants to go, I'll go with her. But I'd rather we both stayed here until Red can reach some conclusions about the prints around that tree outside." He stopped short of mentioning that he didn't really want Genna exposed to the open atmosphere of the outdoor show which would make protecting her very difficult.

Genna glanced at the outline of the holster beneath Andrews' shirt, reminded that he wore his gun even at the dinner table. "We'll stay here tomorrow and deal with Bunny." She nodded to Peggy as she put a forkful of roasted pork and sweet potatoes in her own mouth, smiling slightly at the mingled scents and tastes of tangy cayenne and peppers and the sweet yogurt and mango flavors.

Peggy could be stubborn when she'd gotten an idea into her head. It was sometimes hard to change her direction, so Genna repeated, "You must be exhausted. You've been up since midnight, first with Bunny and then at the show. Tonight you sleep!"

Peggy shrugged but gave up her organizational ideas, since Genna was not going to listen. "Then I'm going to call it a day just as soon as we can get show schedules straight and dinner things cleared away." Peggy forked another piece of sweet potato and garnish by way of indicating that she wasn't ready to end her dinner just yet.

"I'm doing the clean-up," Genna emphasized. "I didn't help at all with the cooking, which is delicious. My thanks to you all, but I can at least clean away the dinner stuff."

Sky put his front paws on the side of Genna's leg in mute pledge to clean anything off the plates that was not wanted.

161

Jean C. Keating

"No, you little beggar," Genna responded. "You are not helping with cleaning dishes. You would eat all the wrong things and I'd be cleaning up messes after you."

"I thought dogs didn't eat things that were harmful to them," Andrews said.

"Oh, but they will. All sorts of things attract them that can be harmful, even fatal. Antifreeze, grapes, raisins, and chocolate, just to name a few. Sky has a real sweet-tooth!"

Peggy and Genna exchanged conspiratory glances. "Can't imagine why!" Peggy's tone held a bit of sarcasm. Neither woman was going to admit to the Almond Joys in the house. Peggy covered their secret quickly. "You always let him have little bites from the table."

"We are not getting into that discussion tonight," Genna responded with a tired chortle. Perhaps to establish her independence, she picked a tiny piece of pork off her plate and transferred it to the eager mouth at her knee. That brought an immediate response from four other Papillons and a larger black shepherd for equal shares. "Whoops! Shouldn't have done that!"

"Jonathan called while I was dressing," Genna said, changing the conversation and ignoring the dogs crowding hopefully around her.

"I heard the phone but guessed you'd gotten it when it stopped during the second ring."

"I didn't tell him about the recent problem in the backyard."

Andrews nodded knowingly. "But you wanted to!"

"Yes ... well ... I knew we could all handle it, especially with you here." Genna could not keep her eyes from drifting to the outline of the gun beneath Andrews' shirt.

"I don't want him to drop the book tour and come

rushing home. He was lucky enough to get the publicity and the chance to promote his books when the original author had to pull out. I don't want him to miss the chance, and he already feels badly that he's missing out on this planned vacation and visit with you all."

"And we will have a wonderful vacation, in spite of all these interruptions." Peggy tried to sound firm but the weary yawn ruined the effect.

"Do you want me to give Muffin a fresh bath tonight?" Shirley offered.

"No. Miss Muffin is fine."

"You're not," Genna smiled warmly at her friend. "Get to bed and let the rest of us deal with things tonight."

"I'll feed Muffin first, and put her to bed in her crate in the dog room if that's okay with you."

"Why don't you let me feed her for you, let her have some yard time, and put her to bed when I go up?" Shirley offered.

Peggy started to object, but a second yawn cut off the attempt. Bowing to logic and the exhaustion of her own body intensified by a full stomach, she nodded in agreement. Reaching over to pat her dog on the head, she excused herself and left the kitchen to the others.

Shirley distracted Muffin with a bit of meat from the table, pulled the little Papillon into her lap to prevent her following Peggy to the stairs.

"Good night, sleep tight. We'll make sure the dogs get settled," Genna called after the retreating back of her sleepy friend.

"I'll get started on clean-up. Then we can get the dogs outside for their last potty break and feed and settle them for the night." Shirley nodded in agreement with Genna's plan.

"I think I'll take a little walk outside first." Andrews

163

tried to sound relaxed but Genna caught his meaning without any trouble.

"Don't use the door from the garage. The lights there are connected to a motion sensor."

"Right."

Shirley caught the meaning finally. She hid her look of apprehension behind Muffin's body as she kissed the wiggling little body and put her on the floor again. "We'll just make sure the water dishes are filled and set out the food and vitamins, shall we?" She didn't wait for an answer.

Andrews quietly exited the door to the backyard, issuing a soft refusal to Blacky when she attempted to follow him.

Genna's hands were almost steady as she stacked and cleared the table, rinsed and loaded dishes, silverware, and glasses into the dishwasher.

Blacky took up sentry duty at the back door. Picking up on the tension, Sky nervously followed Genna from table to sink to dishwasher. After nearly falling over the little red fluff-ball twice, Genna finally ordered him to a sit/stay position by the sink while she finished the job of cleaning up the kitchen.

Andrews and Shirley returned almost simultaneously from work on their separate tasks.

"It's a beautiful, quiet night," Andrews said with a smile and a pat on the black head that happily greeted his return to the kitchen. "You two should join the dogs outside and enjoy the lovely view."

Genna finally was able to breathe deeply. She belatedly realized that her ribs hurt from breathing so shallowly since Andrews had ever so casually indicated his intent to patrol the yard before allowing her outside. Calling Sky to her, she and Shirley gathered the five Papillons and followed the excited pack outside to enjoy the evening's entertainment. When Andrews ignored her pleading look, Blacky

164

decided to join the other dogs and the two women.

Fireflies flickered brightly in the darkness. Solar powered fiber-optics produced ever-changing colors in crystal butterflies which lined the flower beds in the fenced portion of the yard. The scent of stately pines, which reached toward the star-lit sky, mingled with the heavier scents of Genna's prized fragrant irises.

Blacky forgot her attempts to annoy Amber when a firefly illuminated just in front of her nose. Her attempts to catch the little insect resulted in a collision with Pepper and the three dogs engaged in a brief grumbling match before Genna's sharp command reminded them of their manners.

The six dispersed to check out their favorite spots in the yard. Shirley and Genna followed them out to the steps of the deck to enjoy the soft Virginia night.

"My white pants aren't going to remain so for long," Genna observed as she sat on the top step.

"I don't think much could hurt these pants," Shirley added. "Bunny has succeeded in getting his formula all over the front of mine, so getting the seat dirty won't matter much."

Genna didn't answer. After an overlong span of silence, Shirley queried, "Are you scared?"

"A little," Genna admitted. "Murder was a lot more fun when it was far removed in Richmond, and I could treat it as an analytical exercise. The idea of having to check my own yard for intruders before letting my dogs out is giving me a pain in my chest." At Shirley's gasp of alarm, Genna quickly added, "... from holding my breath. I just can't believe this is happening, much less figure out why."

"I suppose it's safe to sit out here," Shirley injected, lowering her voice to a whisper.

Genna chuckled. "Uncle Kevin just checked the woods. Now six extremely alert dogs are playing about us. A stray squirrel couldn't get near the yard without setting off an alarm."

The explanation seemed to satisfy Shirley. She continued in a more normal tone of voice. "I didn't understand much of the conversation about cigarette smoke earlier, but if you want to talk about it, you know I'm always a great listener."

Genna smiled at her friend, her face relaxing a bit at the reminder of the many times they'd laughed together and gossiped about dog related things. "I'm sorry to be such a poor hostess." At Shirley's negative headshake, Genna continued. "No, I am! I invited you for a weekend of fun and shows, and instead you've gotten saddled with a struggling puppy, a murder, and caught up in my professional problems to boot!"

"Well, another way of looking at it is I'm learning a lot about dealing with handicapped puppies that will stand me in good stead when I breed Jessie. I'm seeing the inside of a murder investigation and experiencing even more thrills and chills than *Law and Order*, and I'm learning a little bit more about a friend's career efforts." Shirley reached a hand to lightly squeeze Genna's upper arm. "Not, as I say, that I understand a word of all the cigarette smoke stuff."

Genna laughed. "I don't understand a lot of that myself. A cigarette puts out a lot of heat when it's being smoked. It should have registered on the infrared scanner, and if it didn't, something is wrong. But I don't know how exactly to figure out what's wrong. Besides that wasn't supposed to intrude on our weekend!"

"Oh, and what *events police* dictated that! Remember the time two or so years ago when we were trying to show Sky before he got his championship and the weather was so bad the rain collapsed the side of the tent and you and Sky both got drenched before you could go in the ring. I don't think we planned for that either, but we eventually laughed ourselves silly about it."

"I remember. I wasn't exactly laughing when it happened; I was wet, my new hairdo was wet and ruined, my hair was falling in my eyes, Sky was wet, and his fringes were flat! The show committee finally had to cancel the show because the lightning got bad enough they were afraid it would conduct electrical currents into the pools of standing water. What an awful day that turned out to be!"

"Get out of that hosta, Muffin." Shirley interrupted her reply to admonish Peggy's wayward butterfly who had decided to turn around three times in the middle of the large clump of hosta and make it into a bed, totally ignoring the destruction by her tiny body to the plants. "Maybe the show site is jinxed!"

"Or maybe I am," Genna observed with a grimace. Then she shook her head. "Before we get all maudlin, tell me about the show today. And before we go any further, congratulations on Jessie's major. You must be so happy!"

"I am, oh, I am!" Shirley's white teeth reflected brightly in the dim light from the colorful butterfly lights in the yard as a grin of pure delight stretched her face. "And the judge was so nice. When she gave me the ribbon, she said Jessie had a beautiful head and fringes. She didn't' have to do that, and it just made my day."

"But I wish I could have brought home something on Rusty also," she hastened to add.

"Oh, stop! He got his major yesterday," Genna responded with a grin, which subsided into a frown. "Of course, he never got a chance to try for a best of winners, thanks to a little murder." Refusing to be drawn back into thoughts of the homicide, Genna continued, "So tell me about the rest of the show. You two stayed longer than I would have thought,

167

given that Peggy had been up since midnight."

"Well, she wanted to stay and see toy group, so we did. Though she was a bit grumpy by the time we started home."

Sky wandered over to Genna's knees, looking for a head pat, and then wandered off again to see what Rusty had found and was carrying around in his mouth.

Jessie and Muffin came over together and Shirley absentmindedly reached to pat Jessie's head and to remove a slender frond of white and green from Muffin's back, the residue of her earlier attempt to make a bed in the clump of hosta.

"And the Cavalier winner of Best of Breed asked about you, said to tell you she and her friend hoped you were doing well after all the shock of yesterday. They asked about Rusty and said they hoped his absence today wasn't due to any trauma to him yesterday."

"Do I know them?"

"I think so. They seemed to know you. One named Cindi had a tattoo of her dog in brilliant colors on her arm. Talk about carrying your photos with you to show off! It looked beautiful, sort of like seeing double. The dog in her arms matched the dog on her arm! The other woman was named Linda. Peggy said you spoke to both of them yesterday before Paps went in the ring."

"Oh, yes. They have this beautiful red and white, well in Cavaliers it's called ruby and white, bitch. And she's lovely!"

"That's the dog," Peggy nodded, in total disregard to the incorrect gender tag.

"Did their bitch do anything in group?"

"She took a Group III. The Pap got pulled for a final look in group but didn't get a placement."

Blacky and three of the Papillons had gravitated

to the feet of the two women, which brought an immediate return of a jealous Sky to Genna's side. Pushing through the other dogs, he jumped on the deck between the two women and wiggled his compact little body under her arm and into her lap.

"Possessive, isn't he?" Shirley laughed at the antics of the leader of the pack.

"Oh, yes. He never wants the others to forget for a minute that he is Lord of the Manor!" Genna's laugh came easily as she hugged the five-pound dynamo to her chest. For the first time in a long stretch of hours, the tension in her shoulders relaxed. She planted a kiss on the top of Sky's head and was rewarded with a lightening quick slurp from his wet tongue in return.

"I suppose you guys are telling us it is time for your dinner." Genna's words, especially **dinner**, were rewarded with yodels, whines and chirps from the Paps and a soft woof from Blacky.

"I'll take that as a yes," Shirley laughed, and got up from the deck, brushing the dirt off the back of her hot pink pants.

The legs of Genna's white ones were suitably marked with dirty paw prints in front to match the patch of dirt on the seat. "Ah, another candidate for the washing machine," she observed as she tried to brush the worst of the dirt off both sides of her pants."

The dogs rushed to the door ahead of the two women, crowding each other to be first back in the house.

"I'm glad I already have water and food in each of their crates. Wouldn't want to keep this mob waiting for their dinner," Shirley observed with a laugh. She stumbled over Blacky as she tried to reach the door handle, but five small bodies and one larger one made it difficult.

Andrews opened it from the inside before she could push the milling dogs out of the way. "Ah! I

169

was just coming to get you. Paul Carter is on the phone, wants to talk to you, Genna." He lowered his voice to a whisper as the din from the six canines faded away with their dash to reach the dog room, their crates and dinner. "I don't think you should say anything to him about Swinson's comments or our suspicions until Red and you finish your investigations."

CHAPTER SIXTEEN

Genna's hand trembled slightly and the numbers she recorded in the logbook beside Twinkle's nest were a poor shadow of her usual precise rendering of figures. Bunny's weight was holding but not increasing, and she found her fears for his survival coupled with her growing anxiety over some unknown threat to her home and privacy overwhelming. Tears welled in her eyes and one spilled over to leave a wet track down her right cheek.

The record of figures beneath Tina's name showed the little porker had gained almost half an ounce over the nearly two days since her birth. She was noticeably plumper and longer now than her struggling brother.

"I don't know what else to do for you, little one," Genna whispered to the male she held in her left hand. Eyes and ears sealed shut, tummy hopefully full from his latest feeding, the object of her worry slept peacefully. Twinkle responded with a lick at

Bunny's butt and then an attempt to lick Genna's nose.

Pulling her face back at the last minute, Genna managed a slight laugh that did not soften the stress lines between her eyebrows or lessen the moisture that spilled from her eyes. "Maybe not in that order, Little Mother!"

Sky's whine sounded loudly in the still house. He was protesting his enforced exclusion from the nursery by the half door which barred him from joining Genna. The bond between woman and dog was sufficiently strong for the little canine to pick up on her heightened unhappiness with Bunny's condition and on her general anxiety over Andrews' continuing watchfulness and the threat to her home and privacy that prompted it. Despite Genna's whispered command to be quiet, the little fur ball increased the volume of his whining and added a determined scratching on the doorframe to punctuate his insistent demands to be near her. The slight rocking movement of the door against the frame echoed loudly in the otherwise still house.

"Oh, Sky, stop being such a pest." Genna's voice was harsh with frustration and strain, the strain of suppressing her tears, the frustration of not feeling she could freely take Twinkle outside for another walk around her own yard, and of not being able to cry freely on Jonathan's shoulder.

A softer but more pathetic whine came from the other side of the door.

Genna returned the sleeping puppy to his mother's side and stomped to the doorway, snatching the half-door open with a cross "Will you hush!"

The bundle of fur at her feet looked crushed at the harsh tones of her voice. Ears lowered to each side of his head and tail decidedly trailing behind his body on the floor, Sky cringed at her feet, his dark,

172

liquid eyes pleading with her for forgiveness. Amber and Rusty had retreated down the hall toward the master bedroom with lowered tails and ears, their faces reflecting sadness and anxiety.

Genna's attitude shifted rapidly as she confronted the results of her sharp and ill-tempered responses on her three little dogs. "Oh, my darlings. I am so sorry." Genna reached to scoop the trembling dog at her feet from the floor and cuddle him to her chest.

"I'll be back in a bit, Twinkle," she whispered softly knowing that the little dog in the nursery would understand her soft tones if not her words.

She closed the half door to the nursery, walked with Sky in her arms to the master suite, and closed that door also. Amber and Rusty had joined Kit Kat on the king size bed, but their low ear-set clearly signaled their continuing distress at her early harsh tones.

She carried Sky over to the bed and sat down beside the other two, encouraging them all to climb in her lap.

"I am so very sorry, little ones. I've been so busy worrying about everyone else, I took my fears and frustrations out on you." Her gentle touches and soft tones reassured the three, and they were soon vying for attention for head caresses and ear scratches.

She had exchanged her dirtied white slacks for an azure blue knit lounger with white screen prints accented by white embroidery. Bunny had, of course, added a bit of his formula to one of the geometric patterns on her left cuff. Rusty undertook to lick it clean for her while Amber found the tassel at the end of the attached hood and tried to remove it. The ears of the three little dogs had returned to high alert mode and their tails fanned rapidly, signifying that all was well with their world once again.

Jean C. Keating

Kit Kat, like all cats the world over, was not amused. He responded to being repeatedly bumped by the excited behavior of the three little butterflies in typical cat fashion. He abandoned his favored spot on the middle pillow and stalked to the end of the bed, turned his back on the four, and studiously ignored them. When Rusty's excited romping bumped him again, he refused to retreat further and hissed softly, batting at the smaller dog with his paw, but his claws remained retracted and Rusty paid no heed to the complaint.

Genna took advantage of the cat's move to pile the pillows against the headboard and lounge back against them, swinging her body up to rest along the bed. The three dogs pushed and shoved each other in their eagerness to be the closest to her.

This time, the laughter in her voice was reflected in her eyes, and stress lines between her brows and around her mouth eased. "Here I am, agonizing because I didn't have anyone I could really talk to, really, really level with, and all the time you three were just waiting eagerly to be my listeners." The three reassured her with flashing ears and sweeping tails that this was so.

Keeping her tone soft and low, Genna used both hands to caress the three heads and bodies that excitedly crowded around her. "Well, Bunny is a big worry. We're doing all we know to do, but he's just not gaining weight. And I'm very frustrated with not being able to do more."

Three pair of warm, adoring eyes reassured her that all was right in at least three entities' world. A fourth pair from the other side of the bed said things could be better without all the racket and jiggling of the bed.

"The hardest part of my life, and it's a problem with most humans, is that I can't be honest with anyone it seems." Genna looked directly into Sky's trusting eyes as she spoke. "You three never have that problem. You're always honest and true."

The smile on her face carried over into a smile in her voice, and three plume tails wagged even faster as Genna continued. "I can't tell Jonathan what is going on, can't cry on his shoulder. He'd abandon that book tour and come flying home, and we can't have that. Daddy needs the publicity for his book this tour will give it, and he deserves our support. I can't tell Uncle Kevin that he's scaring the begeebies out of me wearing that gun around the house and wanting to patrol the yard before I go outside. He means well, but he's making my skin crawl. I can't admit I'm terrified, but I am. He's making this murder too real, too close to home."

She'd forgotten to move her hands from Amber's and Sky's heads to give equal caresses to Rusty, so the youngest dog pushed his way under her arm to poke his nose into her face. "Yuck, Rusty! What have you been licking? Your breath smells like you've been in the cat box again."

Rusty jumped away at Sky's low growl of complaint, but wiggled in delight when Genna's hand reached to scratch his back. "Then there's my boss. I talked to him tonight, but Uncle Kevin didn't want me to even hint to him that we suspected the infrared scanner might be flawed based on something Swinson had said at the dog show. So I can't be honest with my boss. Then between Bunny's feedings and ignoring you little people, I've finally found the problem with the scanner. And either Swinson is a dope or he's really dishonest and trying to pull a fast one, because that prototype doesn't respond to signals over the entire range of the infrared spectrum that the design specs require."

Three pair of eyes gazed at her face with

unwavering attention, for all the world as though they understood every word she was saying.

"And what really scares me is that the flaw is so well hidden, I might have missed the intermittent flaws in that instrument's performance had it not been for Swinson's comment about that dratted prototype not responding when someone was smoking near it! I'm not making good decisions right now; look at the way I screamed at you three earlier. So am I making the wrong decision to keep struggling with Bunny?"

Three adoring little bodies wiggled closer, reassuring her of their unfailing trust and love. It was heartwarming and heart wrenching at the same time. "You trust me to play God! And I'm not equal to the task!"

The reminder of her responsibility for deciding Bunny's care brought back tears and an increased sense of frustration and helplessness. Before she could sink any deeper into that quagmire, Genna gently pushed the three furballs away and sat up on the side of the bed.

"Now, I've got to go clean up Twinkle's bed, give Bunny his midnight feeding, and leave good notes for your Uncle Kevin who will do the 2AM feeding. I need you three to be quiet while I'm gone, and I'm going to close the door to the bedroom here. So don't go fussing at the door and awakening the rest of the crew, especially Blacky because she'll have your Uncle Kevin up too early and he won't get enough sleep."

Three fluffy tails wagged furiously but the three mischievous little mugs made no promises about what would happen if she abandoned them in the bedroom.

Her passage down the hallway took Genna past the closed doorway to Andrews' room. A soft snuffle at the base of the door announced that Blacky was alert and aware, but a whispered *shush* at her forestalled any further noise. Jessie and Muffin were asleep in the dog room downstairs, and happily not near enough to react to her late night ramblings. She returned to the nursery, Twinkles and the puppies without any further noise to disturb her hopefully sleeping guests.

She re-closed the half door between the nursery and hall and eased herself into the chair by the table upon which Twinkle's box was sitting. The patient, trusting mother dog acknowledged her return with a slight wave of her tail, and seem pleased when Genna reached to stroke her head and ears. The puppies were almost invisible, tucked securely against their dam's belly with Twinkle's sparsely feathered tail covering them.

Carefully Genna warmed her hands against the water bottles packed around the puppy bed, then removed and weighed Bunny on the digital diet scale. Her heart raced a bit faster when the display showed a flicker and then held on a figure that was one-tenth of an ounce heavier than before. She could barely keep her voice to a whisper.

"Twinkle, he's gained a little. Oh, please let it be real!"

Twinkle took the news with a repeat of her weak tail wag. Genna went about loading and heating a syringe full of formula and enticing Bunny to take it. Only a small dollop of the oyster-white liquid was slung aside by the surprisingly active little puppy.

"Thanks, a bunch, Bunny." Genna 's whisper was a chuckle, "you've now got the right sleeve stained to match the left one. I'm going to run out of clothes soon." The grin on her face, equal parts of cheer and hope, belied any concern for clothing stains.

With Twinkle's help, Genna made certain the struggling puppy was stimulated and cleaned before

177

returning him to his dam's side. Then she happily recorded his weight in the logbook and left a note for Andrews to carefully check the weight gain during his watch. She decided the bedding was still dry and clean and refreshing it was not worth disturbing mom and pups. But she was too excited by the puppy's marginal weight gain to go to sleep, so she sat for a long while stroking Twinkle's head and whispering to her in a soft, sing-song voice.

"I think he might just make it, Little Mother. We're all trying so very hard. And you know you don't have to worry about anything ever again. Kind and caring people will see that your babies and you have a warm and loving home from now on, with people who will cherish you and keep you safe." Genna didn't want to think of the obstacles ahead: surgery to fix Bunny's mouth, surgery to spay Twinkle. Somehow, just being able to voice her fears to her own pack of three had eased Genna's nerves, allowed her to file her worries away in manageable mental boxes. She couldn't solve most of her problems right now, but she could take them out of the mental box separately and deal with them one at a time without being overwhelmed by them all at once. Strange how the spoken language enforced order upon problems when mental processes seemed to swirl about and become hopelessly entangled in each other. She decided to continue that self-help with Twinkle and the puppies.

"You know you don't really belong to me, though I'd be proud to have you in our pack. You belong to a wonderful organization that is dedicated to protecting your kind. So while I'm just your foster mom for now, you're loved and appreciated and provided for. And when the puppies are older, they'll go to their own forever homes," Genna's voice took on an added forcefulness, "and Bunny will live and prosper . . ."

Catching herself before her own voice could disturb her guests, Genna reached to stroke the alert ears that flicked from side to side as Twinkle's intelligent eyes fixed on her mouth. Lowering her voice to the barest whisper, she continued, ". . . and I will screen applicants very carefully, and Sky and I will do home visits to insure that the homes are suitable." All dogs were spayed and neutered before being placed in forever homes, and rigid checks including at least one in-home visit and review would be required before any final placement of Twinkle and her puppies.

"The problem with Bunny is another story." Genna's whisper trailed off into a long pause. Finally forcing herself to voice the dilemma always faced by rescue, "resources are always strained. That's why money applied to near hopeless cases is questioned. Would the money be better spent helping another dog with a better chance?" Her voice broke at putting the problem into words, even admitting the problem. Practically she knew it did. Emotionally she didn't want it to exist.

"But you know what," Genna's whisper came stronger and with a happier lilt, "you and I don't have to make that choice. I just happen to have a rather large endowment of my own, not to mention that I do make a few monetary tokens as a rocket scientist, so his surgery will be just between us. We won't be depriving any other rescues of help because of the expense of this little puppy. And I promise you, he won't lack for anything."

Twinkle pushed her trusting face and muzzle against Genna's hand, reminding the woman that she was failing to provide the proper amount of ear scratching.

"But will I be able to let you or Bunny leave after

179

we've struggled so hard to keep him alive?"

And where is MY chocolate?

CHAPTER SEVENTEEN

Shirley fed Bunny at 6:00 AM, took Twinkle out to potty, entered a delightful note that the scale was flickering toward but not quite reaching a higher weight for the fragile puppy, and went back to bed for a little nap that stretched into another two hours of sleep. By the time she'd showered, dressed for the show, and breezed downstairs to join the rest of the group, Genna was on her third cup of coffee and still not too happy with *her* morning.

Andrews was antsy, sticking his nose in the refrigerator looking for something to add to the unsatisfying portion of cereal he'd consumed an hour earlier. "A fellow ought to be able to get something to at least fill his stomach," he grumbled. Two days of enforced adherence to his point count were producing stress lines in his disposition. "Don't you have any orange juice in this place?"

"Have some of that V8 juice you were pushing yesterday!" Genna snapped. "It has far fewer cal ... points, whatever!" Sometimes she forgot that his new

181

eating plan allotted a point value to food that was based on fat and fiber content as well as calories. This morning she wanted to forget.

He'd come to breakfast in a sparkling clean and yellow, sunny-bright tee over his well-worn jeans. The tail of his shirt was hanging out again but did nothing to conceal the gun he was wearing in his belt. The sight of it continued to rattle Genna's nerves.

Besides, she'd eaten an egg -- without toast or bacon – and a very small apple. She wanted more herself, something entirely inappropriate for Andrews' diet, something like a nice, butter slopped bagel with cheese, or better yet, another Almond Joy. Keeping Andrews on the straight and narrow wasn't doing much for her nerves.

Peggy looked refreshed after a good night's sleep although it had been interrupted by her insistence at giving Bunny his 4 AM feeding. An excellent manipulator knew when to provide guidance and when to keep her mouth shut and Peggy was not getting into the middle of the grousing between Andrews and Genna. She busied herself with stirring another spoonful of sugar in her coffee and scraping the last of her yogurt out of its cup.

"You sure are getting the royal treatment when you visit me," Genna sniped. "I don't think we've used the dining room once, and now you're getting your breakfast out of the package."

"Do I look like I mind?" Peggy said.

"Of course not," Shirley answered for her. "More importantly, what do you think of this outfit? Do you think the judge will like it? Do you think these white shoes are okay? Or will they overemphasize white and call attention to the fact that Jessie has a solid head?"

Her machine-gun transmission of ideas brought a surprised look from Andrews, a sneer from Peggy, and a chuckle from Genna.

"Well, I love the butterflies everywhere," Genna began, "and the purple theme is perfect. I suppose you're trying to send the subliminal message that you're after the Winner's ribbon."

As usual, Shirley's clothes displayed a profusion of butterflies. The solid purple tee sported a large purple, lavender, white and blue butterfly in the center front done in beadwork and sequins. White pants contained smaller matching butterflies randomly placed over both legs. As Shirley turned to display the outfit to her breakfast companions, Genna noted a large purple and blue butterfly hair clip that she'd never seen before holding back Shirley's spill of blond curls. She also noted that one little butterfly appliqué was rather prominent on the seat of the pants. She wondered how comfortable sitting was going to be in the pants, but decided not to raise that issue.

Peggy was not as reticent. "You're going to have a butterfly impression on your butt if you sit in those all day and your feet will be killing you if you try to wear those little heels in those outdoor rings." Her grin was evil. "That's if you don't fall on your face and scare the pants off everyone that there's been another murder at the show!"

Shirley stuck her tongue out and cut Genna off before she could ask about food. "I'll just get a yogurt too, if Ms. Know-it-All there didn't take the last one."

Suiting her actions to her words, she shuffled to the refrigerator, selected a yogurt and brought it back to the table, responding with an affirmative nod to Genna's hand motions regarding coffee.

She pulled the freshly poured cup toward the empty seat at the table and sat down, waving away Andrews' offer of the sugar bowl. "Where are the fluffballs? And Blacky?"

Jean C. Keating

She smiled in greeting to Andrews as he wandered back to the table with a can of V8 juice and glass in hand and a not so satisfied smile on his face.

"Out in the yard comparing notes on the crazy nights around this place. I believe their conversations center on the inability of this household to provide a peaceful and extended period of sleep. Sky looked positively drained this morning, as did Rusty." Genna didn't look all that rested either. Her blue knit lounger looked like she'd slept in it, which she had.

"I checked the puppy log before I came down. Bunny's really gained a little." Peggy's happy remarks finally produced something of a grin from Genna.

"What about today? Are you staying home with the puppy again? And what about Rusty? Is he going to the show with us again?" Shirley rattled on after a brief pause to catch her breath. "Kevin, are you sure you wouldn't like to go with us today?" Age lines around her mouth were accentuated as she sucked on her spoon full of key lime yogurt.

"Yes, yes, and no." Genna finally had to laugh at the bubbling energy that produced additional questions without waiting for an answer from the first? With a nod in Andrews' direction, she clarified, "or is that a yes -- he's sure he doesn't want to go!"

"Eat your yogurt and slow down," Peggy injected, proving that broken sleep didn't improve the dispositions of even tiny dynamos. "Just because I'm not in purple doesn't mean Muffin and I don't intend to get the Winners ribbon today!"

"Well, just because I'm not going to be there, dressed in purple or anything else," Genna snorted, "it doesn't mean Rusty isn't interested in taking a purple ribbon again. He'd like his chance at competing for Best of Winners without some nut shooting up the ring." She was immediately sorry she'd brought up the

184

subject of Friday's horror in the breed ring as the facial muscles on both of her women guests' faces tightened into frowns.

"I'm sorry," she added. "That really wasn't funny." She swiftly changed the focus of the conversation. "What is ring time for Paps today?"

"Actually it is 11:15, so we'd really better get moving." Peggy carefully removed the napkin she'd tucked into the scooped neck of her celery colored, peachskin dress to insure that no coffee or yogurt marred the silky smoothness. The matching short-sleeved jacket bespoke her intention not to be bothered by the humidity at the show today. The outfit looked professional and beautiful with her bleached blond hair.

"I'll help you clean up," Shirley offered.

"Wouldn't hear of it," Andrews injected, a slight red line of a tomato-based mustache outlining the lip he abruptly pulled away from his glass. "I'll handle that and Genna can see to Bunny's 10 AM repast."

"Oh, really!" Genna teased, glad for a further change of subject to something about which they could joke. "Now you wouldn't be planning an unauthorized search of the kitchen for more food, would you?"

"Not me, Madame," he countered with a chuckle. "Haven't got a warrant!"

* * *

Departure by Shirley, Peggy, Muffin, Jessie, and Rusty for the show had been accomplished with a maximum of confusion. Peggy couldn't find her pale green lead at the last minute and had substituted the dark green one she'd used on Friday. Shirley decided a white lead and white shoes would call further attention to Jessie's solid head and ran up and down

185

stairs changing shoes and locating a black lead. Rusty thought all the running to and fro was a new game best played by his chasing after first one human and then the other and had to be physically caught and confined to his crate before he managed to trip someone on the stairs. Sky, Amber, and Blacky lounged under the kitchen table, looking at all the activity with what, on a human countenance, would have been defined as a smug expression of superiority.

When the dust of their departure settled, Genna was glad to leave the kitchen to Andrews and Blacky. She returned to the nursery with Amber and Sky trailing behind. She coaxed them past an instantly alert Twinkle and settled them on the old blue sofa. None of the three Papillons seemed totally happy with her arrangements. Sky grumped softly at not being allowed to settle closer to Genna's feet, but he obeyed her command to settle on a well-worn cushion. Amber locked eyes with Twinkle as though in private communication regarding Amber's distrust of Twinkle's abilities at puppy care.

Genna turned her back to the two on the sofa and toward dam and puppy. She was glad of the peace and solitude she could spend in giving Bunny his 10 AM feeding.

Despite the relative calm in the nursery, she felt oppressed. Laying out the tools and supplies, warming the formula and slowly feeding the wiggling puppy were done on automatic pilot as she tried to arrange her thoughts and analyze her current unsettled feelings. *I should not be sleep deprived,* she told herself. *My guests are taking on way more of their share of puppy care than they should. They came to enjoy the show. Instead they're pitching in to look after me, Bunny, showing Rusty, helping Uncle Kevin with his health regime. And I haven't even had*

186

the energy or inclination to shower and dress this morning! What is wrong with me!

She refused to consider that she was avoiding thinking about the homicide. She felt a fleeting guilt that she did not feel more grief at the death of Edwards. She'd known him only briefly it was true, but he seemed a decent young man just trying to make a life and career for himself. He deserved more consideration than she was giving his death.

She didn't want to think about the prototypes. Between Bunny's feedings last night, she'd run the comparative statistics between heat signatures of burning cigarettes and found an anomaly in the performance of the infrared scanner. It was peculiar and she didn't understand yet just what caused the malfunction, but she had confirmed its existence. If Swinson knew about it, he was a crook trying to pass a flawed instrument off on NASA. It would fly on an unmanned probe, but its failure at a critical time would invalidate a billion dollar project to which thousands of people had devoted their professional lives. If he didn't know, and his comment to Andrews outside the dog show ring certainly sounded as though he didn't, then how did he ever attain the contract to build it in the first place? Poor management and lack of expertise at the upper levels of a contractor's company were something NASA screened for carefully before granting contracts. Each step she took toward investigating the problem seemed to lead to more questions and further and further away from the solutions and closure she wanted.

Genna keyed the digital diet scale to zero out with the tiny basket in place and placed the squirming puppy safely in the basket. The small but positive weight gain only hinted at the night before registered strongly now, and another small fractional gain flickered intermittently as he wiggled. She recorded it as a possibility, but not exactly a true weight gain, despite her desperate need for something to celebrate. Tina continued to widen the gap with her tiny litter brother in both length and breath.

She removed the squirming little body from the basket, returned him to the warmth of her hands and turned off the scale.

Twinkle was dealing well with all the confusion of not one but four humans running in and out every two hours, carrying her outside for potty breaks, and handling, feeding and fussing over her and the puppies.

"You're losing your touch," Genna cooed to the surprisingly active little body in her hand. Apparently full, the pup had been holding a last dollop of formula in his mouth. He flung it out now with a quick flip of his head. The drop landed exactly in the circular decoration on her right sleeve, just on top of the stain from the night before.

"You don't get any points for that stain. You hit it before." Twinkle's ears perked forward for all the world as though she tried to make sense out of Genna's foolish talk.

"Here. Your turn, Mama!" Genna reversed the end of the puppy and angled him so his dam could lick his belly, stimulating and cleaning him. Twinkle made quick work of that chore and moved to lick the sweetened mixture of formula and honey from his mouth and Genna's hand.

"I'm even reluctant to take a bath in my own bathroom," Genna confessed to Twinkle. "You were a lot better at dealing with the stress of being dumped in this strange environment six weeks ago. I know I'm overreacting and I can't seem to help myself. The very idea of someone, some stranger, climbing a tree in my backyard and looking in on me, with or without ill intentions, makes my skin crawl. I've always been able to look out the windows over my bath and enjoy the woods, the sky, the stars, the *privacy*. Now that's gone. And I'm not dealing well with it. I'm not dealing with it at all!"

She'd tried to keep her tone low and soothing, but her anxiety apparently registered with Amber and Sky. A soft whine from behind her brought a soft reinforcement of her command to them to stay. They obeyed, but a barely audible whine suggested reluctance on the part of one or the other of the pair to remain on the sofa.

Twinkle abandoned her attempt to extract the last molecule of formula from Bunny's muzzle and flicked her ears toward the door a minute later. Genna finally identified the cause of Twinkle's attention and increased alert stance when the soft click of Blacky's claws against the hall floor was audible to her far less sensitive ears. An instant later the happy black shepherd loped through the doorway into the nursery with Andrews close behind her.

Twinkle had apparently seen enough of this before that she only woofed once and returned to her licking at imaginary remains of formula.

Andrews came up behind Genna's chair and put his hand on her shoulder, his eyes focused on her latest entry in the puppy logbook on the table. "He's gained another quarter ounce? Well, things are looking up!"

Genna turned her face toward him with a smile of satisfaction that held all the joy she felt in the small but positive progress. "Not much but in the right direction."

She returned the puppy to the sleeping box, and Twinkle happily resettled Bunny along with his sister within the warm and protected area next to her stomach. Twinkle gave one final swipe of Bunny's face with her wet tongue in a hopeless effort at getting just one more taste of honey and formula.

"Kitchen duties all finished," Andrews teased, "and the helpers didn't see the need of raiding the pantry for extras. Although I was sorely tempted," he admitted with a snort. "For some reason I am craving something sweet."

"There are some white grapes in the freezer that are coated in sugar-free lime Jello. Grab a handful when you want. Just don't let any of the dogs get one."

"Oh, it's only MY teeth you want to break!!"

"They remain soft enough to bite, you clown," Genna retorted. "But grapes are dangerous to dogs."

"Oh! But Blacky likes them."

"Well, I don't care if Blacky likes them. They can poison Blacky, so you have to make sure she doesn't eat them." Genna's voice had a sharp edge that she tried hard to suppress. The gun at Andrews' left hip had brushed against her arm as she rose from the chair, painfully reminding her of the murder and the unresolved situation with a suspected intruder on the property.

She tried to cover her shudder by continuing her lighthearted teasing. "Who's in control here, you big pushover, you or Blacky? The snack will give you the sweets you crave and not use up points on your eating plan. Blacky does not need to lose weight nor can she safely eat grapes. Unlike some people we could name who COULD safely eat most anything but who SHOULD not eat most things!"

"I feel the woman has lost it this morning, Blacky." He spoke playfully to the black dog that wiggled around the feet of the two humans standing over her. "Now she's decided to teach me English grammar in a knit robe well decorated with puppy muck that she slept in last night."

Genna managed to rise from the chair more or less gracefully while sticking her tongue out at Andrews. At a hand signal from Genna, Amber and Sky happily abandoned their positions on the sofa and joined Blacky at Genna's side. Twinkle's grumble of complaint at all the commotion accompanied the two humans and three dogs as they left the nursery to mother and puppies and paused briefly in the hallway outside.

"We need to talk about a timetable for your analysis of that instrument's stability. I need to call Red and brief him on anything further you can suggest about Swinson," Andrews said when they paused far enough away from the nursery door to appease Twinkle.

Genna turned toward her computer room, and her four mixed-species companions followed. She went directly to her computer chair, turning it to face outward from the desk and wall to the seating area. Amber and Sky each chose one of the blue velvet chairs. Andrews arrived before Amber could complete her three circles and booted her out of one of the chairs, removing the print pillow from the chair to make room for his ample form. Amber moved to the other chair, jumped up beside Sky and the two of them danced around each other before finally settling with the matching print pillow as their joint headrest. Blacky flopped down at Andrews' feet, resting her chin on his left sneaker.

"Between puppy feedings last night, I had a chance to run some comparative statistics between the heat signatures of a burning cigarette and the response signatures of the infrared scanner. There are some anomalies. I don't know exactly why they exist but I do know that they do, and where the differences are." Genna's words came out with a long, slow sigh. Here in her cozy study with its high windows and completely closed curtains she felt . . . well, safe!

"I don't know that you or Red need know any more. I'm not sure that Swinson even knows this much. His comment to you at the show on Friday certainly seemed to indicate he didn't have a clue that this was a problem." Genna looked puzzled, the drawn look around her mouth making her look even older and wearier than before. "It doesn't make sense that he wouldn't know, but I truly don't think he does."

"How much of a problem is it? From a layman's standpoint, I mean?"

"A non-technical answer? NASA would not fly with this version of the payload!"

"So Swinson's company would be out big bucks."

"Yes. Paul and I will have to do some more work to determine just exactly WHAT is happening, but we could never recommend any payment to Swinson based on this prototype. At least, not on the infrared scanner. The star tracker is fine, but since the two instruments must work together, I'm not certain NASA would be willing to give him any advance payment at this point. "

Andrews was so still for a minute that Blacky raised her head from his shoe to lay it against his knee in silent appeal for an ear scratch. When he finally spoke, his words were low but firm. "I'll call Red and see what he thinks. But I know that I think we should ask Mr. Swinson to come to the station for a little chat."

The big man's left hand reached over to give the black shepherd a caress, and he made no move to follow through on his words. Instead his eyes softened with compassion as he continued to face Genna. "You're feeling violated and threatened by the thought of someone in your yard, someone with

192

possible ill-intentions toward you violating your privacy!"

Genna responded with shock. "How did you know?"

"Don't you think I see far too many victims in my line of work not to recognize the symptoms?"

Genna could only nod, her whole body frozen with a sort of numbness that gripped her mentally as well as physically. "How do you fight it?"

"By trying to get on with your life, but being sensible about altering those aspects of it which might play into the wrong hands! You somehow feel safe in this room. Analyze why and repeat it where you can."

Genna looked at him for a long span of seconds before settling herself against the chair back. When she spoke, her voice lacked its normal forcefulness. "The windows are high and heavily curtained, because I work best without the distraction of an outside view. Jonathan is just the opposite; his study downstairs has huge windows on three sides and he draws inspiration from being surrounded by the sounds and sights of the outdoors." Her voice dropped so low Andrews could barely hear her although he was sitting less than four feet away. "I can't bring myself to use my tub this morning; the big windows behind open on to the tops of the trees in the woods. And I feel . . ."

" . . . your skin crawls and you feel there's a threatening presence behind each tree," Andrews finished for her. "And you're going to do what? Spend the rest of your life in that robe?"

Genna's head snapped up and she looked at him crossly. He could be so, so annoying when he was being so, so *right*. "You might be a bit more sympathetic!" she said.

Her tone was a squeak and both Sky and Amber

raised their heads to look at her, a puzzled expression on their little faces. Blacky rotated her head slightly and cocked her head to look at Genna without moving her ears from beneath Andrews' hand and the fingers that stoked them so soothingly.

Shock, annoyance, determination, and finally humor registered on Genna's face. The look on the dogs' faces finally produced a chuckle, though the amusement did not quite reach her green-banded eyes, which still reflected a haunted look. "No, dammit, I'm going to find my navy silk sheets, make some temporary window covers out of them that won't show shadows, cover those big windows over my bath, and go enjoy a long soak and a change of clothes. Bunny has decorated so many of my outfits with his rejected dollops of food, that I'll be doing laundry soon or I won't have anything to wear. But I'm not going to let any unknown jackleg keep me from doing what I need to. Guess I'll rig some curtains for the nursery room also."

She pushed up from her chair with more energy than she'd felt since Andrews had first entered her study yesterday with the outline of his gun showing beneath his shirt.

The dogs were quick to follow her lead, responding with excited yips and yodels. It took Andrews a bit longer to get his considerably larger backside out of the little blue chair. "While you're redecorating and rejuvenating, I'll go downstairs, call Red on the kitchen phone, and bring him up to date on your findings regarding that scanner."

"Use the phone on the desk there, if you like," Genna said. "I'll be in my *boudoir* hanging sheets."

CHAPTER EIGHTEEN

Once she made up her mind to deal with her fears, Genna lost no time in following through with her plan. It took her more than forty minutes to hang navy sheets over the open windows of her bath, however, thanks to the help from her two Papillons.

Sky rode on the end of the sheet as Genna dragged it across the lavender tiles of the bathroom floor, reluctantly surrendering the end of it only when Genna pulled it into the tub and away from his eager attention. Even after the ends of the sheet were safely away from the two playful dogs, Amber jumped around like a puppy and made a game out of biting at Sky's happily waving tail. Genna completed the project of blocking off the window long before the little butterflies tired of their game. By this time, Sky and Amber had tired of chasing each other's tails and viewed the finished project from the side of the large tub, two pairs of front paws resting on the side of the tub.

Genna found some silk flowers in the linen closet

in the lavender, white, and blue colors of the bath and took the time to decorate around the tops of the sheets so they looked like a plan instead of a temporary fix.

While Sky and Amber found her changed mood a great improvement, the cat did not. Kit Kat had followed the procession of sheets and dogs to the door of the bath, looked in disgust at the exuberant antics of the dogs, and retreated with royal disdain to the soft pillows at the head of the bed.

Amber and Sky were less interested in Genna's next project, a long shower. Not wanting to get their little selves wet, they waited patiently outside the shower stall for Genna to finish, and then tried to ride on the end of the thick, sky-blue beach towel with which she attempted to dry herself. When she dropped the towel and began to powder and spray perfume, Amber had backed away, but Sky persisted in his personal and up-close supervision of her actions. Between laughing at the dogs, teasing Sky for sticking his nose so close to the perfume spray bottle that it gave him a sneezing fit, and enjoying the breezy look of herself in the mirror, Genna felt ready to tackle Bunny's noon feeding, lunch for her and Andrews, and a homicidal nut with confidence. *Well, maybe not the homicidal nut,* she corrected.

She tucked one still-damp strand of dark hair behind her ear, grabbed a light blue printed robe, and headed off for the nursery again.

As usual, Sky and Amber beat her through the door, and Twinkle was standing in the nesting box with one paw outside on the table top exchanging a low growl with Amber when Genna flip-flopped her way through the door. *Maybe sling-back sandals were not the best choice of footwear,* she thought to herself.

"Sofa," she ordered Amber and Sky, reinforcing

196

the command with a hand signal. "I'm ready for you and your little son now," she said to Twinkle as though the little mother understood her words. "I've got this nice little cover here, and you can sling formula all you want, but you're not messing up this outfit." Suiting her actions to her words, she slipped the light cotton wrap over her clothes and snapped it all the way to the top, completely covering her lavender and green printed tee and her lavender pants from the knees up.

Fifteen minutes later she'd gotten most of the formula into the tiny puppy, made certain that Twinkle had cleaned and stimulated him, refrained from weighing him again – although she badly wanted to – removed her wrap and left it on the back of the chair by the table. Twinkle resisted her encouragements to go outside for a potty break, so she left the little mother to rest with her puppies, collected Sky and Amber who were only too happy to leave the sofa and mill around Genna's feet again, and headed off downstairs to consider lunch for her and Andrews.

Even in laced tennis shoes, she could never match the two tiny dogs' descent of the stairs. With her feet in flip-flops she took even longer with the descent, and the two Papillons along with Blacky were milling impatiently at the foot of the stairs long before she joined them. The four entered the kitchen together in a noisy mass.

Andrews was sitting quietly at the kitchen table.

"How do you like the new me?" Genna's tone was breezy and she did a little turn to show off her cool and casual outfit. Her purple flip-flops were a tone darker than the lavender slacks, but picked up the darker purple overlays of the lavender flowers in the white printed tee. "Shirley's not the only one who can wear purple today, even if I'm not sporting butterflies

197

everywhere."

Andrews' response was a weak attempt at a smile. Only then did it register with Genna that he was overly solemn.

"What's wrong?" Genna's good mood evaporated at the glum expression on her companion's face. Sky and Amber seemed unaware of her change in mood, dancing in place around the back door, yipping and yodeling their need and expectations of being allowed outside. Blacky had separated herself from the two small dogs, and was continuing her excited dancing under the table near Andrews' feet.

"Just a minute while I let these two monkeys outside," she said, opening the door and re-closing it behind the two eager Papillons.

"Now! What's wrong?" She swiftly took in the empty table, and the time on the kitchen clock which registered twenty minutes past noon. Andrews would normally be raiding the fridge for something to eat by now. His coffee cup was sitting in front of him, still half full. She eased herself into the seat beside him, put her hand over his, and repeated her question. "Whatever is wrong? You look like a thundercloud!"

"I talked to Red -- twice." Andrews face was drawn, eyelids narrowed over eyes that looked pained and defeated. "The young detective he put in charge of shadowing Swinson followed him to a motel in Hampton a few miles from the research facility. He did what he was supposed to do. He notified the police for that district. Only trouble was he decided to trust that Swinson would stay put and he left briefly to meet with the local officers out of sight of the motel."

"And Swinson took a powder while this young detective wasn't observing him."

"Worse," Andrews said. "The young guy called for back-up and everyone swears that Swinson's motel room door was under observation all night."

"But . . .?"

"I called Red this morning while you were redoing the bath and yourself, and he decided to pick Swinson up for questioning about the instruments. He'd hoped it might lead to some further information about Friday's homicide." Andrews dragged his words out so slowly that Genna had a difficult time not squirming and verbally urging him to come to the point. She knew most of this. They'd talked about it before. What was making Andrews so depressed -- almost haunted?

"After my first phone call, Red had a police unit from Hampton meet him at the motel and went in to arrest Swinson." A long sigh marked another hesitation. Just when Genna thought she might scream, he added, "... and they found him dead."

"Dead? Swinson?" All of Genna's recaptured sense of control washed away like rain off a greasy outdoor grill. Both of her hands reached unconsciously to cover her mouth. "Oh, how can this be happening?" The question was rhetorical. She didn't expect an answer and she didn't get one.

"The youngster didn't do anything wrong, but Red is ready to explode this morning." Andrews picked up his coffee cup and took a sip, made a face and spit the cold, unappetizing liquid back in his cup. "Yuck!"

Glad for something to do while she tried to settle the fearful inertia brought on by sheer terror, Genna grabbed the cup and jumped up to replace it with something more appealing. "Here, I'll get you some fresh coffee." The knot of panic in her chest and stomach returned and increased so that even her breathing was shallow and restricted. All the attitude adjustment efforts of the morning were nullified by this newest tragedy. She felt closed in and threatened, all the more terrified because now, once again, the enemy had no face.

She returned to the table and set the fresh cup of hot coffee in front of Andrews. Neither spoke for some long, poignant minutes, each busy with their own thoughts. Finally Genna could no more keep her fears to herself than she could relax the tight bands of muscles around her torso, which kept her from drawing a full breath. "I thought I had my nerves under control. I thought I could block out the trees with a sheet and get on with my routine. I thought the threat had a face."

It was Andrews' turn to cover her icy-cold hand with his large, blunt fingered one. "The unknown! Somehow it always holds more terror than the enemy we can identify."

Blacky deserted her post of keeping Andrews' foot warm and pushed her black muzzle into Genna's lap from under the table, offering her mute assurance of sympathy and affection.

Genna squeezed Andrews' hand in gratitude for his sympathetic touch and used the other to absently scratch Blacky's ears. "What happened? Do they know?"

"Swinson was shot with a different caliber than that which killed Spratt. This one looked to be a handgun. No one heard the shot, so the killer probably used a silencer, the same as when Spratt was killed. Swinson was shot from close quarters, but the crime scene crew thinks the perp came and went during the interval when Red's young colleague was discussing the situation with the officers from Hampton and out of sight of the motel. It's the only time the front door of the motel wasn't under observation after Swinson went in. And there's not a back door or window. They think the perp then drove away on the service road behind the motel. So the

200

surveillance team didn't see or hear anything."

Andrews voice ceased, and the two sat in frozen silence for long minutes.

"Where does this leave us? We'd sort of decided that Swinson and the defective prototype of the infrared scanner might have been behind Spratt's murder, that it was an attempt to get me and keep me from finding the problem." She hoped Andrews failed to notice the increasingly higher pitch to her voice as it shifted to something resembling a squeak to her own ears at the mention of someone feeling strong enough animosity toward her to want to kill her. "But we also hadn't ruled out that the killer might have been after Harper."

"Do you think we were wrong? That maybe . . ." Her voice trailed off because she couldn't think of another explanation, however badly she wanted to.

"Swinson's murder sort of confirms our theory that the motive concerns the prototypes. But we now have to assume that we're dealing with someone other than Swinson, someone who considered him a weak link in the chain. And given the man's slip to me about the cigarette smoke, he probably was a danger. Trouble is we don't know who that shadow individual might be."

Genna shook her head in frustration. "I feel like I've got *restless leg syndrome* all over my whole body. I want to run around and scream and do something. But I can't figure out, for the life of me, what to do."

"You can't do anything but stay away from the windows, stay tucked in and safe and let Red and his team sort this out." Andrews patted her hand once again before adding. "I like that young detective. He has a good head on his shoulders and he'll sort this out. In the meanwhile, woman, you can feed me. It is long past my lunch hour,"

Genna smiled weakly, recognizing the attempt at misdirection for what it was. But it was later than normal for his lunch and allowing him to become too hungry was a sure way to have him eat the wrong things. "I like him too. Maybe it's because he has a dog named Junket that he's not at all reluctant to discuss. And lunch, at least, is something I can handle."

Andrews pushed himself away to help. "I'll fix our drinks. Would you like lemonade, tea, or what?" Blacky added her bulk to the organized chaos by whirling around first Andrews' feet and then Genna's as Genna pulled cold cuts, cheese, bread, mayo, mustard, lettuce and pickles from the fridge and arranged them on a sandwich board.

"Maybe just a glass of cold water for me. Want some soup with your sandwich?" Genna's voice regained some of its normal tone as routine activity loosened her tight muscles and allowed her to take a deep breath of air.

"Nope, think I'll stick with just a sandwich and some lemonade." Andrews gave the backyard a careful scrutiny while he busied himself with getting down glasses, filling them with ice, and filling them with their drinks.

Sky and Amber did not indicate any concern for intruders in their outside world, either animal or human. They seemed happily engaged in rooting under the mulch that protected the roots of the beautifully blooming azaleas in the yard. One orchid-like blossom from the large plant by the gate had fallen on Sky's back and looked like a fragile white, pink, and magenta garden hat atop his rump.

Andrews turned from his inspection with the drinks in his hand, stepped around Blacky and put them on the table without spilling either of the overfilled glasses. "At least Sky and Amber seem to

202

be enjoying life. Whatever they've found in your mulch has them enthralled and entertained."

Genna glanced into the back yard and chuckled. "Oh, great. Heaven only knows what they've found this time. Hope it isn't squirrel poop. I'm the one who gets to brush their teeth after these adventures in eating!"

She added her loaded tray to the middle of the table, followed closely by a highly attentive and pathetically pleading black head. "Hope springs eternal doesn't it, girl? Well you can't have this. Neither your dad nor I want to clean up the mess you'll make tonight if you get any of this fat loaded human food."

"Well, let's hope it isn't too fat loaded," Andrews injected as he pushed his way back to his seat. "Right now I could eat the whole plate, and that would not be good for my weight."

"You won't have a chance to eat the whole thing with Blacky around." Genna chuckled as she glanced at the two Paps in the yard. She made another short trip between counter and table, returned with two small plates and joined Andrews at the table.

"I think I'll leave the little ones outside since they're enjoying themselves so much. Two less beggars to deal with," she added as a black head tried to insinuate itself between her elbow and side.

In spite of their recent shock, or maybe because of it, the two assembled hearty dishes for themselves, garnished their plates with pickles and some olives that Genna had added as an afterthought, and continued their earlier dissection of the shocking events with their mouths full of bread and sandwich fixings.

"Where does this leave us?" Genna, at her most controlling, was already seeking a way to bring order out of the shambles. "I mean, if I'm ever going to sleep tonight, I have to try to put another face or several faces on this unknown threat!"

"Us? We stay right here and keep a low profile. And *we* let Red and his people do their job." Andrews was quick to respond and squash any suggestion that Genna would decide to get herself as involved as she had on the earlier case which had brought Blacky into both their lives.

"Oh, I don't intend to go skipping off after anyone. But I think we have a better view of the problem than anyone else." Genna's voice sounded almost normal as she fought to control her earlier attack of sheer terror by channeling the energies into action directed at solving the problem. "Swinson was so perfect as the candidate for Spratt's killer."

Andrews interrupted her. "Except we both know he couldn't have concealed a rifle in that tight outfit he was wearing at the show ring, and he didn't have time to get one and set up for Spratt's murder."

Genna nodded in agreement between munches on her sandwich. "But," she injected, "he was supposed to be an ex-Army Ranger. He'd have known about rifles, and climbing trees to shoot them from."

"You've become an expert in that now, have you?" Andrews chided her. If he'd hoped to turn her attention aside from what was fast becoming an unhealthy trend toward meddling in the investigation, it didn't work.

"I did some research on the internet while I was pondering how that dratted instrument could be so flawed."

"So how did you find out about his being an ex-Ranger? Was that in the resume and material you gave to Red?"

"No. Someone told me, but I don't remember who."

"Did they tell you anything else? Like what unit?

Beguiling Bundle: Death Takes Best of Breed

And when he served? That might be helpful to Red. I know from bitter experience that getting information from military data banks is likely to be a long dance with Army bureaucracy and require the next thing to a dispensation from the Pope."

"Not that I remember." Genna mumbled into the second half of her sandwich, which she'd raised to her mouth to bite. Blacky had deserted her earlier after being offered a pickle instead of the meat and cheese she'd smelled, but Andrews had proved to be even less responsive to his dog's pleadings. So she'd returned to finally put one paw on Genna's knee and reach with the other to pull the hand containing the half sandwich down near her own mouth.

"Oh, stop that, you big mooch! Get down! You'll spit out the lettuce, and smear the mustard and mayo all over my pants." She pushed the dog away with more than a little feeling of guilt. Soft liquid eyes followed her hand and the sandwich, though the gentle dog obeyed her command to sit.

"Well, try to remember where you heard that. Ex-Rangers would know other ex-rangers. Red will certainly be interested in any of Swinson's friends who have experience with firearms. Whoever is responsible has knowledge of weapons and access to both weapons and to silencers which isn't your general run-of-the-mill citizen." Andrews stuffed the last of his sandwich in his mouth to avoid any further chance of weakening and sharing it with the pair of pitiful brown eyes, which gazed at it so hungrily.

Sky and Amber interrupted any further conversation with an all out assault on the back door. The sound of their yips and barks was augmented by the sound of the claws from four tiny feet scratching on the outside of the door.

"I guess the squirrel pellets are exhausted and now they want a part of our lunch. So much for the new paint job on that door! Jonathan will not be pleased to come home to the same scratches that he just finished filling, sanding and painting before he left for the other coast." Genna reluctantly put her unfinished sandwich-half on her plate and rose to open the door to the tiny tyrants. "Better let the kids in before they put matching grooves on the door jam to match the ones they've already made on the door."

Blacky scrambled to follow Genna and greet her two little friends who tumbled over each other in their excitement to get in the house.

"Now, everybody be good, get under the table, lie down, and be quiet."

"I don't think I'll fit," Andrews quipped. "I ate too much to bend."

"Oh, Smarty. Just for that I should make you clear the table." Genna slipped into her seat and stuffed the remains of her own sandwich into her mouth before either of her four-footers could forget their manners and join Blacky in begging for table food.

"What! No dessert?"

"There's a low-cal ice cream bar in the fridge. I think it says it will cost you only two points."

Andrews gathered up both plates, rinsed and loaded them in the dishwasher on his way to the freezer. "Want one?"

"No." She had plans of snagging another Almond Joy when Shirley came home and offered it, but she wasn't about to share that news with him.

The phone rang just as Andrews started back to the table so he checked the Caller-Id on his way by the handset.

"It's Jonathan," he announced.

Genna bolted out of her seat and reached for the phone. "Don't you dare tell him about this latest killing. He'd be on the next plane and I don't want his book tour disrupted," she whispered sternly.

"Okay. But . . . don't you think he's going to be a bit miffed when he finds out all the stuff we haven't been telling him?"

Genna croaked an emphatic denial, brushed three dogs out of the way, opened the communications on the phone and cooed a soft and sultry greeting to her mate. She acknowledged Andrews' selection of an ice cream stick from the freezer and his hand signals of going outside to enjoy it with Blacky. The silky voice that sang in Andrews' ear as he and Blacky let themselves out the back door was hardly recognizable as the high pitched, stress-filled one of an hour earlier.

"Ain't love grand!" Blacky seemed to agree as she frolicked ahead of him out into the backyard to check out the site beneath the azalea that Amber and Sky had found so attractive. "And don't go eating any squirrel droppings, you naughty girl," Andrews called after the exuberant shepherd. "I am not brushing your teeth again this morning."

Jean C. Keating

CHAPTER NINETEEN

Genna had finished her phone visit with Jonathan and had put away any remains of lunch when Andrews and Blacky returned to the kitchen. Amber and Sky greeted them at the door, touching muzzles and exchanging greetings with Blacky as through she'd been away for days rather than the short span of minutes the two had been in the yard.

"How are things going with the book tour?"

"Wonderful! Jonathan says hello, and he's sorry he didn't have time to wait and talk to you too, but he's been asked to do a side appearance with a local Science Fiction and Fantasy club this afternoon and he's rushing off to that." Genna patted the black head that pushed its way into her lap, and then had to provide equal time to Sky who demanded her attention. "He's really beginning to enjoy the trip and to see some rewards for all the effort. I'm so glad for him!"

The phone rang again. Genna checked the Caller ID again, before nodding to Andrews with a smile. "Shirley."

She grabbed the handset and acknowledged her caller with a light and breezy tone. "Hi, Pal. How are things going at the show?" Her smile widened as eyebrows lifted and her shoulders relaxed even more. "Rusty took Winners Dog," she repeated for Andrews benefit, although he didn't look like the words conveyed a whole lot of meaning as he eased his bulky figure into an empty chair at the table.

"...and Muffin finally took the points today and Breed in addition to Best of Winners! How did Jessie do?"

Genna paused to listen, nodding her head as she absentmindedly patted the red-and-white head that pushed its way into her lap.

"Well, you couldn't both win," she laughed into the phone. "And living with Peggy might just be a bit easier tonight, now that Muffin finally has some points."

"No, Uncle Kevin and I are doing just fine. Bunny is stable; we've just finished lunch. I wish we could have been there, but congratulations to Muffin and Rusty." She shifted the phone to her other ear, giving a thumbs up sign to Andrews with her free hand. Some of the stress lines around her mouth and eyes softened as she listened to Shirley's excited voice on the other end. "I'll be glad to tell Sky that his son has another major to his credit, but somehow I don't think he's going to care."

Whatever her excited friend was saying caused Genna to laugh aloud before continuing. "Don't worry about being late. Uncle Kevin and I will snack our way through the afternoon and have something good waiting for you all whenever you get here. Congratulations and best of luck to Peggy and Muffin in Group."

She stretched to return the hand set to the wall

unit. "Toy Group is last today, and Muffin will represent the Papillons, so they'll probably be six or so getting back.

He settled on the point of keenest interest to him. "I like the idea of snacking our way through the afternoon."

"Right! And undo all your efforts at healthier eating!" Genna pushed her chair away from the table. "We seem to have the afternoon to ourselves. And it's a beautiful day. What would you like to do on your vacation here?"

"Well, if you wouldn't think it too rude of me, I'd like to take Blacky and go for a long walk in your woods. The dogwoods are still making a beautiful display along the path to the river, those azaleas with the huge pink and white blossoms are spectacular, it looks like there's all sorts of colors where the tree line ends and more sunlight is available near the river, and I don't usually get to see this kind of display of nature's beauty in the city. Don't get to go for long walks either."

Genna was nodding in agreement long before he finished his list of scenic interests. "Nothing rude about that! Those big blossoms are the George Lindley Tabor variety. They are rock solid gorgeous." It was a beautiful day outside and she'd eaten enough at lunch that a long, stroll would be just the thing to relax tensions, work off the normal lethargy which accompanied a heavy lunch, and provide the opportunity for a nice visit with Andrews as well. She was a little nervous at the idea the woods might shelter the unknown killer, but she trusted the dogs to give warning and Andrews to provide protection. "The little guys and I could use a nice nature walk."

"But ..." he paused, exhaled loudly, and then charged ahead. "...I don't want you going with me. I don't want you out in the open woods just now, not until Red and his team can dig into Swinson's background, can narrow the list of suspects down so we know a bit more about what is going on."

"Great! Now I can't even go for a walk in my own woods!" The three dogs were milling around her feet. She curled her fingers into fists, but she wasn't really too disappointed. After not one but two unexplained homicides, she was not about to argue the wisdom of his cautions. "Okay, I need to feed Bunny in another forty minutes or so anyway, and I could always use some more time on the analysis of that infrared scanner. And I really should call Paul and tell him where things stand." "No." Andrews reply was swift and emphatic. "You cannot, must not tell Paul anything about what you've found."

"But, he's going to ask where I am with the analysis." Genna was taken aback at Andrews' sudden response. "It's Saturday and I promised to have an answer by Tuesday."

"It's a long way till Tuesday. Until Red gives us the clearance, I don't think we should mention anything, not even that we know anything about Swinson's death. We don't want your boss to say something that would compromise the investigation."

Genna began to pace back and forth across the kitchen, her left hand rubbing her left temple. "This is all getting to be more than I can keep track of. Are we not going to tell anybody the truth about anything? Not Jonathan! Not Paul! I'm getting dizzy just trying to keep all the false stories straight."

Andrews did not remind her that the choice to keep Jonathan in the dark about events in Williamsburg had been hers. "Well, just don't mention anything to anybody about the murder or what you've discovered about the scanner. It may be very important in tripping up the shooter."

"Are we not going to tell Shirley and Peggy

when they get back tonight that we know Swinson is dead?" Genna looked very near rebellion at the idea of not being able to talk freely in her own home.

"Not unless Red shows up again and includes them in his discussions. And then let him do the explaining. Don't contribute any more to the conversation than he covers."

The conversation was doing nothing for Genna's frustration level. The three dogs were responding to her anxiety by tumbling over their own feet and getting under hers as she paced back and forth across the kitchen with no purpose.

"Well, I think Blacky and I should take ourselves off for a nice nature walk," Andrews said, heaving his still-substantial bulk out of the chair. "Do you have a retractable lead I can borrow? I'd like to give her a bit more freedom at running to and fro than her regular lead, but I don't want to let her run totally free. Without the little ones around, she might just take off and decide to go for a nice swim in the James River. My exercise plans for the afternoon do not include getting sloppy wet retrieving her and then giving her a bath."

This latest direction of conversation at least eased the tension in Genna's face and shoulders. "There's three of them hanging on the wall beside the dryer," she responded, pointing toward the laundry room. "Neither has that heavy duty hook of Blacky's lead, but don't worry. Any of those lighter ones will still hold her. I think the blue one is the easiest to set and release, but you're welcome to use any you like."

Andrews returned with the blue retractable lead. "You're sure this light thing is going to hold her if she decides to take off after a rabbit or something?" He sounded very doubtful.

Genna had gotten a hearty laugh out of Andrews' choice of collar and lead for Blacky, and chided him on an earlier visit about his selection. Not having owned a dog before, Andrews had compared Blacky's size to Genna's Papillons and selected a collar and lead, which he judged to be proportionally sturdier and larger. The results were a beautiful black and white braded leather lead and collar that would have held a male newfoundland or a mastiff and represented much more than needed for the gentle, female shepherd. Between the huge and heavy hook at the end of the lead and the equally sturdy and heavy hook on the matching collar, Genna teased that Blacky would need a neck brace with wheels to compensate for wearing such heavy gear.

Andrews leaned over and clipped the tiny hook of the retractable lead to Blacky's oversized collar ring. "All right, but if it doesn't hold and she goes in the river you're going to have to help me bathe her."

The phone rang again as he straightened up. "Some days I hate Alexander Graham Bell!" Genna grumbled as she crossed the room to check the Caller ID. "Oh, great! Paul! And I can just guess what he wants."

"Well, just remember what NOT to tell him," Andrews cautioned and ducked out the side door with Blacky before she could make a cutting remark in response.

* * *

Blacky did a brief check of the site within the fenced yard that had received so much attention from Sky and Amber earlier in the afternoon, but it seemed to hold far less fascination for her than it had for Sky and Amber. She happily responded to Andrews' urging to follow him out the back gate toward the woods and the bank of the James River. The longer reach of the retractable lead allowed her to dash from one side of the lane to the other, checking all the scent-mail with happily waving tail.

Dogwoods created an apple-green canopy under taller pines and tulip poplar trees. Their beautiful white and rarer pink blossoms had long since fallen to nourish the woodland floor, but the low spread of their artistic branches resembled beautiful lighter green umbrellas against the upper level of larger trees. The floor of the wooded area and the path were dotted with pinecones and needles colored randomly with the fallen blooms of late blooming azaleas and rhododendrons. What looked like a natural mixture of nature's beauty was, Andrews knew, the work of a very dedicated team of Jonathan and Genna. One obvious give-away was the wood markers placed to the side of some of the large displays of blooming bushes.

It was a restful and serene space, and should have left Andrews more relaxed than it did. He was unable to truly enjoy the pleasurable sights and smells of the woods. A mental alarm seemed to sound, just barely discernable, and the reason for that alarm seemed just beyond the reach of his memory. All his instincts and training were telling him there was something he needed to recall, consider, but he couldn't remember what.

Several impressively large-leaved bushes dotted the path on both sides and sported the huge light pink patterned flowers. The white-banded flowers with the darker magenta blotch that covered the plants were identical to a much smaller version of the bush within the fenced area of the yard. Blacky found a particularly interesting scent-mail to read at a nearby tree and Andrews bent to read the wooden markers by the bushes. *George Lindley Tabor* and a date appeared in front of at least five. This was, he knew,

215

one of Genna's favorites. He could see why. The few blooms that remained on the plant resembled a beautiful orchid.

Another large plant was heavy with buds that were just beginning to open. *Martha Hitchcock,* according to its wooden marker, was a bit on the slow side in adding its showy color to the landscape, while huge expanses of *Delaware Valley Whites* had come and gone. It made a slow and beautiful stroll along a rustic path that was a treat for a city dweller like Andrews.

Blacky's progress was one of fits and starts, as she dashed from side to side of the path investigating new smells that attracted her attention. By the time she finished her inspection of yet another tall pine and dashed off toward the sunny end of the trail which opened on the banks of the James River, Andrews was ready to find a resting spot on the seat of a picnic bench just past the tree line.

Increased sunlight here encouraged the profuse growth of day lilies (according to yet more wooden markers) and Andrews marveled at the multitude of names. As yet, there was little to distinguish one stand of green leaves from another but the many colors that appeared in the names promised a showy display of rainbow colors when the blooms did appear later in the summer.

After a few unsuccessful attempts to reach spots further than her lead would allow, Blacky had finally satisfied her curiosity and flopped down near Andrews' feet.

For a space of time he allowed his mind to drift, enjoying the smooth slap of the water against land. Gradually he focused on his current situation and mind set.

I'm still wearing my weapon. And just why do I think that is necessary? He reached to pat a black head that shifted closer, but that movement was unconscious. The conscious portion of his mind was focused elsewhere. The walk had been an excuse to get away, to retreat to a quiet place where he could contemplate the nagging sense that he was missing something.

It wasn't the gun he wore or the reason he wore it. Thoughts focused on those topics brought no sense of linkage to the nagging alarm bell in the back of his mind.

It was something he'd heard, something to do with the telephone. It didn't mean anything especially connected to the murders. Of that, he was sure. Otherwise his training would have clicked the facts into focus for immediate consideration. But it was an anomaly. And he didn't like anomalies anymore than he liked coincidences.

An anxious mockingbird sounded her challenge in triplicate to the intrusion into her nesting territory by Andrews and Blacky. She flew a low and challenging trajectory that missed the top of Andrews' head but not by much.

"Ah! So you think you own this space, do you, old girl?"

Mockers were at least familiar to city dwellers like Andrews. The tree in his front yard in Richmond was 'owned' by one, who spent much of the late spring fussing at him each time he tried to walk beneath *her* tree to get to his front door, and marking his car with her deposits when he dared to park it nearby.

"There's a killer around. So, of course, I'm keeping my weapon close. Genna is in danger. We know that. Just don't know why!" Vocalizing his thought, to Blacky and the determined mockingbird, did not help at all with the illusive memory that he sought to retrieve.

217

Jean C. Keating

The sun moved enough to put the bench and table in direct sunlight, and his full stomach left him sluggish in spite of the walk. A flicker of concern penetrated briefly about Jonathan and Genna's phone conversation. *But she wouldn't give anything away,* he assured himself. He put his head down on his crossed arms, and closed his eyes to rest at the picnic table.

CHAPTER TWENTY

Amber had tired of trying to follow behind Genna as she paced around the great room with the phone pressed to her ear. The little dog chose a comfortable wicker rocker and plopped herself in the middle of the blue print cushion – after the prerequisite three full turns of course.

Sky continued his duties as shadow and faithfully followed every turn and twist of his mistress' feet.

Genna's right hand kept the phone headset pressed to her right ear. Her left hand was in constant motion, as she frantically flicked it nervously at the wrist. Sky apparently did his best to interpret the hand motion as some sort of command, though he knew not what. He sat briefly, lay down, and then tripped himself up trying to regain his feet and follow Genna's rapidly moving ones.

Dealing with her boss was proving to be very difficult for Genna. Paul was forcefully pushing his position. He was trying to be helpful, offering to take the load off her of evaluating the infrared scanner.

219

She had the raw measurements made by NASA technicians of the prototype and he couldn't very well ask NASA to redo them. He was pressing Genna to release the raw measurements to him. She'd already found the flaws in the instrument. She knew anything he did would be wasted and repeated efforts. Nothing else was needed for the evaluation. She already knew the anomalies and the troubles, but she wasn't supposed to tell him.

I am getting very, very tired of trying to keep so many different stories straight. How do liars ever get anything done? How can you keep so many scenarios running in your head without confusing to whom you told what?

"I know you're trying to help us both. And I appreciate what you're trying to do. I just don't see any reason for your having to deal with the infrared scanner data. I'll get to it by Tuesday." Her voice in the phone was louder than she'd meant. Her frustration was increasing by the minute. Paul was being perfectly reasonable, if – and it was a big, fat IF – she had in fact not already done the analysis. But she had! She wasn't allowed to give him the reason she didn't want him to waste time with duplicating what was already done. She couldn't even hint at the reason. She could only refuse to give him the raw measurements. And sound like a bitch doing it.

"I know Swinson needs the advance. I know he's a nice man. He'll get his answer on Tuesday," she said, struggling to remember to keep her verbs in the present tense. Paul didn't appear to know about Swinson's murder. So the police had managed to keep it quiet. It might be on the evening news. It might not. They might fall back on not releasing names until next of kin could be notified. She twirled about on her left foot, slapped her left hand against her thigh in frustration and nearly stumbled over the tiny red-and-white companion that followed her frantically, agitated by the state of his mistress, the continual hand signals which he couldn't interpret, but equally determined to shadow her no matter what. Flip-flop sandals were not the best footgear for rapid movement and directional changes and Genna stumbled more than once in her frantic pacing.

"But it isn't more than I can handle." She wanted to scream in frustration. "I've already told you that validating the star tracker was a breeze. I've had lots of help here from my guests with Bunny, and the methodology I used made the navigational displays for that prototype a snap to validate." She nodded impatiently, as she listened reluctantly to her caller's response. "Well, you ought to learn haversines and their usage then. You'd find it a lot easier to do two and three body motion problems."

Finally, she threw up her free hand, causing the tiny dog at her side to flinch. Realizing that Sky had momentarily feared her agitation was directed at him, she made a conscious effort to soften and lower her voice, while she leaned over to caress the top of his head. "Look, Paul. Thank you, but no thank you. I don't want help. I will have the evaluations done by Tuesday morning. Now go away and enjoy your weekend. I'm hanging up now, because I have to go give Bunny his 2:00 pm feeding."

The voice in the phone continued to drone on but she talked over it with a firm signoff. "Good bye, Paul."

Her purple sandals slapped against the floor as she stomped back into the kitchen and slammed the headset of the phone into the wall mount. "Oh, how frustrating!"

Amber tried to lower her head even further into the pillow of the chair in which she'd chosen to hide.

Sky faithfully followed her, standing just beside her left ankle and regarding her with a hurt expression on his little face. "I'm sorry, gang. I'm just about to the end of my rope trying to deal with all this. I can't tell Paul why I don't need him to help with evaluations. I guess I can't blame him for trying to hurry me along when I'm not telling him the truth about any of this. About the only thing I seem to be able to control at the moment is to give Bunny his feedings, and I can't see whether that's helping either."

She stooped and gathered a puzzled Sky into her arms. Amber immediately deserted her hiding chair and came over to share in the petting.

She returned Sky to the floor and patted Amber on the head. "Come on, you two. It's almost two o'clock. Let's go bother Twinkle and give Bunny some more food."

The two little dogs understood the direction of her movements if not her words, and scrambled for the second floor, reaching the hallway of the upstairs before Genna could manage the first two steps with her floppy sandals.

Sky wheeled in place and then led the way down the hall toward the nursery once Genna managed to join them in the upstairs hallway. Amber seemed to need a bit longer to recover from her dash up the stairs, but after a brief bout of coughing, she followed Sky toward the nursery at a more sedate rate.

By the time Genna and her flip-flops made it to the nursery, both Sky and Amber were standing just inside the door exchanging yips and barks with an ever-alert Twinkle, who did not appear happy to have her afternoon nap disturbed by the intrusion of the two.

Genna sent her two escort Paps to the cushions of the old blue sofa with a soft command backed by hand signals and took the chair at the table holding Twinkle and the puppies. Sky was swift to respond to a hand signal he could finally understand. Amber followed at a much slower pace.

Genna gently caressed the ears and head of the mother dog, marveling at the changes six short weeks of love and proper care had brought. In spite of the confusion of three strange humans caring for her, she was trusting of Genna and her three guests around her precious puppies. "You have a wonderful temperament, Little Mother," she cooed to Twinkle. She reached beneath the table, removed formula and fixings from the tiny refrigerator there, turned on the portable apparatus that heated the water to warm the formula, and reached around Twinkle to pick Tina up from the ball of intertwined puppies.

"I can't resist weighing your little ones every time I get ready to feed Bunny. I know it's silly and it only makes sense to compare weights at the same time each day, but I just can't wait." Genna kept her voice soft and soothing. The words didn't matter, but Twinkle's tail waved gently at the tone and the affection it conveyed.

The digital scale at the side of the table was already set up with a flat tray lined with a tiny scrap of fleece displaying baby rabbits and lambs and readjusted to show zero. Genna laid Tina in the tray, noted the reading with her hand just above the puppy to guard against any sudden attempt to flip out of the tray, and managed to get a valid weight in spite of four tiny legs that waved energetically in the air. She retrieved the puppy and returned her to her bed after first planting a soft kiss on the top of her head. Opening the logbook tucked between the scales and the puppy basket, she entered the new weight and shared the news with Twinkle who observed it all very attentively as though she understood each and every action. "Well, as you might guess, the little porker has gained another ¼ ounce since last night. You must have some high-test milk there, Twinkle. Too bad Bunny isn't able to get his share."

Twinkle tensed and turned with a low growl toward Sky, objecting to his appearance at Genna's side. The little red-and-white dog had deserted the sofa to quietly seek Genna's knee, attempting to push his head under her left elbow for attention.

"It's all right, Twinkle," Genna soothed the mother dog. "Sky, go back and sit down over there." Genna turned in her seat and motioned her jealous shadow back toward the sofa. Amber had remained sitting on the sofa but seemed to be shaking.

"What is wrong with you two? You know better than to upset Twinkle. Sky, you get back on the sofa and sit down." She motioned the little dog back to his assigned place, and returned to repeat the weighing process for Bunny.

"Well, you have not gained anything. But you haven't lost anything, so I'll take what I can get." She warmed formula in the water she'd heated, fed a surprisingly hungry Bunny, insured that Twinkle had cleaned and stimulated him before returning him to his nesting area. The bedding seemed a little soiled and damp, so she exchanged it for fresh blankets and toys, gathered the soiled pads, blankets and one slightly soiled stuffed toy in the shape of a blue rabbit, returned any hot or hazardous stuff to safe areas under the table, and gave Twinkle one last caress before rising and calling Amber and Sky to follow her out of the nursery.

Amber was slow to rise and jump down from the sofa. When she landed on the floor, her front feet collapsed and she tumbled awkwardly to the faded blue scatter rug that was spread there. Sky followed more gracefully, but his legs were visibly trembling.

Beguiling Bundle: Death Takes Best of Breed

"What is wrong with you two?" Genna's voice fairly squeaked with alarm, as she suddenly realized that something was very wrong with her two darlings. She wheeled to thrust the dirty bedding into a hamper beside the little refrigerator, and rushed over to kneel down in front of two distressed little dogs.

Amber's tail was down and her beautiful ears were sticking straight out from each side of her head as though their normally erect position was too much for her to handle. She struggled to regain her feet, stretched her head toward Genna seeking solace and affection, and immediately gagged and threw up on the blue rug.

Genna picked her up and returned her to the blue sofa, then repeated the process with Sky. Crossing rapidly to a supply table set to one side of Twinkle and the puppies' area, she returned with a roll of paper toweling and spray, quickly cleaned up the mess, removed the rug and added it to the laundry basket. Then she picked up both Sky and Amber and carried them down the hall to the master bedroom along with the soiled paper towel containing the debris from Amber's accident.

Kit Kat had been taking yet another of his many naps on the king size bed in the master suite and was not at all happy to have his rest interrupted by the abrupt intrusion. Genna ignored his hissing and gently deposited Sky and Amber on the bed and followed that intrusion by flopping herself down on the near side of the bed also. It was too much for the disgusted cat, and he stalked to the far side and jumped off to find a quieter spot in a cat bed behind the chair in the corner.

"What have you gotten into, Amber?" Genna made certain her voice was under control and the tone was comforting in the hopes of calming the two little dogs beside her on the bed, but she felt anything but calm. Examining the debris in the paper towel, she found it contains dark chunks of some material she couldn't identify. She remembered the two had been digging in the mulch beneath the azalea in the yard, but wood chips would have been stiff and solid. These chunks could be pressed and left a dark smear when she rubbed the toweling together.

"There's no plant material in the yard that should be poisonous to either of you. Jonathan and I made sure of that. But I don't know what you've gotten into. " Rabbit or squirrel poop would not have resembled the large, dark chunks she was viewing in the paper towel.

Sky flopped where he'd been placed on the bed, stress beginning to show in his eyes and expression. He was panting rapidly although it was not warm in the room. He whined pitifully and pushed himself to a sitting position, front legs shaking as he began to gag. Genna jumped up and raced for the linen closet, returning with a towel just in time to put it between the bedspread and the gross gunk of debris that spewed from his mouth.

She'd lost one of her floppy sandals on the run to the linen closet. She kicked the other off and crossed to her closet, extracting a less decorative but more serviceable pair of white tennis slippers that would allow her to move quickly in an emergency. Once she had the towel safely beneath Sky and Amber, she wiggled her feet into the sneakers while she consoled her extremely depressed dogs, both of whom were now shaking and gagging.

A brief examination of the gunk, which had been ejected from Sky's stomach showed the same dark chunks of matter she'd seen only minutes before from Amber's. Whatever it was, it was acting like poison to both dogs, and she was not about to deal with this

226

alone.

Crossing swiftly to the phone on her nightstand, she put in an emergency call to her vet. As usual, he was still at his office, although office hours had officially closed more than an hour before. He concurred that it sounded like some form of poison and directed her to bring them to him immediately.

She transferred the towel piece containing the gunk from Amber's stomach to a plastic bag from the bath and stowed it in her pocket to show to her vet, and ditched the dirty towel in the laundry hamper. Kit Kat would have been very offended if a soiled towel had been left on HIS bed, no matter what extenuating circumstances existed to warrant it.

She retrieved a fresh towel from the linen closet and wrapped it around the two trembling little bodies, gathered them up and struggled down the stairs holding the two tightly in her arms. By the time the three reached the downstairs and headed into the kitchen, Amber had managed to throw up on her left shoulder and Sky was contributing some unsightly additions to the flower print on the right hand front of her shirt.

She stopped in the kitchen and put the soiled towel and two trembling dogs on the floor briefly while she opened the back door and shouted for Andrews. When she received no response to her cries, she returned to the kitchen, grabbed a pad and pencil from the holder on the refrigerator and scribbled a note to him that she was on her way to the vet.

She invented a few new curse words when she couldn't locate her purse with the car keys. Someone had pushed it into the opposite side of the kitchen cabinet from its usual place, and it took her extra time to find it. In her state of fear it seemed like hours.

Amber or Sky had created a bigger mess on the towel during her brief activities, so she cleaned the little ones as best she could with more paper toweling, sponged her own tee-shirt in spots, and kicked the dirty towel into a corner. Kit Kat and Andrews would just have to live with the mess until she returned.

Frantic now, because Amber was beginning to tremble uncontrollably, she grabbed several fresh towels sitting on the top of the dryer, bundled the two sick dogs in them and raced for her car. She slammed the door between the laundry room and the garage hard enough to shake a rake off the wall holder in the garage, but managed to hit the automatic garage door opener with her elbow on the first try.

It took two tries to get the car door opener to release the passenger door. As she tried to ease the suffering pair down on the seat and keep them covered with the towels, she realized that Blacky's lead was entangled in the towels. She spent an extra few seconds getting that separated from the toweling so that the two trembling dogs were not resting on the thick braid of leather and the heavy metal hook. She briefly considered not bothering with the padded car seat Jonathan had created especially for the dogs, but finally decided that the two were so weak they could not balance on the seat otherwise. Begrudging each second it took, she moved the flat padded arrangement into the front seat, transferred the two dogs with their towels to the padded box and strapped it securely down with the seat belt. All the time, the little voice in her head was urging *Hurry! Hurry!*

This fortunately gave the garage door time to elevate to its full position, because she ran around to the driver's side, secured her own seat belt out of habit, cranked Pee Wee, slammed the little PT Cruiser into reverse and backed out of the garage without bothering to look behind her.

She squealed the tires loudly, throwing dirt and debris in all directions and went tearing off down the long drive leading to Route 5. Mid-afternoon sun filtered through the canopy of tall deciduous trees overhead, which were just beginning to develop their full summer foliage. Random rays of sunlight penetrated to the lower treetops, reflecting as shimmering waves of multi-colored green. For once Genna had no eyes for the beauty of the Virginia spring.

Sky whimpered softly. The noise cut through Genna's nerves like a knife. Amber was lying on her side now and trembling in what might be a mild seizure. It seemed as though the drive was miles long and the ticking clock in her head was hurtling toward disaster.

Something pinched the underside of her right thigh, and she reached with her right hand to feel between her leg and the seat cushion for the cause. The heavy medal hook of Blacky's lead was wedged somehow under her leg and the lead to which it was attached seemed to be hung around the gearbox between the seats. She struggled with little success to extract the worrisome metal without letting up on the gas. She almost overbalanced the car in trying to extract the bothersome lead as she pushed the vehicle to a speed far in excess of a sensible one for the turns in the long, winding driveway.

A bright ray of sunlight reflected off something shiny in one of the trees along the drive just as Sky whined pathetically. The distraction and temporary blinding by the light seemed to come at the same time. She jerked the steering wheel sharply to one side, overcorrecting it, and suddenly the car was out

229

of control. She heard a loud pop as something hit the windshield. She couldn't see for the many lines of fractured glass that had an instant ago been a clear span of glass. She jammed on the brake and tried to recover control but she could no longer see the drive through the now opaque glass. Her forward motion was abruptly halted as the car hit a tree alongside the road. Airbags deployed on both driver and passenger side and absorbed much of the shock of impact, but the sudden force of her head hitting the airbag stunned her for a brief time and created an instant headache. She struggled to recover and react. Her concern was less for the car and the bruises she would likely have from the seat belt straps and more for the lack of breathing space the bag was likely to allow the two already sick dogs at her side.

In spite of the shock and the hammering in her head, she remembered the safety tool in the map box between the seats. "Thank you, my darling Jonathan," she whispered aloud at the memory of her mate's insistence that the compartment between the two front bucket seats must carry an emergency cutter to allow rapid deflation of the air bags and a cutting blade tough enough to cut through a seat belt strap. Her right hand fumbled for the tool, and found it after some anxious minutes. It allowed her to puncture the air bags, first the one braced against the dogs' travel box, and then her own. She weakly tried to unbuckle her own seat belt and was pleasantly surprised to find that she could.

The door presented a more difficult problem but some determined pushing managed to get it to open and Genna put a shaky leg out and managed to get the rest of her shaken body to follow, high adrenalin levels and shock serving to mask any thoughts except concern that the two little bodies in the passenger seat were not further injured.

Beguiling Bundle: Death Takes Best of Breed

Blacky's lead was hopelessly tangled in the seat belt release for the dogs' travel box, and she grasped it in one hand while she tried to angle the cutting tool she'd used on the airbags to cut the lead and seat belt away from the dogs. She was stopped by an angry voice close behind her.

"Dammit, Genna. You have more lives than a cat!"

She wheeled in surprise, the sudden motion making the pounding pain in her head even worse.

"Paul? What are you doing here? Never mind, where's your car, I need . . ." Her befuddled mind finally took in the oddity of the situation. Her boss was standing somewhat unsteadily on his feet, with a rifle in one hand while his other hand struggled to put a silvery cylinder in the pocket of his jacket. His hair and jacket were covered with leaves and woodland debris.

"Just shut up!" Anger and frustration made Paul Carter's voice huskier than normal, and gave his face a deeper flush of red to go with a bloody scrape mark on the left side of his chin. "You are more trouble than anyone I've ever met!"

Genna's brain tried to make sense out of his presence here in her drive and with a rifle in his hand.

"What happened to your face?" she stammered to gain time from her thundering headache to allow her brain cells to communicate.

"Thanks to your terrible driving, you smashed into the tree I was in and I fell. Woman, you've already cost me one good rifle, and now you've ruined the silencer for this one. You are not going to cost me my business." Carter sputtered in rage. But his fall had obviously unnerved him also, and Genna struggled frantically to try to keep him talking to give her time to figure out what was going on.

231

"Are you talking about the rifle found at the scene of the homicide at the dog show?"

"Never mind." He pointed the rifle at her, eyes squinting with anger. "Just come away from the car and walk ahead of me toward the road." He motioned with the end of the rifle toward the direction he wanted her to take.

"I can't. My dogs are very ill. I have to get them to the vet." She tried to keep her voice as calm as possible though her knees were trembling and her fingers hurt from being clenched so tightly around the cutter and Blacky's lead.

"Do you think I give a damn about those dogs except as a useful tool to get you away from the house and that nosy bodyguard of yours?"

A few more lines of information finally connected in Genna's swimming head and she sputtered, "You left something in the yard to hurt them, didn't you?"

"Never mind, just move." Carter moved the muzzle of his rifle menacingly. But the only motion he got out of Genna was a tightening of muscles around her mouth and jaw and the slight forward thrust of her square chin.

"What did you throw in my yard, Paul?"

"Hunks of baking chocolate. It's supposed to be very bad for dogs. Now move before I shoot you where you stand."

"Oh, you don't want to do that, do you, Paul? Uncle Kevin is close, and he's armed. And that thing you put in your pocket was a – what did you call it, a silencer? So you don't want to shoot me because Uncle Kevin will hear the shot and be here before you can get very far."

"It won't stop me from knocking you in the head and dragging you off, if you don't move." Carter moved a step closer to Genna, rifle still pointed

232

steadily at her chest.

She backed up a half step, but the side of the car blocked any further retreat. She wasn't going anywhere with him, she was certain of that. But if she could keep him talking, Andrews might have heard the noise of the crash, and come to check. She wished she knew where he and Blacky had gone. She didn't. Not only her life, but also Sky's and Amber's depended on her out thinking the dazed but dangerous man facing her now.

"Why would you want to hurt my dogs, Paul? They've never done anything to you." The tone was reasonable, conversational. Anyone who knew her well could, however, have read the menace in her voice. Genna's dogs were her children. Although the man facing her was too focused on his own deadly intents to realize it – and she now was certain that he had probably been responsible for both Spratt and Swinson's murder -- he had just become public enemy number one for daring to threaten her fur children.

"To get you away from the house so I can make certain you never get to the analysis of those prototypes."

Genna opened her mouth to contradict him, but he seemed to want to vent his frustration with further complaining. Since that was exactly what she wanted him to do, she closed her mouth again and let him rant on.

"You were only supposed to deal with the star tracker. I'd never have asked you to work for me doing this contract in the first place, if John Hunter hadn't been so difficult. Narrow-minded old fart! He wasn't about to trust the validation contract to someone who was extremely qualified on paper but who had no prior experience with NASA. So I had to add you to the mix. I managed to keep him mad at you for leaving government service, but he still trusted you and only you to deliver quality service." Carter rubbed his jaw with his left hand which was visibly swelling around the bloody scrape along the jaw line. Slight shakes of his head suggested to Genna that the same drummer that was making life miserable in her own aching head was contributing a great deal of discomfort to Carter as well. "Bloody bastard! He always made me feel as if my training and experience didn't mean shit! If you hadn't been trained by NASA, you didn't know what you were doing."

"He certainly managed to conceal any of that admiration from me!" Genna injected. "And I really thought you wanted me as your partner."

"I wanted you to do the evaluation on the star tracker. You were reported to know your stuff around navigational astronomy. You weren't supposed to get your nose into the infrared scanner. But you wouldn't let things alone, and you wouldn't release the raw data, so you left me no choice."

Genna was beginning to understand a few things, but not all. Spratt had been killed long before Carter made any overtures to obtain the raw data. Sky whined weakly, reminding her that his and Amber's lives still hung in the balance while she tried to deal with the angry and threatening human facing her across the wrong end of a rifle. "You're a bit late if you think I don't already know the scanner doesn't work, and more importantly, that my Uncle Kevin and the police don't know that as well."

It was a mistake. She could see it in the tightening of his facial muscles and in the increase in redness in his face and neck. "Liar," he screamed. "I just talked with you not thirty minutes ago and you haven't had time to do any of that."

"I told you a lie, but it was to deny that I'd

234

already evaluated the scanner and found it defective. I wasn't allowed to tell you on orders of the police!"

Sky whimpered a bit louder but Genna could not take her eyes off Paul Carter's face. *How could I have missed the ugliness in this man's nature? I've been working with him for months. How could I have been so blind?*

Carter's seething anger seemed to shake his shoulders but the hand on the rifle held it steady on Genna's upper torso and she realized his finger was tightening on the trigger. He was so lost in fury at her and frustration in his inability to control the situation that he no longer cared that the sound of a shot would bring a witness to his deeds.

The cavalry isn't coming over the hill in time she reasoned and threw the cutter she'd used on the airbags and seat belts at him with all the force her cramped hand could manage. She flung herself to one side and swung the hook-weighted leash at him with all the fury and desperation she felt, just as the rifle roared loudly in her ear and a shock wave hit her shoulder with enough force to spin her further around. She wondered briefly if a bullet shouldn't hurt, but her legs collapsed and took her into blackness before she could come up with an answer.

CHAPTER TWENTY-ONE

She was dimly aware that she hurt all over. Sharp and unpleasant smells attacked her nose, but her eyes felt as though they were glued shut. She seemed to be resting on a smooth surface, but the hard pillow which supported her head did not remind her in the least of her own bed. She favored soft down and feather headrests that smelled of lavender not the crinkle of plastic beneath harsh cloth that scratched her cheek when she turned her head.

The headache she remembered seemed to have moved lower, to the region of her right shoulder. Some sadistic drummer was definitely pounding away with red-hot rods in that region.

Then the images of two little suffering faces, whining and shivering, crowded out all other memories.

"Sky. Oh, my God! Amber!" Her eyes weren't completely glued together she decided because there was moisture on her cheeks that had to be her

236

own tears. "Oh, my poor darlings!"

"They're fine. You're fine." A soft voice at the right side of her bed was accompanied by the soothing contact from gentle hands, which gathered her right hand in their own.

"Shirley?"

"Yes, sweet. I'm here, Jonathan is on his way home, Amber and Sky are going to be fine." One of the gentle hands released her own and moved to brush a lock of hair away from her forehead. "Do you feel like opening your eyes?"

"I hurt!" Genna's croak was little more than a whisper, but she did manage to crack her eyelids enough to confirm that she was in the quintessential hospital room, though she could not tell what time of day it was.

"I'll get someone in here to fix that," the gentle voice continued.

Genna turned her head with some effort. The spill of blond curls about her friend's face brought a wave of peace to her spinning thoughts.

Shirley reached gently over the metal railing between them to fiddle with the bulky control unit dangling near her hand. When it squawked something unintelligible in response, Shirley responded with a request for pain medication. "Hang in there, Sweetie. Help is on the way."

"The cavalry didn't come over the hill," Genna whispered weakly.

"Cavalry?" Shirley patted her hand, her face trying to keep a bland expression that hid puzzlement and fear that Genna was conscious but not lucid.

"Uncle Kevin. I'd hoped he'd hear the noise from the wreck and come to check, get there in time to get Carter . . . save my dogs." Tears she didn't want but couldn't stop coursed down her cheeks, following the track of earlier ones.

"He got there, Sweetie, in time to mop up. You took pretty good care of Carter all by yourself. And the dogs are going to be fine." Shirley squeezed Genna's hand in a comforting hold with one hand while she reached for a tissue from the bedside table with the other. Gently brushing the tissue against Genna's eyes and cheeks she continued. "Now just try to relax and let the medications and the medical people do their jobs.

A white-clad figure came in so quietly it was as though she'd simply materialized out of thin air at Genna's bedside. The voice was crisp, assured, and comforting. Her smooth chocolate skin showed no signs of wrinkles or aging, though the hair that was brushed back from her face into a neat bun at her neck was almost totally white. Three black bands on the white cap perched on the top of her head made cap and hair sparkle in contrast in the subdued light of Genna's room. She uncapped the needle of a syringe in her hand, checked the thin tubing that was attached to Genna's left arm, and inserted the needle into the mechanism with a speed and self-assurance that bespoke much practice. She recapped the empty syringe and transferred it to her pocket. The motherly voice was as gentle and comforting as the reassuring squeeze she gave to Genna's left hand. "Now, that should make you feel a lot easier in just a few minutes. Just give me a call if you need anything else."

She was gone before Genna's dry mouth and sluggish tongue could find the words to thank her. Shirley's soft "Thank you" followed her out of the room.

"Jonathan?" Genna picked up a thread of the conversation that had brought both a sense of guilt and of comfort. "I've ruined his book tour."

"You've done no such thing, although I have a

238

feeling he's going to give Kevin a hard time about keeping him in the dark for so long about the troubles here."

"That was my doing," Genna whispered. "He needed this book tour. And I didn't want him to worry any more about me and Uncle Kevin, and your visit and all. But . . . I'm so glad he's coming home. Does that make me a bad wife?" She turned a worried face toward her friend, seeking forgiveness for her weakness, for her admission of her need for the comforting presence of her mate, for giving in to her own needs and failing to be supportive of his.

"I hardly think being targeted by a fanatical boss constitutes normal. Jonathan won't either. His only regret is going to be that he wasn't told sooner. He'll probably never say a word to you about that – at least not any time soon -- but I'll bet he and Andrews will have some very lively conversations." Laugh lines about Shirley's mouth and eyes aged her gentle face a bit, but the accompanying twinkle in her eyes suggested she'd like to be within hearing distance when the two men argued the issue.

"I never wanted to have my career interfere with Jonathan's. He's always been very supportive of mine." Genna's voice gained a bit in strength as the mad drumming on her shoulder retreated a bit into the distance.

"Stop buying trouble! You're glad he'll soon be home. You need him, and he needs to be here with you. End of conversation!" Shirley could play the role of dominating mother when she chose. Genna found it soothing now.

"What time is it?" she asked, changing the subject to something less emotional.

"Sunday morning, almost lunch time."

"Good grief! What happened to yesterday afternoon and last night?"

239

Jean C. Keating

"Well, hitting a tree with your car and then getting a bullet crease that plowed a groove in your right shoulder afterwards sort of put you in need of rest and recuperation!" Shirley patted her hand gently while she tried to put a light spin on recent events in Genna's life. *That explains the throbbing and burning sensation in my shoulder,* Genna reasoned. *I suppose all the other aches and pains are from the impact.* She remembered that her seatbelt had performed with forceful efficiency in slamming her back against her seat just at the airbag exploded in her face to jam her face and shoulders against the headrest. No wonder she felt bruised all over. Better that than going into the steering wheel or worse still, through the windshield.

"I'm sorry. I can't seem to keep my eyes open," she whispered weakly.

"I think that was the idea of that last shot. Go to sleep. Everything is under control."

"You're sure Amber and Sky are okay? And Bunny . . . what about Bunny?

"They're all fine. Now rest!" Shirley's voice came from further and further away as Genna seemed to be floating toward a shadowy cloud of welcoming softness.

* * *

The soothing murmur of multiple voices drew her back toward awareness. Her right hand was held in a strong one, the thumb of which gently and rhythmically stroked her wrist. The familiar touch brought her comfort and a spreading sense of safety even before she identified the source.

"Jonathan!" Genna opened her eyes on the face of her mate. "Oh, I'm so glad to have you home." The response of need and happiness at having the strong

240

figure at her bedside to lean on came out before she could worry about what might have been compromised to have him here at her side.

"And I'm glad to be here, though we will have some words later about it taking so long for anyone to level with me about what has been going on." The mock severity of the oval face was ruined by the gentle look in his jade eyes and hound-dog appearance caused by the sandy shadow of facial hairs on a chin and upper lip that were overdue for a shave.

"I don't even know what day it is, much less what time." Genna didn't really care much either. Her Jonathan was here, and she could cease to be strong, and brave, and in control. She could trust everything to his broad shoulders now. But there was time for curiosity, starting with how her cherished mate could be here, at her side holding her hand, when she'd last talked to him an entire span of the country away. "What have I missed?"

"Well, to take your questions in order: it is about three or so on a rainy Sunday afternoon, and other than a few choice remarks about being left out of things, you haven't missed very much! Uncle Kevin called me yesterday afternoon, just after your dramatic confrontation with the tree and your boss. I got the red eye flight back to the east coast and got in about an hour ago. I came straight here and we've all just been chatting while we waited for you to wake up, oh sleepy one."

"The little drummer isn't very active any more!"

Jonathan looked at her rather fearfully, as though she'd started spouting Martian.

Shirley chuckled from her chair on Genna's other side. "She jumps around in her conversation a bit, but she knows what she means even if no one else does!"

241

"I'm sorry. My shoulder felt like someone was beating on it with hot pokers the last time I woke up, like some drummer was pounding on it. But it's dulled now. That's all I meant."

"Well, I should hope with all the medication they've been giving you that it was improving something," Jonathan replied with a relieved chuckle.

"Did you catch that rat-fink boss of mine?" Genna had spotted Andrews standing at the foot of her bed and blurted out the one subject that remained unresolved in her mind. "I hope you've got him in jail."

Andrews shook his head in disagreement, but before she could express alarm or disgust he continued, "He's down the hall in another room under heavy guard. Though I don't suppose he'll be going anywhere any time soon. He's too busy screaming about his injuries and the damages to his looks."

"I hope you had to shoot him to catch him." Turning to Jonathan for sympathy and support, she continued, "He deliberately poisoned Sky and Amber. He ..."

" . . and he deliberately shot you, but I think you got even with him for both." When Genna turned back to face Andrews, she found his eyebrows were elevated as he tried to twist his face into an expression of mild disapproval, but the corners of his mouth flickered upward in something that resembled more of a smile. "I don't suppose you were at all thinking of the fact that he'd already killed two men in his mania when you decided to attack him?"

"He was going to shoot me," Genna snorted. "You don't mean to tell me I really hurt him with that cutter I threw at him?" She considered stopping to thank Jonathan for the cutter being in the car in the first place but this didn't seem like the right time.

Beguiling Bundle: Death Takes Best of Breed

Jonathan and Shirley both smiled and glanced at Andrews, willing him to answer Genna's question.

"No, my dear child. Jim Bowie you are not! I don't think you even managed to leave a bruise with that. But you are hell on wheels with a weighted dog lead. Your cutter distracted him, but the swing you took at him with that weighted dog hook on the end caught him just right on the side of his face to do a lot of damage."

"How much?" Vindictiveness and a savage desire for revenge lent strength and power to Genna's voice.

"Well, you took out his right eye, cut a ragged tear across the front of his face and managed to break his nose. I'd call that one well-placed swing!"

Only Jonathan was aware of the shock value of Andrews' news from the tightening of the hand he held in his own. Genna's voice was sure and unrepentant. "I'm glad. I hope you don't expect me to say I feel sorry for the jerk."

"I'd be very disappointed if you did," Andrews admitted with a grin.

"He as much as admitted that he killed both Spratt and Swinson, but I never understood why. He was ranting about my keeping the raw data from him, and needing to keep me from finding out about the flaws in the scanner, but I didn't understand why that would be important to him at all, especially to such a state of frenzy that would drive him to murder two people."

Andrews responded with one word, "Greed!"

"But how did the failure of the scanner impact him financially? He got paid whether it worked or not. We were hired and would be paid to evaluate it. It didn't work, but we would be paid just the same!"

Andrews drew a noisy breath before responding. "It took a lot of digging and we're not through yet. Some offices are difficult to deal with on the

243

weekends, but we'll eventually get it all unraveled. However, thanks to the shock value you created with that dog leash and from learning that the police already knew about the defective scanner, Carter has been giving us a lot of details that fit with the bits and pieces we knew but hadn't yet tied together."

Three heads nodded at him in encouragement. None of his listeners interrupted him with so much as an audible sigh.

"Carter and Swinson were partners in this venture. Carter created the scanner through a third company, which we're tracing now. Swinson created the star tracker and supposedly put the two together into the interrelated payload through his CS Industries Company – which as it turns out doesn't represent Carlton Swinson at all but Carter/Swinson. Then the plan was that Carter would bid very low and get the contract to evaluate the instruments. So whether they worked or they didn't the CS Industries would get a clean pass and no one would be the wiser until the payload was flown and failed or didn't."

Genna nodded knowingly. "Look for some company with 'C' in the name. Paul had an ego the size of Jupiter and always wanted his mark on things. The company that employed me was named Ctimes2. Now you say that CS was his. So I'm guessing he managed to put a C in the name of the one under which he created the scanner even if he needed to hide his relationship to it."

Jonathan frowned at several points during this flood of information, but wisely decided not to ask for clarification. Much of the explanation seemed to be more than Shirley needed or wanted. After Genna's side observation about company names, all three faces maintained a respectful silence and expectant encouragement for Andrews to continue.

"Yesterday afternoon when I went for a walk, I

was trying to remember a little point of inconsistency that I'd heard. It was a vague sense of something that didn't quite fit, but I couldn't clearly retrieve it from memory. Unfortunately the sun, the walk, and a heavy lunch produced a snooze on the picnic bench rather than a recollection of what was nagging at my brain."

Genna squirmed on the bed, impatiently willing Andrews to get on with his story and seeking a more comfortable position for her hips and back which were beginning to complain.

"You'd made some telling remarks on Friday night during a phone conversation with Carter. It didn't seem to mean anything at the time, except for being an oddity. There seemed to be some difference in who told whom about Swinson being an ex-Army Ranger. Do you remember, Genna?"

The question and the point caught Genna by surprise, but after a brief pause she managed to stammer, "John Hunter said Paul had told him of Swinson's military service. But when I mentioned it to Paul, he said Hunter was the one who had mentioned it first."

"But you didn't find it in the bio of CS Industries or in Swinson's?"

"No, but Swinson could have mentioned it in conversation with Hunter. They would have reasonably been expected to have had phone or face to face conversations after Swinson was awarded the contract to build the instruments that would not have been in any paper shared with Paul or me." Genna's left hand gestured her lack of appreciation for any importance of the conversation. Her right hand held firmly to Jonathan's.

"Exactly! So it was just an oddity. But one my aging brain was trying to get me to remember and follow up on." Andrews' grimace indicated he was disgusted with himself. "Unfortunately, I didn't see the significance."

He paused for breath. This time, an impatient Genna could not contain herself. "And?"

"Fortunately we don't need to depend on the Army for conformation or we might be forever in getting the information." Andrews' tone reflected the usual complaint voiced by one bureaucracy about the inflexibility of data sharing with another bureaucracy. "According to Carter, both he and Swinson started in training together as Army Rangers.

"So that's where Carter got his training in weapons!" Jonathan could finally understand that portion of Andrews' explanations, even if some of the previous facts and connections were a bit obscure for him.

"Well, sort of," Andrews nodded at his god-son. "But Carter washed out. It seems he was bold enough but not exactly disciplined enough to complete the training as a Ranger. And he wasn't exactly the greatest marksman in the world either."

"So the two maintained their association after Carter left the army!" Genna was quick to connect the dots.

"Yes. Carter had the scientific and engineering training, Swinson the business sense. So they worked out this arrangement to play both sides of the government contracts to their advantage. It was a workable plan. Until things started to go wrong."

"When?"

"Well, Carter's ranting would suggest that he felt somewhat out of control from the start. Despite your frustration and anger with John Hunter – which I suspect was fueled by Carter's careful manipulation – he wouldn't accept Carter's low bid without more experience on his team. So Carter had to court and hire you. Hunter was the one who knew your capabilities with navigational astronomy. Carter really didn't. That didn't worry him at first. He struggled with trig all his life, so he figured he could keep you occupied with the star tracker evaluation and you'd never notice anything amiss with the scanner."

"Silly man!" Genna snorted with a quick side glance at Jonathan.

"Then he vastly underestimated the cost to produce even a defective version of the scanner. Apparently producing an instrument to respond over the entire range of infrared frequencies would have been very expensive. But Carter had outlined in his proposal to do the evaluation in only a selected number of frequencies. He figured he could easily – and cheaply -- produce an instrument that would work in just those specific frequencies. Since the frequencies chosen for evaluation were supposed to be random and unknown by the supplier, he sold NASA on the idea that that method of evaluation would be acceptable. But it turned out to cost way more than he'd figured. All three companies were heavily in debt, and facing collapse."

Genna coughed harshly. Shirley quickly moved to lift a cup of water from a side table and position the straw for her to easily get it into her mouth. Andrews paused in his lecture, a look of concern on his face.

"Are you sure you're up to listening to all this now? Maybe you should just rest. This can all wait until you feel better."

"Oh, no! I'm dying of curiosity," Genna gurgled between long draws on her straw. "I thought he was a dedicated business man and engineer. I can't believe I was so stupid, but I've got to know what set the jerk off to go shooting up my handler and his partner."

Jonathan laughed and patted Genna's had that

247

he held in his own. "If I could measure pulse in my dear lady's wrist, I could probably assure you that your engaging commentary is probably doing her more good than any three drugs these medical marvels could provide."

Andrews nodded his acceptance of Jonathan's comment but disgustedly injected an aside. "Well, hopefully it is more useful than my gun-packing guard duty was. I'm guarding the rear of the house, even if I was napping, and she goes flying out the front and nearly gets herself killed."

"I didn't even think about your cautions to be careful. Sky and Amber were ill and needed help. And I was rushing them off to the vet. You can't guard against my failure to think about unknown killers when I know my dogs have been poisoned," Genna said.

"Which was exactly Carter's thinking in attacking the dogs in the first place, " Andrews added.

"Don't even go there. It was not your fault or omission. And it all turned out fine."

"She says," Andrews joked, "from a hospital bed with a bullet crease along her shoulder that could have gone three inches lower and killed her."

"We know all that. What happened to set Carter on a killing spree?" Genna's voice came back strong and determined. Any concerns for aches and pains were momentarily forgotten as she encouraged Andrews to share what he'd learned about the Carter she'd never realized existed.

"Swinson insisted on presenting the prototypes early and trying to rush through a payment that would keep the companies afloat."

"And Carter had that tooth replacement and couldn't be there," Genna augmented his tale for him.

"Oh, that was deliberate. You were intended as the fall guy when NASA found the prototype failed,"

Andrews said. "But you wouldn't cooperate. You'd insisted on having time off for the weekend, for your guests, for Twinkle's delivery."

"The reason I left NASA was because I didn't want the restrictive nine to five, five days a week routine. I wasn't about to let Carter and Ctimes2 interfere with my life style."

"Well, Swinson was very confident of his people-skills, and he came to the dog show to get you to rush through the evaluations. He and Carter had conferred briefly and agreed that they could not ever appear to know one another. But Carter was nearby when Swinson made the comment about the response of the scanner to the individual smoking around it. Swinson was a business type. He really didn't understand the implication of his error. Carter did. And he knew you would pick up on it if you ever heard it."

Andrews fixed Genna with a stare that plainly charged, I told you so. "And then you really sent him over the edge when you mentioned using haversines. He didn't exactly remember what they were, but unlike Swinson and yours truly, he knew they meant you'd speedily finish with the star tracker's evaluation and be messing around with the scanner.

Genna snorted in exasperation. "You mean that comments about the cigarette smoke not hurting the scanner and my saying I'd use haversines pushed him over the edge? I don't believe it."

"Having all of his companies on the brink of failure sent him over the edge. Those two indicators made you an immediate threat," Andrews said.

When Genna shook her head in disbelief, Andrews continued with his tale. "So he decided on direct action. He had a rifle with a silencer in his trunk, and he decided you were too much of a liability. He found a tree along the sheltered back road, and tried to kill you. But Sky jerked you to the side at the last minute and the bullet hit Spratt instead. Someone started down the road toward his tree about then with a dog, and he left the rifle in the tree, got down and away before he was spotted. Red followed the trajectory of the bullet back to the source and found the rifle, but Carter was long gone by then."

"So Spratt's death had nothing to do with him or with Harper." Genna's response was soft and sad.

"No. The poor guy was just in the way when a bad marksman tried to take you out. And Sky probably contributed to saving your life by jerking you around the ring," Andrews said.

"But I saw Carter a little later. He came over and spoke to me right after Spratt was killed."

"He told me about that. He'd brazenly come back and mingled with the crowds at the show. He wanted to make certain Swinson didn't get close enough to you to make any more stupid slips about the scanner."

Genna puzzled over this for a long minute before nodding. "That's right, I remember. I saw Swinson in the crowd but he went the other way when I saw Carter."

Andrews nodded his agreement. "He went back to the show on Saturday, and was frantic when you didn't show. He was afraid you might be getting into the scanner performance stats. He came to your house with another rifle, he was getting frazzled by then, but the dogs made such a racket that he went away again. But he remembered your fear of chocolate around dogs, and came back sometime we didn't catch and threw a large quantity of it into the fenced area of the yard under the azaleas so you wouldn't notice."

"But why did he kill Swinson?" Shirley had been

paying more attention to Genna's condition than to most of Andrews' story, but she remembered the evening she'd returned home with Peggy and found Red conversing with Genna and Andrews around the kitchen table. Swinson had been the topic of conversation then. She'd not known of his death until last night when she'd returned home to another shock, that of learning of Swinson's death and Carter's attack on Genna. She had met Carter at the dog show, and was shocked, as was Genna, at the thought of his being a callous killer.

"He only meant to visit Swinson at his hotel, upbraid him for his stupid remark about the cigarette smoke and repeat his warnings for him to stay away from you. When he spotted the tail Red had put on Swinson, he panicked. He was fearful of what else Swinson might say. So he went around to the back of the motel room while the police were covering the front."

"And went in while the police were conferring nearby but not observing the door to Swinson's room?" Genna's puckered eyebrows were the result of puzzlement not pain.

"In and out again. He was very brazen – at the dog show, and again at Swinson's room. Carter had no trouble getting Swinson to open the door. They were partners remember? He could have told Swinson about the police tail out front and shot him with a pistol with a silencer while they were talking. We haven't gotten all the details yet, but we know he killed him to prevent the police from questioning him. Carter has told us that much."

"He seems to be babbling more than Swinson did," Jonathan observed.

"He's got more at stake now. He's very concerned about getting a replacement eye, thanks to the leash-swinging Wonder Woman there in the bed!"

251

"I was just trying to protect myself," Genna said, "and my poor, helpless little dogs. How did you deal with Carter and get Sky and Amber to the vets."

"Your vet came charging up your drive when you failed to show at his office. He heard all the sirens with the police and ambulances that came with Red in response to my phone message." Andrews shook his head in mock horror. "That man stomped all over the crime scene getting Sky and Amber out of your car, into his, and back to his office."

"Fortunately Red is a dog lover and sympathized with the need to get expert help for Sky and Amber. It was utter chaos there for a while, with two ambulance crews trying to deal with you and Carter and your vet fretting over Amber and Sky. Red put up some token resistance about your vet mucking up a crime scene, but he really never tried to prevent him stabilizing and removing the dogs. But since Carter was conscious, babbling by this time, and screaming over the loss of an eye and damage to his pretty face, it wasn't hard to reconstruct what happened even if you were not able to contribute your side of the story."

The chunky figure at the foot of her bed did not fool Genna with his feigned grumbling. The old Andrews, the one she'd known BB (before Blacky took over his life) might not have understood. She knew this Andrews was not surprised at the single-minded devotion of her vet.

"And you're sure they are going to be fine? And Bunny! What's happened with Bunny?"

A fourth visitor breezed in through the doorway in time to inject her voice into the conversation with a response. "Mr. Bunny has gained a half-ounce since yesterday. At your dear vet's instruction, I added a drop of dark molasses to his cuisine. And except for the decidedly darker mess he makes the area around him, especially my clothes, he is growing stronger with each passing hour."

Peggy's entrance, as always, was achieved with rapid and self-assured footsteps. She was dressed in the same outfit she'd worn to the dog show on Friday, but now the sage green jacket was dotted with water spots from the downpour that was only dimly audible in Genna's room. She managed to move with her usual whirlwind speed, despite the oversized navy purse she carried slung over her left shoulder. She pushed up beside Jonathan and leaned over the bed railing to say hello.

Genna dropped her hold on Jonathan's hand to grasp the one Peggy extended toward her in greeting. "Hi, Pal! Is the show over already for the day? How did Muffin do in group yesterday?"

"Well you certainly sound a lot more alert today than when I saw you last." Peggy said as she smiled back at Genna. "Muffin managed to take 4th place yesterday in Toy Group, but none of us were in the mood to go back for another try today with all this rain and with everything else going on. I've been playing with Bunny and bothering Twinkle and keeping track of the rest of the brood." She dropped Genna's hand to brush at her green jacket, calling attention to all the water spots that still lay like dark dots on the fabric. "Besides, I was tired of getting sprinkled with the 'slight chance of rain' your weather channel keeps predicting. Don't those people have windows in the studio? This is nothing short of a downpour!" Peggy snorted.

"Amber sends her love," Peggy continued. "She's still a little wobbly, but she's on an IV and improving steadily. Sky apparently played the gentleman and let her have more than her share of the chocolate,"

"Sky?" Genna's fears showed clearly in her face, and the age lines around her mouth suddenly appeared deeper and more extensive.

Peggy did not answer immediately. Instead she turned slightly to look directly at Andrews.

"You are about the biggest guard we have here. How about closing the door so Genna can have a little privacy and leaning against it for a little bit."

Andrews hesitated for a moment. He was a very good detective. It didn't take him more than two nanoseconds to figure out the situation. The law enforcement officer in his nature started to lodge an objection. The dog loving human in his nature won the argument, but he had to pay lip service to his other half. "Are you sure this is wise?" he asked Peggy.

"Of course! Hospitals are cesspools of bacterial infections and germs, but they are unimaginably prejudiced against the single most important medication for Genna's ills." Peggy motioned him toward the door and his assigned task with one hand while she swung her large navy pocketbook over the railing to sit it on the bed beside Genna.

Andrews backed toward the doorway, closing it and leaning his substantial bulk against it to block unwanted visitors. Peggy unzipped the top of the bag she'd just placed at Genna's side.

A tiny red and white head pushed its way through the opening and an eager moist tongue excitedly licked the hand that Genna extended happily toward it.

"Sky would like to present his best wishes to you in person," Peggy chirped, "and reassure you that he is doing fine."

Beguiling Bundle: Death Takes Best of Breed

Jean C. Keating